THE WILD

A KING SISTERS NOVEL

THE LAS VEGAS LOVE DUET
BOOK 2

PENELOPE BLACK

for the girlies who love a good surprise pregnancy trope

AUTHOR'S NOTE

Please note that The Wild is a dark mafia romance and has some darker themes some readers may find triggering.

Please message me if you have any questions:
penelopeblack.pa@gmail.com
Happy reading!

PLAYLIST

"Shut Up and Kiss Me" by Angel Olsen
"July" by Noah Cyrus
"Bigger Than The Whole Sky" by Taylor Swift
"Family Line" by Conan Gray
"Possibility" by Lykke Li
"Heavy Weather" by Billie Marten
"All The Flowers" by Angel Olsen
"Bored" by Billie Eilish
"Only" by RY X
"Vigilante Shit" by Taylor Swift
"I Should Live in Salt" by The National

1

MAEVE

I OPEN my eyes to an endless blue. Soft wispy clouds trail through the sky, and if I squint one eye closed, I can almost see them moving across the sky.

I wonder what they're going to look like when they reach their destination. Will they have dissipated by then, shed their water droplets on the dry land? Or maybe they'll have joined together, swirled into one and then unleashed their fury with thunder and lightning?

Mum always told my sisters and me that we're stronger together than we'll ever be apart.

My eyes burn with long-buried emotion, so I close them against the bright blue sky and let the sun warm my face. And if it dries the tear that slides down my temple, then it's a coincidence. My eyes are dry, gritty feeling from looking at the sky so long, that's all.

I hear a twig snap, and my eyes fly open. Planting my palms on the grass beneath me, I push to a sitting position. My head swims and so does my vision. Bright white dots dance behind my eyelids.

"Damn," I mutter, pressing my palm to my bowed forehead. "I must've been lying here longer than I realized."

Another twig snaps, and my senses tingle. My extra sense, as Mum taught us. It's hard to explain how I developed it, only that I did, and it's come in useful more times than I thought it would.

I shift my weight to my knees and push to stand up slowly, spinning to take in my surroundings. I raise my hand to my forehead, shielding my face as I wait for my vision to clear.

I'm in a familiar meadow, concealed within expansive woods. Trees make a semicircle behind me, their leaves lush and green and their branches full. I've spent countless hours playing in these woods with my sisters, exploring trails, and playing spy.

I'm at Grandda Charlie's house, I realize.

A flush of confusion rolls down my body, and I sweep my hair off of my neck and beg for a swift breeze. I should've put it in a high ponytail before I came out here.

Where is everyone?

I spin around, expecting one of my sisters to jump out and scare me. They don't. But what I find stops my heart all the same.

Hair the color of leaves in Central Park in October. It's wavy, hanging halfway down her back. It's the deep shade of red that looks almost amber in the right light, always a little darker in the colder months.

A gentle breeze sweeps across the open land, rustling the leaves of the surrounding trees and making the wildflowers around my ankles dance. Strands of hair slip free and tickle my cheeks.

But the warm sunshine and the soft breeze can't steal my attention from the figure in front of the small pond ahead of me.

"Mum?"

The wind snatches the word, carrying her name across the

patch of grass separating us. She doesn't turn around at the sound of my voice.

"Mum?" I call her name louder this time, urgency pounding against my skin. She still doesn't acknowledge me.

I take a hesitant step toward her, my shoes squelching as they slowly sink into the grass. My chest tightens and sweat breaks out on the back of my neck.

Why isn't she turning around? Why can't she hear me? Is this another game of spy?

I bet I'm the first one back, like usual. And she probably has her headphones in because she wasn't expecting anyone to finish so soon. She likes watching the ducks in the pond while listening to her favorite playlists.

My muscles coil tight as I take another step toward her. My shoe gets tangled in something, stopping me from taking a full step. I glance down, expecting to see an errant tree branch or a tall weed with those prickly burrs that sink into clothes in a second or something.

Instead, I see a white skirt.

No, not just a skirt. A wedding dress.

"What the hell?" I press my hands against my stomach, the satin material soft against my palms.

My eyebrows slam together as I rack my brain, trying in vain to remember why I'm wearing a wedding dress. I don't remember this from any of Mum's little games. I must've hit my head. Actually, that explains why I was on the ground.

It doesn't really matter why I'm wearing it, though. The only thing that matters is getting to Mum. My gut is warning me that everything isn't as calm as it initially seems.

I haul the layered tulle and satin into my arms, hiking the skirt up high enough so I won't trip over it as I run and yell her name again.

"Mum!"

Finally, she responds. She raises her right hand and waves, but she's still facing away from me.

Who is she waving at? Who else is here?

Confusion bleeds into fear. I can't explain it, and it doesn't make any sense because Grandda Charlie's is a safe space for me —for all of my sisters, actually. It's the place we roam without a care in the world.

I look around as I high-step it over the overgrown meadow grasses. Where are my sisters? I don't see them anywhere, so this must be part of Mum's games.

"Mum! I'm behind you," I yell, but she still doesn't turn around.

I jog a few paces to the left and squint to see if I can spot anyone on the other side of the pond. But either they're too far away, I need glasses, or there's no one there.

I'm three feet away when she lowers her arm and abruptly spins to face me. She lunges for me, digging her fingernails into my skin on my shoulder.

"Ow, Mum. What are you doing?" I try to recoil, but she catches me by surprise when she yanks me toward her.

"Get out of here, Maeve," she yells.

My chest tightens as my gaze bounces over her features. The whites of her eyes look pronounced against her stormy gray irises, they're so wide. Her laugh lines look less joyful and more severe, like she's been fretting for hours. Lips chapped and hair wild around her face.

She doesn't look like herself, and that frightens me more than waking up in a wedding dress with no recollection on how I got there.

"What's going on? Are you okay?"

"It's not safe for you here, my love. You have to leave." She walks me backward, keeping her grip on my shoulders.

"Okay, I will," I assure her, trying to plant my feet. "But not yet. I want to stay with you for a bit."

"No, no, no. You have to leave. Now, Maeve." Her words are hurried as she walks me back another couple of steps, frantically glancing over my shoulder. Her fear permeates the air around us, and my own rises in response.

I drop my skirts and throw my arms around her shoulders. I yank her to me and squeeze her tight. "It's okay."

She maneuvers her arms around me and murmurs, "I love you, my brave girl. But you can't stay with me. You're still needed out there."

"My sisters," I reply, nodding against her shoulder.

"Aye, your sisters. Among others."

My face is buried in her hair, the tickle against my nose a familiar feeling. I inhale the scent of lime from her favorite shampoo. The citrusy-sweet smell sends a deep pang of longing through my gut.

My arms tighten around her reflexively.

"Come with me then. We can find them together. I bet Rosie's in that spot by the kittens in the barn. She always hides there."

Mum's chuckle warms my soul up from the inside. "Ah, if it were only that simple. I'm sorry, my love, but you must leave. Now."

She pulls back, her hands sliding to rest on my shoulders once more. Suddenly, she shakes me. Hard.

"Wake up now, Maeve. Wake up, wake up, wake up!" Mum yells, wrenching my shoulders forward.

My head snaps forward from the jarring motion, and I bite the tip of my tongue. My neck feels like a wet noodle, incapable of standing tall and weathering the force.

"Mum, what are you…" I trail off as the trees around us start to melt. Streaks of green run down the sides of my vision like condensation on a glass on a hot day. Confusion and terror seep from my pores, forming this nearly tangible slush around me.

My vision starts to swim again, and Mum goes blurry in an instant. My head aches, and I try to hold onto one of the two figures weaving in front of me. "Mum, wait."

"Wake up, you stupid fucking Irish cunt. You don't get to die so easily."

The unfamiliar voice from Mum's mouth catapults me from the melting scenery of Grandda Charlie's property.

And I slam straight into hell.

2

MAEVE

AN EARSPLITTING SHRIEK reverberates through the air, shivering my bones until I can feel it in my teeth. A ringing so loud it stabs at me eardrums, threatening to burst them open. I shake my head to the side in a vain attempt to clear it as tremors course through my veins.

A woman's face looms above me, flickering and doubling before my eyes.

I try to focus on her face, her moving lips swimming in and out of my vision. I can't focus on what she's saying, my gaze drawn to the inferno within the church.

Tall flames lap up the brick walls like angry tongues. They lash the air, reaching toward the sky like a fiery staircase.

Heat radiates from the building, and I can feel it on my skin despite the distance. With a fire that size, I'm not surprised the heat radiates this far.

The window I escaped through is unrecognizable. It's a gaping maw of fire filled with billowing smoke that stings my eyes and crawls down my throat, squeezing around my chest like an iron fist.

Pieces of brick and rebar litter the ground, turning the parking lot into a battle zone.

"What the fuck?" I whisper. Disbelief and horror war for dominance.

There's no way this is from Keira. She didn't have the right materials to cause this kind of damage. She planted smoke bombs and one tiny peacock bomb. The kind that's more pomp and show than damage. It was designed to cover up my escape, leaving what's-his-name at the altar. Not explode with me still inside the church and take half of it down.

Which means that someone else wanted this wedding to end. Right?

The woman grabs my shoulders and yanks me hard. I cry out in pain, and that's when I really notice her.

Black hair that hangs pin-straight and frames her pinched face. Her dark brown eyes are harsh and accusatory, which doesn't bode well for me. She doesn't seem like she'd be inclined to listen to any explanation I have.

I try to fling my arms up in a desperate attempt to push her off of me, but she easily dodges my weak efforts and continues to sink her nails into my shoulder. My movements feel sluggish and slow compared to hers.

"My stupid fucking idiot cousin just had to marry the Irish. Fucking dumbass motherfuckers deserve what they got, but that doesn't mean that I'm not going to exact revenge in their honor," she grumbles, yanking me to my feet.

She grabs me with a strength I wasn't expecting. I'm not what I would call petite exactly, and this monstrosity of a wedding dress weighs a ton. Yet she hauls me up without much effort.

The world tilts, and I sway and lean on her. She huffs and shoves me a step away with a disdainful grunt. My head feels heavy on my shoulders, but a wave of clarity washes over me with every jolt of movement and helps bring me back to center.

"Of fucking course, you had to pick a ballgown skirt," she snaps, shoving the errant layer of singed satin away from her legs.

"Who are you?" I manage, wobbling on my feet as I regain my balance.

"Fuck you." Her reply is instant.

A laugh rattles in my throat before I have time to stop it, and it quickly morphs into a cough. As acrid smoke wafts from the burning building around us, I feel its icy grip piercing through my layers of torn satin and lace.

The air is so thick with haze that it appears to be reaching for the stars. As it clings to my skin like an invisible fog, my head starts to spin. All I can see are swirling shadows of revelations and turbulent flame.

With trembling hands, I grasp my knees through the dirty and damaged layers of satin and tulle as I double over. My head feels foggy, like it's stuffed with cotton and then shaken up, and I struggle to catch my breath.

"Oh for fuck's sake. Mattia, get over here and carry the princess to the car," she yells.

I take a slow breath through my nose as I assess the damage as best I can. A sharp pain throbs in my head, and I gingerly touch the worst of it along my hairline. My fingers come away stained red. Shit. Head wounds are notorious big bleeders, but it isn't synonymous with serious trauma. My ribs feel tender and so does my right hip, but nothing bears the sharp agony of a fractured bone.

"What about this one, boss?" a male voice says from behind me.

She leans to the side, enough for me to steal a look at her expression. She rolls her eyes so hard, I'm surprised they don't fall out of her head. She clucks her tongue with a scoff. "I bet that's her lover. The dumbass is probably the one who set the church on fire and blew her up."

"Probably," he says with a chuckle.

"Though." She drags the word out slowly. "He might be useful as a tool to torture her."

I take advantage of her distraction to look her over again. My eyes scan her face, trying to recall any detail from the last three days, but coming up empty-handed. Her voice doesn't sound familiar either, but that doesn't mean much. I didn't exactly commit any of his family to memory in the last three days. As far as I was concerned, it was a waste of brain power.

Hindsight is a joke, and I'm the current punchline. If only I had paid more attention, maybe something could serve as my ticket out of this mess.

A sudden thought screeches across my brain, sinking talons of fear into my very marrow.

It's not just my fate that hangs in the balance.

My fingers tremble, clutching the fabric of the dress near my stomach.

The baby.

Oh god. Oh no, no, no.

My mind splinters as unadulterated terror floods my system, turning the saliva in my mouth into something acidic. My heart beats double-time and a fresh wave of adrenaline floods my veins. I need to get the fuck out of here and find a doctor. Someone I can trust.

Right now.

I stand frozen for what feels like an eternity, letting my panic bleed all over my visions of my future. I've only known I was pregnant for hours, and yet, I subconsciously already started planning for a life with a baby. This baby.

I shuffle back a step. The first thing I need to do is put distance between us. I can't outrun her, not dressed like this and with a likely concussion. But I have other means to protect myself.

Her arm shoots out before I can get far, and her hand clamps down on my bicep like a vice. "Where do you think you're going, bitch?"

"I don't know who you are or what you want, but I'm leaving. Now." I do my best to let her feel the full weight of my glare, but it's more scared woman than badass right now.

She narrows her eyes and tsks. "Leave him, Mattia. We don't need him. She's the one who's going to serve us our vengeance, so get the fuck over here. She's fucking heavy with this abomination of a dress, and I don't think she's going to come willingly," the woman grumbles, adjusting her hold on me.

The taste of bile rises as I breathe through the urge to vomit and sweat beads on my forehead. The heat from the fire is a constant reminder of how much danger I'm currently in.

Either I have a concussion, or I'm so goddamn scared that I'm going to toss up the minuscule lunch I ate earlier.

How am I going to get out of this without incurring more harm? Each second that ticks by feels like an eternity, the hands of father time cruelly taunting as they pass me.

My mind feverishly races with the thoughts of escape plans and contingency strategies. None of my carefully laid plans—and definitely not my hastily made ones—have ever a deviation to account for this type of situation.

Actually, this entire plan went to shit quick. All thanks to someone else's handiwork, too.

A misstep I'll be sure to remedy in the future.

My vision blurred slightly before slowly coming back into focus as I realized that I could use my nauseous state to my advantage—if I could just distract her long enough to make a grab for either the blade concealed in my thigh holster or her gun. I'm sure she has one tucked into the back of her pants.

With no time to waste, I force myself into action.

"I'm going to be sick," I moan out before I let myself become dead weight. Predictably, she stumbles forward and loses her grip on my arms.

My knees collide with the unforgiving cement, but I ignore the pain and press my palms to the ground in some messed-up version of tabletop position I remember from the couple of yoga classes I took.

"Oh, fucking gross," the woman says but she doesn't back away. Good. The closer she is, the easier it'll be to knock her out or subdue her long enough for me to get to the car.

I'm regretting parking it four blocks away now. I can't afford to be slowed down by fatigued or a concussion or fifty layers of burnt tulle.

Strength and determination begin to swell within me. I have a responsibility now that extends beyond mere vengeance.

A little life, unseen but still so loved already, was blossoming inside of me. And heaven help anyone who jeopardizes its safety. The attachment I feel toward this miracle is unparalleled, and I will do whatever it takes to protect it.

If I had any questions about this pregnancy, I suppose this moment answers them.

I stopped being offended by others' estimation of me or my abilities years ago. Instead, I leaned into it. Being underestimated has served me on more than one occasion, and I already know it's going to be her downfall. It's only a matter of how far she's going to fall.

The rage in her eyes is unmistakable, though her vengeance is misplaced. She doesn't strike me as the questions-first kind of person, so I'm going to extend the same courtesy.

I bite back the guilt that creeps up my throat and remind myself that it's a fight for survival, and no one gets to win without a few scrapes.

And me? I always play to fucking win.

3

MAEVE

MY FINGERS CURL around the jagged piece of brick in front of me, the sharp edges cutting into my skin. The pain is welcome amidst the chaos—a reminder that I have power here. I'm not helpless and I can get out of this.

If I strain my hearing hard enough, I can almost hear Rosie's words of encouragement in my ear. I imagine her sitting at her desk in her dorm room, six computer monitors strategically set up in front of her and the sound of her fingers flying across her keyboard as she finds me an exit strategy. She's always been our eyes in the sky. Right now, she'd tell me to get my head in the game and not to miss my opportunity.

I take a deep breath and shift my weight to the balls of my feet. My boots slide under the pebbles as I shuffle a little to make sure I'm not stepping on any layers of my skirt. The last thing I need is to be thwarted by tulle.

The wind swirls around, bringing a thick smoky fog that paints the courtyard in grim shades of gray. The stench of fear bleeds into the air and seeps into every crevice.

Hers, mine, his. All of those people inside the church. It

doesn't really matter who it belonged to. It's an electric charge that runs through us like lightning, coursing through our veins, and settling heavily in our limbs.

There's enough of it to leave a permanent stain on the ground. An eternal reminder of the choices made here.

My heart hammers in my chest as I take a step forward, my eyes locked on the woman in front of me. She's still reeling from my feigned sickness, her face scrunched up in disgust.

Fuck it. Now or never.

I hike up my skirt with one hand, my fingers seeking flesh underneath the eighteen layers that make up my skirt. I shift my hand higher until I feel the cool steel of my favorite blade.

I slip it free from the thigh holster and spring to my feet in the next breath. My legs are unsteady, and I use it to my advantage. I twist to the side at the same time the woman turns toward me.

With a grunt, I lunge forward. The woman tries to sidestep me, but I've got the element of surprise and the deep-rooted desire to walk out of here alive. My arm swings, and I slam the piece of brick to the side of her head.

The soft thud is enough to turn my stomach, but I try to shut off that part of my brain. I didn't use enough force to kill her, but definitely hard enough to stun her. Adrenaline pumps tenfold in my bloodstream, granting me that temporary strength I so desperately need.

"You fucking cunt," the woman seethes as she presses her palm to the gash on her head. Blood starts to pool between her fingers, almost a mirrored image of my own head wound. Irony is a real bitch sometimes.

"I'm going to fucking enjoy killing you," she grits out between clenched teeth,

She reaches behind her, whipping out a gun and pointing it at me as she lunges. Time stops, a split second in time where my brain agrees to take a backseat and let my body act on instinct.

Time is a funny concept. Sixty seconds ago, I could've sworn an eternity of time had passed while I all but drowned in realization. But it was maybe thirty seconds in reality. And now, now it feels like time has slowed down, showing me frame by frame how it's going to play out.

There's only one way I walk out of here. I make my peace with the reality of what I have to do, and I shut everything else down.

I don't think about the resistance her body offers as I jab my knife into her gut. I don't think about the way her pupils dilate in surprise or the way her lips part on a disbelieving sort of laugh.

I don't think about anything other than the cold determination to survive. And in a situation where it's kill or be killed, I don't think about what that means for my conscience.

"I'm sorry." They're the only words I can offer her as I pull my blade out. If it was just the hit on the head, she would've been fine. But a stab wound to the stomach lowers those odds drastically.

"Ginny!" the man yells as he barrels toward us.

The woman, Ginny, stumbles backward before her back collides with the small brick retaining wall. She sinks to the ground slowly as he reaches her, her eyes wide and tight with pain.

Her hand goes to her wound, but as soon as she touches the blood that pools thickly in her palm, she cries out. Her gaze flies from her hands to the man in front of her.

And then she pins her disbelief on me. An incredulous accusation.

"You should've let me go," I murmur. Regret shakes my voice.

I hesitate for a second, indecision drowning me. If Keira were here, she would tell me that I can't leave him alive. He's seen my face, fleeing the church as it collapsed. But more importantly, he saw me stab her. He'll come for me, and I'll be looking over my shoulder for the rest of my life.

Until I ultimately find him and end our misery.

Still, I can't bring myself to kill him. Not right now. I let my gaze fall over the pair of them, and that's when I see it. Something shifts in his shoulders, fury rolling off of him in waves.

Fuck. Time to go.

I haul my skirt up again and start to run. I jump over a pile of bricks, and my ankle rolls when I land on a patch of small pebbles.

"You motherfucking bitch," the guy yells.

I look over my shoulder and see him standing over Ginny, gun in one hand and fire shooting from his eyes.

"Get her to a doctor, you fucking idiot," I snap. I left her alive for a reason.

But I can already tell he's not in a reasonable frame of mind, which is understandable. But that's the thing—I'm not feeling fucking reasonable either.

I feel like a cornered tiger, and the closer he circles me, the sooner I will take him out too.

As much as I want to disrespect him, I don't give him my back. He seems like the cowardly type, and I'll be damned if I'm going to get shot in the back.

I pause next to another body. He's lying on his side, facing away from me, arm thrown over his head.

It hits me then. I saw his face, right before everything went dark. It was only a flash, a single moment in time. But I'd recognize the dark hair and shoulders and tattoos in a crowd.

It's Santorini.

But more importantly, he's possibly the father of my child.

4

ROMEO

I'D BARELY RECOVERED from the shock of seeing my Juliet at the end of the aisle, when the dumbass next to us opened his mouth. I can't be held responsible for what happened afterward. Though, I admit I got a little carried away.

I rub my sore jaw, the splatter of blood on my knuckles catching my attention. "Oh, fucking gross." I wipe my hands off on the robes and glare at the motherfucker. He sucker-punched me and bled on me when I returned his sentiment.

I was going to let Nic take care of him after I chased him outside, but then he called my girl a cunt.

So now I'm going to kill him with my bare hands.

And if I happen to find satisfaction in permanently eliminating the possibility of him ever speaking about her like that again, then that's an emotion between me and god.

I look around, the irony of my thoughts not lost on me. Smoke rises and wafts toward the back of the nave, no doubt whisking away into the evening.

If I had to guess, I'd bet this asshole's life that those smoky distractions were planted by my girl. And I want to know why.

I nudge him with the tip of my boot. He groans and curls inward a bit. Still alive, then.

I feel the explosion before I hear it. This pulsating wave of force that rocks me back on my heels. A thunderous boom slams against my eardrums with a force that has my hands clamping over my ears in protection.

A rapid shiver runs through the church, creaking and groaning before settling back into stillness. I don't trust it though.

I exhale, forcibly releasing the tension from my body. But it only lasts a moment before fear floods my veins.

Juliet.

Her face flashes before my eyes, pulsing in line with the whooshing sound in my ears. Where is she?

I twist left and right in frantic semi circles, desperately searching for a flash of her white dress. My heart beats against my ribcage, a violent demand to lay eyes on my girl.

I thought—fuck, I don't know what I thought. That she'd wait for me, give me a chance to explain or something.

But that's not her style.

"Fuck this."

I tug at the rip in the chest of the borrowed chasuble, and the threads burst apart as the tear widens into a jagged hole. I reach inside and grab my favorite gun from my shoulder holster.

Nic scoffed when he saw me put the holster on, said it was sacrilegious or some other bullshit I tuned out. And thank fuck I did. Wait until I tell him how useful it was too. I'm going to enjoy watching him eat his words.

Rage slithers up my spine, demanding we take our pound of flesh from the motherfucker sprawled out in front of us. Time isn't on my side, and in a choice between vengeance and my girl?

Well, that's even a real choice, is it?

I choose her. Every single time.

And right now, I need to find her more than I need to make him suffer.

So I assuage my rage by reasoning that he'll die by my hand either way. In one blink, I raise my arm and squeeze the trigger.

The sound of my ragged breath echoes around me, mocking me amidst the ominous creaking from the building. Keeping a tight grip on my gun, I step over him and sprint down the aisle.

The robe gets tangled between my legs, enough to slow me down not so much that I risk the precious seconds it'll take to stop and take it off.

I push open the heavy wooden doors, momentarily blinded by the sunlight. I pause on the top stair and shield my eyes as sweat drips down the back of my neck.

The sleeves of the chasuble are smudged with dirt and blood, remnants of this afternoon's battle. I don't even know if I can constitute what happened here as a battle, but it sure as fuck feels like one.

And I can't risk leaving it here. That stupid motherfucker sucker-punched me, and I can't be sure there isn't a trace of my blood on these things. I don't trust these assholes not to get creative with my DNA.

Well, as creative as they can, I suppose. I don't peg the Milanos as an exceptionally creative family.

A connected family of Italian winemakers who smuggle drugs and guns in their crates of wine? Please, it's like they're begging the ATF to raid their little homestead.

We did them a favor, really.

My gut tightens at the sight of so many bodies in the courtyard. I'm not surprised it's only men. My brothers are both excellent shots.

I don't know what's worse: coming up with this idea to take out all the men or pulling the trigger that takes them out.

They're equally soul-staining, I think.

None of us wanted to fucking be here, but in a situation like this there are no happy outcomes. Only tragedy and catastrophe.

I look forward to the day where the toughest decision is what ice cream flavor I want and not choosing who dies or how.

A whistle splits the air, and my head snaps up. I narrow my eyes and see Nic waving his hand from his crouched position between two SUVs.

It's the reminder I need to bring me back to the present. There will be plenty of time for me to let today's events haunt me.

I sigh and shift my weight from foot to foot. Nic stands up from his crouched position between the cars and jerks his head toward me.

"The bride?" I call out.

Nic jerks his head to the side. "He went that way."

He means Tommy. Why the fuck would Tommy go around the side of the church? Him leaving was not part of the plan.

I shake my head. "No, the bride. Where is she?"

"What?" he yells.

I sigh and pitch my voice louder. "The fucking bride. Did you see her?"

"No." He raises his voice to match mine.

I should be jogging toward him, and then the three of us should be getting the fuck out of here. That's the next step in our plan.

But everything changed once I saw her at the end of the aisle. I'd recognize her anywhere. Even in an over-the-top wedding gown that looks like one of those fancy tiered cakes.

My Juliet.

Rage reignites underneath my skin, bubbling up and compressing my veins when I think about why the fuck she was here.

Now it starts to make sense.

I thought she left because she wanted to play, and fuck, maybe she did. Maybe she was waiting for me to rescue her from this arranged sham the whole time.

I intend to ask her all that and more—as soon as I find her.

"Get him and meet me out back in five," I yell.

I shake my head once at Nic and spin on my heel, entering the church once again. If she's not out front, then she either went out the back, or she's trapped inside somewhere. And I can't shake this nagging feeling that she needs me.

I hear Nic yell something, but my determination drowns out the sound of his voice. I've had months of practice in finding my girl. This will be a piece of cake.

5

MAEVE

A GUNSHOT RINGS through the air.

It's the kind of noise that I've never grown accustomed to. Not in all my time shooting at my grandda's house or in any of the scuffles we've been in over the years. Not even hearing them when I'm visiting the South Side of Chicago, where guns are drawn over the smallest infractions sometimes.

I freeze, stuck in a halfway crouch that I didn't even realize I was doing until this moment. My right hand rests on Santorini's bicep, my left hovers a few inches above him, still firmly clutching the handle of my blade. I subconsciously planned to turn him over. Check his pulse, look at his face and see if my eyes were playing tricks on me.

"Stand up. Slowly," Mattia commands.

"You're wasting time, Mattia. We need to go," Ginny pleads. Her voice doesn't sound like it belongs to someone hanging above death. She sounds annoyed and in pain, sure, but like she's knocking on death's door? Not so much. Maybe she'll pull through, and I'll end up looking over both shoulders.

Jaw clenched and teeth gritted, I conceal the blade between

the folds of my shredded skirt and slowly stand to my five foot four height. My body trembles as though lightning has shot through it.

I've unknowingly brought a knife to a gun fight. And it doesn't matter how good my throwing skills are, I'll never be able to throw the knife and hit him before he can pull the trigger.

Those are just the cold, hard facts.

"Turn around, bitch. Slowly. I want you to see our faces when you die, to know it was me who took your life from you."

I do as he asks, spinning around at a measured speed as he continues his little speech.

"It was me who reaped vengeance for your actions against our family today. I'm going to enjoy showing you off to the remaining elders, to proclaim our victory for the family," Mattia says.

It reminds me of the kinds of things you see the villains do in the movies. They spill their guts and map out their entire plan just in time for the good guys to win it all in the end.

I keep my chin raised high, shoulders down, and channel my sister Fiona. She's learned from her experience with the snooty uppercrust of society to never let them see you sweat. Since I can literally feel the cold sweat currently coating the back of my neck, I'm going to have to fake it a bit. "I don't even know who you are."

His face turns a mottled shade of red, and Ginny groans behind him from her perch against the wall.

I jerk my head in her direction. "You have a choice to make. Either you claim your misplaced vengeance or you save your friend's life."

He takes two big steps toward me, shaking his gun at me. "You don't tell me what to do. I'm the one with the fucking gun. I'm in charge here, not you—you-you fucking bitch."

I shrug my shoulders and let them fall back down, maintaining an unaffected posture and neutral expression. It's not like I haven't heard that name before. His words are meaningless to me. It's his gun that I'm concerned about.

Movement from over his shoulder catches my eye. I glance as quickly as possible to the left, over the little brick retaining wall, and refocus on the asshole waving a gun at me.

I'd recognize that messy blonde bun anywhere.

Gratitude so profound snaps the band of fear around me, and I almost slouch in relief. My chest feels lighter than it was moments before. I'm still ill-equipped for this fight, but it's no longer two against one.

I've never been happier for my headstrong sister to ignore my instructions in my entire life. It was the very top of her head and only for a second, but I know it was her.

I just need to keep his focus on me to give her time to get us out of here. Hopefully, without another explosion.

Ginny's still on the ground, clutching her stomach with a grimace. Her eyes are squeezed shut, and she's breathing heavily. I almost feel bad for stabbing her, but not bad enough to regret saving myself.

"Leave it, Mattia. We'll get her another time. I need a doctor," Ginny grits out, her eyes still closed.

Mattia starts to turn around just as Keira's head peaks over the wall again.

Shit.

I lick my lips and widen my stance, preparing myself for anything. "It sure didn't seem like you were in charge earlier. Ginny called the orders out, remember? In fact, I thought you were her little errand boy, ferreting around on her every whim."

He grits his teeth as he charges toward me in menacing, measured steps. "I'm the fucking boss, not her. Women aren't allowed as leaders in the Outfit."

"Sure, sure." I let the sarcasm drip from my words as I look over his shoulder and wink at Ginny. Not that she can see it behind her closed lids. But he doesn't know that.

"You disrespectful fucking bitch—"

"Your insults are old and unimaginative," I interrupt him. It's enough to stop him in his tracks for all of three seconds. I stare at him dead in the eye, willing my hands to stop trembling. "If your plan is to kill me by boring me to death with mediocre insults, then you might actually succeed at something."

He raises the gun, and my heart slams against my chest. It beats in an irregular rhythm, cursing my brain for letting my mouth run away from us. Sweat collects along my brow, and my breaths come in fast, choppy inhales.

C'mon, Keira. What are you waiting for? I mentally urge her.

Blood sludges down the side of my face, that in between state of wet and dry, where it's tacky to the touch and starting to itch. I exhale the need to brush it off. I don't want to make any sudden movements and spook him.

He flashes me a grin that's all teeth. It's a drugstore version of the malicious smiles from the Syndicate's men. It barely scratches the surface of intimidating.

"I'm going to enjoy this," he snarls, stepping over a small pile of bricks.

I see a flash of blonde in my peripheral vision, and I tense my muscles and shift to the balls of my feet. A gunshot cracks through the air, and I flinch. I drop down into a crouch, antici-pating Mattia to pull the trigger on reflex.

He doesn't.

His hand holding the gun falls to his side, his grip loosening enough that the weapon clatters to the cement. His hands reach up to press against the center of his chest. Blood blooms under-neath his palms, spreading wide across his shirt at a macabre speed.

He looks from his bloodied fingers to me, his brows crushed

together over his accusatory glare. "What the fuck?"

He starts to spin around, but before he makes a half-turn, his shoulder jerks with the impact of another bullet.

"Enjoy hell, you misogynistic fuck," Keira says.

My sister stands on top of the retaining half-wall, her feet planted wide and her left palm supporting her right-hand grip.

Wisps of her blonde hair whip in the breeze, a dirt smudge darkening her forehead. She looks like a badass action hero from those movies Ava likes to watch.

Her lips flatten into a line of determination, but I know her well enough to recognize the zeal of excitement in her gaze. Not that she's excited to extinguish someone's light, more like she leans into the opportunity to enact her own version of justice. I half expect her to pull out a sword from behind her back like a lethal medieval magician.

I blink, swaying slightly on my feet as my shoulder throbs on cue with my heart thundering against my ribs.

Mattia stumbles, his feet barely staying underneath him as he shuffles forward a few steps. He mumbles something too low for me to hear as he trips over debris and falls to his knees with a bone-jarring thud. He stares at me, shock and surprise splashed across his face.

Keira jumps off the wall and lands on her feet with the gracefulness of a cat. She's so fucking agile, I sometimes wonder if she should've been the thief in the family.

But she likes blowing shit up too much. Her words, not mine.

"Maeve!" she yells, desperation making her voice shrill. She sprints toward me, her blonde bun bobbing as she jumps over piles of broken bricks with ease.

I swallow down the sob of relief at seeing her beautiful face. I don't know how much longer I could've held him off.

Not for the first time, I thank the universe for giving me my sisters.

6

MAEVE

KEIRA CRASHES INTO ME, throwing her arms around my neck and pulling me into a fierce hug. "Fucking hell, you scared me."

My arms fly around her, and I hug her tight, maybe tighter than I have in years. I ignore the way my ribs protest the pressure, stuffing the pain in a box and burying it somewhere until I can safely let it resurface. "Even though I told you to leave, I'm so glad you're here."

She pulls back and scans me from head to toe, her gaze frantic. "Where are you hurt?" She prods the gash on the side of my head with gentle fingers.

"I'm fine." I push her hand away. "But we need to find a doctor, and we need to leave. Now before anyone else comes."

She brings her left hand to cover her mouth with a gasp. "The baby?"

I bite my bottom lip, my eyes widening. "I—"

Garbled laughter cuts me off. Keira spins around, gun pulled and raised at Ginny in a heartbeat. "You're pregnant?"

I'm going to blame the concussion for the fact that I completely forgot about her.

"Who the fuck is this?" Keira asks.

I shake my head. "I don't know, not really." I place my hand on her shoulder and tug her back a step. "Let's just go. Quick, before anyone else comes looking for them."

"I'm guessing it's not my cousin's?" Ginny says though a crazed laugh.

Keira jerks her head back before glancing at me. "Who the fuck is her cousin?"

"God, you Irish bitches are dumb." She huffs. "Milo Milano. This one's fiancé," Ginny says, raising her hand and pointing at me. Blood drips from her fingertips and lands on her thighs. "Or dead fiancé, I assume. Does that make you a widow? A widower?"

She's rambling, which tells me she's liable to run her mouth as soon as she sees someone. I sink my teeth into my bottom lip and try to think through the best next step.

"That fucking name," Keira says with an exaggerated shudder. "You dodged a bullet with that one, sis." She pauses and raises her brows. "Too soon?"

Sirens sound in the distance. Shit. My pulse flutters as I wrap my hand around Keira's bicep, right above her elbow and tug her. "Time to go."

Keira dislodges my hold on her and gestures to Ginny. "We can't just leave her, Maeve. She's seen our faces."

"She caught the end of my blade. She's as good as dead," I murmur.

Keira stares at me for a beat before looking at Ginny. She stomps over to her and crouches down so they're eye-level. "I'm sparing your life today. Don't forget that, or I'll make what happened here today look like fucking playground politics, aye?"

Ginny laughs again, this painful, watery sound. "Bitch,

please. We both know I'll never make it. Besides, it's her that spared me, not you."

"Aye, she's kinder than I am, too. Something else to keep in mind." Keira delivers the threat with such ease, pride pierces my heart like a sharp lance.

A sprout of warmth blossoms in my chest, bolstered by her devotion to me and our sisterhood.

Groaning from below steals my attention from whatever else Keira says. I twist to look behind me in time to see Santorini roll onto his back.

Holy shit. It really is him.

I bend down and pat his cheek a little. "Nico? Wake up!"

Keira's next to me in an instant, gun aimed at his head. "Who's this now?"

I look up at her, beseeching her with my gaze. I don't want to say too much, not while we're in the open. "He's coming with us."

"The fuck he is! I don't know him, and I can't carry him and help you," she snaps, shifting her weight from foot to foot.

The smoke steadily fills the air as the fire rages inside the church. Crackling and popping form a crescendo, and I tense, waiting for the moment it caves in.

We cannot be here when that happens. Urgency pounds against my bones, commanding we move. I shift and adjust my weight.

"Then I'll fucking carry him." My voice has more bite than I intended, and I close my eyes for a second. I blink them open and push to my feet. "He's coming with us, Keira. I'm not asking."

She exhales a big breath and glares at me. Her amber-colored eyes are so hard, they remind me of the marbles we used to play with as a kid. I had this one that looked like a tiger's eye—amber with a black almost split in it, like a stripe.

If I think of myself as a tiger, then Keira is a lion. Capable of stealth and brute force. Destructive, intense, viciously loyal.

She doesn't censor herself, and she's always going to choose the most impactful retribution, which usually includes violence.

I think it's one of her most endearing quirks.

"Seriously?" she snaps, cocking her head to the side.

"Yes, and we're wasting time now."

Her gaze ping pongs between my eyes, her eyes narrowing and her mouth flattening. I see the moment she cracks. The tension slowly bleeds from her face but her shoulders never lose their taut frame.

She sighs. "Goddammit, Maeve. Stay right here."

She hands me her gun with one hand and slips another gun free with the other. I don't even know where she hides all of her weapons, but I knew she had at least two guns on her.

She never leaves home without them, like a security blanket for a toddler. I wouldn't be surprised if she has three more weapons hidden on her person right now.

I let the familiar weight of a gun in my hand settle my mounting anxiety, even if only fractionally. I like my blade better, but I've already made that mistake once today. And I'd like to think of myself as a fast learner. "Where are you going?"

"To get the car. I'll be back in a couple minutes." Her voice is clipped but not unkind as she watches my index finger settle over the trigger as I hold the gun to my side.

"Okay," I say with a decisive nod.

"Don't fucking move until you see me. Shoot anyone else who wanders over here. These people are not our allies, aye?" She points with each sentence. At me, then toward the street, and finally, toward the church.

"Aye, I got it. You don't need to baby me." There's no frustration in my voice, more like a neutral reminder.

I know she's not doing it for any other reason than to soothe her own anxiety, but I wish she'd just hurry up and go already. We're wasting time talking about shit both of us already know. After all, I'm the one who taught her the rules.

"I'll be right back," she assures me again.

"I know, Keira. Go already before someone else comes." There's a little heat in my voice, enough to light a fire under her.

She nods and spins on the ball of her foot and dashes back the way she came—over the piles of broken bricks, around the retaining wall, and disappears from sight.

I exhale, my cheeks puffing out with air. I can hear my pulse thrumming loudly in my ears, increasing with every second the sirens get louder. We don't have much time now.

Soft groaning hits my ears, and I squat closer to him. "Nico? Can you hear me?"

His long black lashes flutter a few times before he opens his eyes. Dark brown eyes peer at me beneath a furrowed brow. I was so caught up in the moment back in Las Vegas that I didn't have time to appreciate how beautiful his eyes are. A deep, rich shade of brown with flecks of whiskey-brown and a hazel starburst.

I scan him for injuries. There's a small laceration above his eyebrow, but there's nothing else visible, at least on his face.

"*Piccola seduttrice*, is that really you?" His voice is low, gravelly and rough.

I smooth his hair off his face and bite back the small smile. "Aye, it's me. Can you stand?"

He blinks, a slow exaggerated lowering of his lids. When he looks at me again, his pupils are dilated. "I must be dead, right? And you—" He reaches toward me, his fingers stopping shy of touching the strands of hair that came loose. "You're a figment of my imagination. You're not even real." The corners of his mouth turn down as he focuses on my hair hanging off my shoulder.

Feminine laughter splits the air, the maniacal edge raising the hair on the back of my neck. I glance over my shoulder to see Ginny with her head tipped back, caustic laughter spilling from her lips.

"Oh my fucking god. This is amazing. You let the Las Vegas scum knock you up, didn't you? God, you really are a whore."

I don't say anything, just watch as her mirth tapers off into a coughing fit. Once I'm satisfied she's not going to run her mouth again, I look back at Santorini. Only his eyes are closed again.

Panic seizes my chest with an iron fist, and I gently shake his shoulders. "No, no, no. Wake up. I can't carry you."

He doesn't open his eyes, but a groan falls from his mouth. It's honestly music to my ears, second only to the sound of tires crunching on gravel.

That better be Keira, or our body count is going to go up.

7

NICO

I KNOW this plan of my brother's was held together on a wing and a prayer, but I thought he'd have more fucking sense in that big brain of his. Only a fucking idiot runs into a burning building.

I hear the wail of a siren in the distance. I wouldn't say that I'm nervous exactly, but I am fucking uncomfortable. I don't like executing plans without contingency plans. And this half-assed plan of Rome's was thrust upon me at the eleventh hour.

I have no idea what he's doing.

Was running in part of the plan? Why does he need to find the bride? Did he ditch his clothes or is he wearing them under that gold robe?

And where the fuck is Tommy?

I shake out my hand in some vain attempt at shaking some of my irritation loose. This is why I make the plans. Following isn't part of my fucking DNA and neither is being left in the dark.

I command the dark like it's my own personal Crayola color.

I give him five more seconds. Five more breaths to come out before I drag him out by the collar of that ridiculous robe.

Sweat beads on my brow as it furrows. My muscles pull tight, preparing to dive into motion in an instant.

I can't imagine why he's shouting about the bride. Women were never the targets, so she's a nonissue.

Surprisingly, once the Milano men started hitting the ground, the women fled. There wasn't nearly as much wailing fanfare as I expected. Either they know the score, or they weren't sorry to be free of the men in their lives.

Knowing the connected lifestyle and their enemies, I'd guess probably a bit of both.

I inhale and trap the breath in my lungs as I strain to hear the sirens. I can't tell if they're getting louder or my imagination is playing tricks on me. Either way, I've had enough of my brothers fucking around.

First, I need to get Rome. Then we'll find Tommy, and the three of us can get back to Las Vegas and move forward with our plans.

It's time for our ascension.

A renewed sense of purpose invigorates me. I toss the gun that I used in the car next to me. My hands steady as I douse the fabric upholstery with lighter fluid. One swipe from my thumb across the little metal wheel, and a small flame dances in front of me. I toss it on the front seat and watch it catch instantly.

A gunshot cracks through the air. Panic traps the air in my lungs, only jump-started by my racing heart. I can't tell where it came from, not over all the moaning and groaning from the church and the siren that gets louder with every second.

"What the fuck?" I whisper harshly.

Dismissing the car on fire next to me, I heard toward the front of the church. I pull my favorite gun from the back of my pants and carry it at my side, my index finger hovering over the trigger.

My gaze swivels from one side to the other for the longest

thirty feet of my life. I assure myself that it was probably Tommy taking care of a straggler. But Rome still hasn't come out, and something is off. I can taste it in the air.

My brothers can handle themselves just fine, but I'm feeling twitchy as fuck.

And I'm fucking done with this plan.

I pick up my pace and cross the courtyard in a blink. Wiping my free hand across my face, my foot hits the bottom stair at the same moment Rome bursts through the doorway.

"Jesus Christ, Rome! Why the fuck did you run into a burning building?"

"I have to find her," he mumbles, scanning the parking lot.

I shake my head a little. "What? We need to get Tommy and get the fuck out of here."

"She's gone," Rome yells, damn near frantic.

"Who?"

"I need my computer. I can track her, I know I can," he says, ignoring my question. His shoulder brushes against me as he sprints through the courtyard.

"Where the fuck are you going?" I jog after him, annoyance prickling my skin as my shoes slam against the cracked concrete. "Hey, wait." I reach out as we turn the corner and grab a fistful of the priest's robe. "Would you just stop for a second and tell me what the fuck is going on?"

He skids to a stop, and I nearly bowl him over. We jerk back in unison as a wave of heat slams into us. My fingers tighten on his robe as I take in the full scope of what happened.

He stills, his body rocking back and then forward again. He glares at me over his shoulder, unconcerned about the flames licking up the side of the building.

"I love you, Nic, but if you don't let go of me right the fuck now, I'm not going to be held responsible for what I do next."

I release him instantly, my mouth parting in surprise. "What the fuck, Rome?"

The hard look doesn't leave his eyes, but he doesn't run away again, so that's something. I'm acutely aware of the sirens bearing down on us, adrenaline sliding up against my skin like one of those innertube tunnel water rides at a water park. It speeds through my body, washing up on the left and then right, heightening my senses.

"I need to find her, Nic."

I shake my head a few times. "The bride?"

"Yes," he says through clenched teeth. "I don't have time to explain, but I'm not leaving her here."

I've only ever seen my brother so intense on a handful of occasions, and the last time was when we found our long lost sisters.

"Alright," I say with a decisive nod. I clap him on the shoulder. "Then let's go find her. Preferably before the cops get here or our day is fucked."

He doesn't respond, taking off and rounding the corner. I'm a step behind him, both of us giving the wall of flames a wide berth. It looks like half the wall got blown out toward the back. I whistle under my breath and side-eye Rome. I didn't realize he was so proficient with explosives, but I guess I shouldn't be surprised. He can do anything he puts his mind to.

"No wonder I couldn't get through. That fire is raging inside the church," he mutters.

The fire feels like a threat but not the biggest one, the pulse of danger radiating everywhere. I scan the small area, looking for the source through the piles of broken bricks and debris.

Rome and I both spot the body at the same time, the jean-clad legs visible around a pile of crumbled concrete and brick.

"Fuck," he curses quietly before jogging toward it.

As soon as I see the dark-haired head face-down on the

ground, I inject my legs with a burst of speed with my heart in my throat. I beat Rome there by three steps, and I'm bending over and wrenching the man over in one breath.

"Oh thank fuck, it's not him," I breathe.

No sign of him here is good. Then I know he'll stay out of trouble if the cops catch up to us. A cough from behind us tears me from my thoughts of Tommy.

I stand up and turn around, gun aimed at the person coughing. A woman sits propped against the retaining half-wall. She clutches her gut, her face pale and sweaty.

Rome stalks toward her. "Did you see a woman back here? Black hair, wedding dress?"

She smiles at him, blood staining her teeth red. "God damn, she really is a whore." Her words are punctuated with a wet coughing laugh.

Rome raises his gun at the same time I lower mine. Who the fuck is this bride he's obsessed with?

"Where'd she go?" he presses.

She tilts her head back against the wall. "And why the fuck would I tell you anything? You're probably with them."

"Them?" I take a step toward her. "Who?"

She switches her gaze to me, her grin growing wide. "Another Santorini? What a fucking lucky day today is."

Rome stalks toward her, pressing the barrel of his gun against her forehead. He applies a little pressure, tipping her chin back. "Tell me where the bride went."

Her eyes deaden. "Or what? I'm already dead." She moves her hand away from her stomach, blood bubbling up right away. She covers her wound quickly.

His finger rests against the trigger. "You're right, I'm going to kill you either way. But if you don't tell me what I want to know, I'll find every person you've ever loved and every person you ever thought you could love, and I'll make sure they suffer the most painful existence before I kill them too."

Outwardly, I remain motionless like my brother delivers death threats every day. But inside I'm looking at him out of the corner of my eye, torn between proud and concerned.

Her eyes fill with angry tears and she glares at Rome. "Yeah, I saw the bride. She took off with her sister. And they took your brother."

"How'd you know who we are?" I ask as Rome puts a little space between his gun and this random woman.

Her shoulders drop as she stares at me. "We were given information that you might make an appearance."

"Who received the information?" I ask while Rome shifts from foot to foot, his impatience palpable.

"The only person who could answer your questions is probably dead." She stares at me knowingly.

Rome pulls the trigger while she's looking at me. Apparently, he had heard enough. He doesn't spare her a glance as he lowers his arm and says, "Let's go. She's not here."

8

ROMEO

"WHERE ARE WE GOING?" Nic asks.

"I don't know," I say, balling up my chasuble and stuffing it in one of the plastic bags in a plastic tote in the trunk. I grab my laptop and jog around the SUV to slide into the passenger seat.

"Should we head north?"

"I don't know." I open my laptop, my knee bouncing with anxiety. Every second, she gets further and further away from me. The thought of that being the last time I see her feels like a third-degree burn in my stomach lining.

"Why the fuck didn't we pick a meeting spot in case shit went sideways? Shit always goes sideways," Nic grumbles.

"I don't know," I answer again, my words curt.

"Well, what the fuck do you know? Because from where I'm sitting, we lost our brother to some mysterious woman, who you still haven't explained."

"What do you want me to say, Nic? That when I saw the bride walking toward me, I forgot that we were there to wipe out an entire line at Vito's request. For the briefest moments, I thought she was walking toward me. Or maybe you want to know that I wish she was."

Nic's quiet as he maneuvers us out of the immediate radius of the church. I pointedly ignore his intrusive stare.

"Who is she?"

There's no point in hiding it from him any longer. He's heard me talk about her in an abstract sort of way for months—years, even. "The Wren."

I brace myself for his judgment, prepared to let it wash off of me like a summer rain. But to my surprise, he only nods.

"So, you've met her before then—in person, I mean."

I nod, my mind already distracted as I try to think of what I can do on my limited access to my normal programs since I only have my laptop. It's bulky and offers only a fraction of the capability as my setup from home. But it's better than nothing, and it's literally the only thing I have right now.

While I can piggyback my setup at home, it takes almost all my laptop's battery to do it. And since I have no way of knowing how long we'll be driving, that's a last resort.

"I thought . . . I thought you were in a relationship or something with the Wren." His cadence is cautious, like he's bracing for me to blow up.

I grit my teeth. "We are. Or we were. I don't know, man. It's confusing how it ended. I was always going to find her again. I just didn't expect it to be like this."

"But she was going to marry someone else? How does that come into play?"

I stop what I'm doing and glare at my brother. "I don't fucking know, okay? We didn't exactly have a chance to exchange stories tonight before she ran off."

"Well, if you love her, why the fuck didn't you chase after her in the church?" He's incredulous, his right arm hanging in the air, his palm slightly upturned.

Shame wraps around my throat. "I was preoccupied teaching the groom a lesson. And I never said I loved her."

Nic scoffs. "Come on, man. You forget I had front-row seats for the months you obsessed over her. And all the days you spent glued to your phone with that goofy-ass grin on your face. Or how about the time you just fucking ghosted us for four days?"

My shoulders rise with each sentence. "I didn't realize you noticed."

"You're my fucking brother, of course I noticed. Plus, we live together, dipshit."

I sigh. "Yeah, well, I am a dipshit because instead of catching her before she left the church, I beat the shit out of the groom and then shot him."

Nic nods like all of this is completely reasonable. "Alright, so how are you going to find her? According to that woman, she's with Tommy."

I snap my fingers. "Yes, fuck yes. I can track Tommy's phone. I'll have to piggyback off my server at home, but if I can time it right, then it should work," I mutter to myself, already pulling up the necessary windows on my screen. "He has to be on the phone, though."

"What? Can't you track it as-is? I don't understand why he has to be on his phone," Nic grumbles.

He tsks. "I don't have time to explain the complexities of how I altered our phones so they're not instantly trackable to anyone with beginner-level hacking skills."

He huffs and takes a sharp corner. "Seems like you summed it up pretty fucking easily."

"Just call him."

Ringing fills the stifling air of our SUV. It rings out until the voicemail picks up. Nic hangs up and looks over at me. "Now what?"

"Call him again," I snap. My fingers fly across the keyboard of my laptop.

After the fourth time Tommy's voicemail picks up, my frustration boils over at the sound of the automated voice, and I reach over and press the end call button on the dash without taking my gaze from my laptop.

Fuck, this better work. I don't have the time to fly all the way back to Las Vegas just so I can find her.

9

MAEVE

"START TALKING," Keira says from the driver's seat.

I ball up excess fabric from a torn part of my skirt and press it to the back of Santorini's head. He's crammed into the backseat with me, his head on my lap and facing me.

How we even got him in the car is a miracle, honestly. The sirens were ear-splitting by the time Keira pulled up with the SUV. She pulled out of there with thirty seconds to spare, spitting gravel as she gunned it.

Normally, we try to lie low when it comes to the illegal shit we get into. We have a lot of connections in the states for those times where we need a little sway. But we're in Milano territory, and I'm a runaway bride last seen fleeing a burning church. Overall, not great odds.

We've tested the fates enough for one day.

Thank god Keira had the foresight to grab the SUV I stashed a few blocks away. She drove it back to the church before doubling-back to the block over when she realized I wasn't alone.

We could've left it, but considering it has all the things we need to disappear for a while, it just makes our lives a little easier.

I brush Santorini's hair off of his forehead, watching the way his eyes move underneath his closed lids. I don't realize I'm holding my breath until Keira calls my name again.

I meet her gaze in the rearview mirror. "What?"

One of her blonde brows arches. "Why are you looking at him like that?"

My fingers still in his hair, and my shoulders settle lower. "It's him. Nico Santorini."

The car jerks to the right before Keira centers us. "I'm sorry, but did you just say that Nico Santorini, the same Nico Santorini that you were supposed to poison but ended up fucking instead, is sitting in your lap right now?" She whisper-shouts the word fucking like we're pre-teens gossiping in my bedroom during a sister sleepover.

My shoulders hike up, along with my eyebrows. "Yes?" It comes out as a question.

"Why was he there? Was he stalking you?"

A police car with rotating lights and a blaring siren flies past us on the opposite side of the freeway, probably heading toward the church. But my mind snags and promptly fractures when realization dawns.

I twist in my seat as much as I can to look out of the rearview window. I was so consumed with not dying that I completely forgot about him.

My stomach churns, acid splashing along the sides and making me feel like I'm going to be sick. I face forward and squeeze my eyes shut, tight enough until they ache.

The need to demand my sister turn the car around and go back for him hits me with such force and it hurts. I'm used to denying my wants for the betterment of everything and everyone else, but I can't just brush this away.

Romeo—my Romeo—was there. The man I despaired over

leaving and never seeing again was at the church that just practically exploded.

And I shouldn't have fucking left without him. My eyes burn with a fresh wave of emotion.

I don't understand why he was there or why he was dressed as a Catholic priest. There's no way he's an actual priest, given the many, many sinful acts we did together.

No, I think to myself, shaking my head. No way. There must be another reason.

But that's not the worrisome part. The question that circles around and around inside my head is: why were Romeo and Santorini at the church?

My brain aches as excuse after excuse tumbles around my head like dryer balls in an empty dryer.

I settle back in my wedged position between the seat and the door and breathe through my mouth to ease the sting. "Do we know where we're going yet?"

"Aye. Rosie called, said she—"

"You told Rosie?" My voice is shrill.

"Aye!" Keira snaps. "We needed the help, and someone needed to know what really went down in case Da reaches out."

"Oh, fuck," I say with a sigh. In all the commotion, I'd forgotten about Da and his role in everything. It seems I've forgotten about a lot of things in the last couple of hours. "Oh, fuck. Have you talked to Ava? Goddammit, Keira, what did I do?"

She meets my gaze in the rearview mirror. "What you had to." She focuses back on the road. "The girls will understand. And as far as Da is concerned, it was a terrible, freak accident at the church." She pauses and looks at me again. "One that might've even claimed your life too. If you want."

I falter, blinking slowly a few times. "I hadn't thought of that."

"We have time. Not a lot, but enough for us to make a plan. We'll worry about that after we see the doctor."

I'm not used to being taken care of, and this is the second time in as many months that Keira has seamlessly stepped into the role. It's a little unnerving but not unpleasant. Mostly I'm grateful to not have to make all the decisions right now.

"How did she find a doctor?"

"Rush vouched for Matteo Rossi, and Rossi vouched for Dr. Clemente."

I nod a few times. I don't trust Rossi like I trust Rush—and I don't even trust him all that much. But in this, I'll take his word for it. He knows better than anyone what happens to those that cross us.

"How far away?" We've been driving for what feels like forever, but I know that's my anxiety talking and not the clock. I bet it's only been ten minutes, tops.

"Not far now. Maybe another seven miles or so."

I lean back against the headrest and let myself rest for a few minutes. My eyes burn behind my closed lids. The bitter smell of smoke lingers in the car—from my dress to my hair to Santorini in my lap. We're all coated in the scent of destruction.

My hurried plan from earlier can still work, I just need to fine-tune it.

Later. After I talk to the doctor.

Ten minutes later, Keira pulls into a small parking lot. It wraps around one of those houses-turned-businesses. It's a two-story Cape Cod with gray painted wood siding and black shingles. A bright yellow door sits squarely in the middle of the house with big double-hung windows on either side.

A row of squat bushes wrap around the whole house, trimmed within an inch of their lives. It's a little alarming how perfectly square the top and sides are.

"How do we know this person again?" I don't bother concealing my skepticism.

Keira swings the SUV into a parking space on the side of the building, one spot away from a matching yellow side door.

"Stay here." She shifts the car into park and pushes open her door before I even process her request.

If I wasn't pinned to the seat by over two hundred pounds of tattooed, muscled man, I'd jump right out of the car and nudge her behind me. But I can't muster up enough energy required to shift him off of me and dash after her.

She pounds on the door three times with a closed fist. It sways open outward, something they must've changed when they converted the house from a residential home to a commercial business.

I watch my sister's mouth move but I can't read her lips at this angle. She takes a step back and the door closes once more. She waits a beat before jogging over to my car door.

I pull the lever and open the door, doing my best not to fall out of the car. I'd been half-leaning against the door and back-seat the entire ride.

"You okay?" Keira asks.

"Are you okay? Who was that?" I jerk my chin toward the door.

"Joseph Clemente. He went to get a wheelchair for this one." She nods at Santorini in my lap.

If I ignore the head wound, he almost looks sleeping. He's too rugged of a man to ever be considered soft, but I'd be willing to bet that he would loathe it if I called him soft. I adjust my hold on the fabric, keeping the pressure on his wound. "Don't you think he should've woken up by now?"

"Do I look like a fucking doctor, Maeve?"

My neck twinges from how quickly I look at her.

61

She sighs and closes her eyes briefly. When she opens them again, she nods. "I'm sorry, okay?"

"It's fine." I lift his head off of my lap and try to scoot out of the seat. This dress is big and cumbersome and fucking stuck somewhere. I yank on the skirt, ignoring the sound of fabric ripping. The sooner I get out of this dress, the better. "Let's just get him inside, aye?" I say around a grunt.

Keira reaches over me and grasps a handful of the fabric. We pull in unison, and two tugs later, the fabric rips, and I'm free.

"Shit," I grumble, my palm covering my shoulder where it slammed into the window.

"Here, let me help," a masculine voice says from behind us. I look through the darkened window and see an older man pushing a wheelchair.

I step back and let him and Keira maneuver Santorini into the wheelchair. My heart skips a beat when he groans and grumbles, his eyes fluttering open.

"Where am I?" Santorini's head lolls back a little.

"Follow me," the man says, pushing the wheelchair.

Keira waits for me to take a step before she closes the car doors and follows me into the building.

10

MAEVE

"WHERE AM I?" Santorini asks as he pushes up from the wheelchair.

"Please stay seated," the doctor says, placing a hand on his shoulder. "We're going to get you checked out."

Santorini stills and shakes his head. "Nah, I'm good."

"You arrived at my practice unconscious. It's my duty to make sure you're not hurt," the doctor says.

I wait in the hall as the doctor wheels him into the last open door on the right. The lights in the hallway are dim, and I don't hear the low murmuring of anyone else. Hopefully, we're alone.

"Fine, but let's make it quick, yeah, doc? I got people waiting on me. And where the hell is my phone?" Santorini's voice gets quieter the further the doctor wheels him in.

I take the room across the hall, wandering around the perimeter. It's a spacious exam room with three chairs along the wall opposite the door, a privacy screen in the corner, and the classic sink and cabinet combo along one wall. It looks almost exactly like every doctor's office I've ever seen.

A fact that should ease some of Keira's worry. But judging by the way she's shifted so she's in front of me, I'd say it did little to assuage her.

I have to roll my lips inward to stifle the smile. She's protecting me, and I fucking love her all the more for it.

I'd already decided I was going to get her a new tropical flower, but now I kind of want to get her a whole greenhouse full of her favorite tropical plants. Maybe a flamingo flower or a bird of paradise.

The doctor strolls into the room and closes the door behind him. I'd put Dr. Clemente in his fifties. Close to six feet tall with salt and pepper hair cropped short and styled to the side. He's wearing a black quarter-zip pullover and black slacks.

Honestly, he looks exactly how I'd expect an on-call doctor with ties to the mafia would look. I only hope for his sake that he's as good as Rush said he is.

I take a step toward him, nerves writhing in my belly like a nest of snakes. "Is he okay?"

He nods. "I'll need to run a few tests, but he should be fine."

I cock my head to the side. "Why did it take him so long to wake up?"

He offers me a ghost of a smile. Thankfully for him, it doesn't feel condescending, or I'm sure Keira would introduce him to her favorite weapon. "I'm sorry, but I'm not at liberty to discuss another patient with you. No matter who you know."

I dip my chin and hold his gaze. "Alright."

"Dr. Clemente, is it?" Keira asks, stepping in front of me completely and folding her arms across her chest.

He inclines his head. "When Mr. Rossi called, he only mentioned the girl."

"Consider this a change in plans. You're going to check her out first, then him." Keira shifts and lets her arms fall to her sides. I don't need to look down to know she's pulling her favorite gun from the back of her pants. She casually holds it at her side, her index finger resting along the side of the gun, just a twitch away from the trigger.

Dr. Clemente arches a brow at her obvious display. "It'll cost you extra."

"Fine," she says through gritted teeth.

"And tell Mr. Rossi this makes us square for my niece," Dr. Clemente says.

Keira shakes her head before he even finishes talking. "I don't get involved in the Five Families business. You'll have to take that up with Rossi."

He inclines his head and pivots to face me. "Alright. Now, want to tell me what happened?"

"It's better if you don't know the specifics."

I'm not going to incriminate myself by spilling all the details. I don't care who vouched for him or how good he is, I don't know him. Which means I don't trust him with the truth.

Well, almost all the truth. If I wasn't sick with worry about the baby, I wouldn't even be here right now. Distracted people make stupid mistakes, and I'm not in a position to make any kinds of missteps right now.

He tips his head to the side. "Miss . . ."

I only arch a brow at his fishing. "Let's keep names out of this, aye?"

He sighs and raises his hands up, palms facing the air. "Look, I don't know how you expect me to treat you if you won't tell me what happened."

I slide my tongue across the back of my teeth, debating on how to put this.

"There was a small . . . explosion of sorts, and I think I have a concussion," I hedge.

"She's pregnant," Keira blurts.

I cut her a look but she's unrepentant. "Frankly, it's why we're here. As you can see, my sister is seemingly fine, but we need to be sure."

Dr. Clemente inclines his head. "Alright. How far along are you?"

I shift from foot to foot and do the math in my head. "Not long. Maybe ten weeks?"

"And you've had it confirmed with a blood test by your doctor?"

I bristle a little, even though there's no judgment in his tone. "No, I just found out."

"Let's start with an over-the-counter test and then some bloodwork," he says.

"No bloodwork," Keira and I say at the same time.

"Do you have a portable ultrasound? Or one of those Doppler things to listen to the heartbeat?" Keira asks.

If she feels my gaze on the side of her face, she doesn't show it. I didn't think my sister knew anything about that kind of stuff, but clearly I was wrong.

"Let's move to one of the patient rooms at the other end of the hall. We have a few things in there for expecting mothers," Dr. Clemente says.

FIFTEEN MINUTES, a change of clothes, and one positive pregnancy test later, I'm sitting on the examination chair. My black leggings are rolled down low on my abdomen, exposing the area for the handheld doppler.

Dr. Clemente stepped out to give me privacy, and presumably, to check on Santorini. I'm not really sure what he's going to do. It's not like they have an MRI here or whatever else he would need.

Just when I feel my impatience rising, I hear the synthesized tune of the chorus of a Hamilton song. I look around for Dr. Clemente's phone, maybe he left it on the counter in the corner or something.

The only thing on any of the counters are boxes of blue latex gloves.

My sister pulls out a phone from her back pocket and stares at it, her lips pursed to the side. Huh. I don't think I've ever heard her ringtone before. She's more of a vibrate-only kind of woman, much like all of my sisters.

My brows dip lower the longer she takes to answer the call. "What's wrong?"

She turns the phone around and shows me the screen. It reads "Nic" at the top.

"Since when did you exchange numbers with him? Honestly, when did you even have time for that?"

She takes a step toward the bed just as the call times out. "I didn't. This isn't my phone—it's his."

"Whose? The doctor's?"

"No, Santorini's," she says just as the phone starts ringing again.

"Okay," I drag the word out. "I don't know why you took his phone, but what's the big deal?"

"I took it because I don't trust him." She raises her hand higher, the one holding the phone. "Before you say anything, yes I know you fucked him in his house. But do you know him enough to trust him? To trust him with our lives?"

The words I was so sure of ten seconds ago get trapped in my throat. I don't know how to answer that. There's a certain level of trust simply because I was able to infiltrate his home—it gives me reassurance almost, despite the fact that I didn't look around much.

I can't say for certain that I trust him, and definitely not with our lives.

I also can't deny that a small speck of me desperately wants to trust him. What if he is the father? Am I really going to raise a child with someone I don't trust?

"Exactly," my sister says slowly with a deliberate nod. "Plus, Nic seems like it would be short for, say, I don't know, Nico."

"Or it could be anyone named Nic or Nicolas." The ringing ends and immediately starts again. "Why don't you answer it and see?"

Keira slides the bottom bar to accept the call, and I hear voices immediately. She pulls the phone away from her ear instantly. Whoever this Nic is, they're yelling like crazy.

"Tommy, thank fuck. Where are you?"

11

MAEVE

I SUCK in a sharp breath and trap it in my lungs, watching the phone like it's going to sprout horns and suddenly start talking.

The person on the phone pitches his voice louder still. "Tommy? Can you hear me? Goddammit."

"Did they just say—"

"No." Keira interrupts me and ends the call. Her eyes are wide, the whites tinged pink from the smoke or the stress of the day. I can only imagine how bloodshot my own are.

We look at each other, and I'm sure my eyes are as wide as hers. Neither one of us speaks. The phone rings again, the song piercing the unstable bubble of unspoken thoughts formed around us.

Her thumb hovers over the accept button. I should tell her to answer it again. It's on the tip of my tongue, but I can't shove the words past my teeth.

The phone stops ringing, and Keira blinks. She flicks the button on the side, silencing it.

The silence grows once more. Thicker, louder than the electronic version of whatever song that was.

I clear my throat. "Why did you hang up?"

Her fingers tighten around the phone, her knuckles turning white. "I don't know."

"Okay." I nod like that makes perfect sense. Like it's not out of character for either one of us to let something like that go. "Give it to me then." I hold out my hand, palm up, and wiggle my fingers.

I swallow roughly. I don't know if I have it in me to unravel another mystery right now, no matter how simple it might be. Fate doesn't really give a shit though, and she dishes out problems and hurdles with abandon.

But fate also gave me sisters. Four of the best goddamn people in the world.

I see the refusal on her face before she opens her mouth. And I might let myself feel the shame of it later, but I already know I'm not going to push her on this. Not right now.

A knock on the door saves us both.

"Come in," Keira calls.

I observe my sister as she watches the doctor wheel in a portable ultrasound machine. I can't put my finger on why, but everything about the phone call seems off. Well, more unusual than any part of this already unprecedented day, at least.

Maybe it's not just me who's afraid to find out why someone named Nic called Santorini's phone and called him Tommy.

"You found it, then," she murmurs, hovering over his shoulder as he parks it on my right.

"I did. But I have to warn you: without bloodwork to confirm conception dates, I'm not sure that we'll be able to hear anything." He holds a hand up to ward off whatever interjections from my sister. "But that doesn't necessarily mean there's anything wrong. These doppler wands only really work best when you're at least ten weeks along. However, we do have the option of a transvaginal—"

"No," my sister and I reply at the same time.

I know enough to know that there's no way I'm letting some random doctor Rush second-handedly vouched for get up close and personal with me like that. The relationship a woman has with her gynecologist is cultivated over time, not something hastily done in a back alley deal.

Dr. Clemente holds up his hands. "Just offering you all the options."

"I appreciate that, but let's try listening first." I scoot back further on the exam table, adjusting my weight on the hard cushion. My hip aches from sitting in this position, and I curb the twitching desire to get up and shake my sore muscles out.

"Of course." Dr. Clemente nudges a swivel rolling stool with the tip of his boot, stopping it before it hits the exam table. He adjusts the height using the lever on the side before he sinks into the seat.

Keira slips a phone from her back pocket. A frown tugs her lips downward as she stares at the screen for a moment, and my heart thickens in my chest.

"Are you going to answer it now?"

She flips it around so I can see it's her phone. "A text from Rosie. She's checking in."

"Oh okay." My anxiety doesn't lessen as I watch her thumbs fly across the screen with a response. "Is it still ringing? The other phone?"

"Nah, it's fine." Keira flashes me a tight-lipped smile and stuffs her phone in her back pocket once more. She folds her arms across her chest and stares at the doctor.

"Well? We're on a tight timeline here, doc. Can we pick up the pace a little?"

Her reminder of our predicament is a necessary if unwelcome one. This isn't how I ever envisioned finding out I'm pregnant. I mean, what the hell am I going to say to him or her one day?

Sorry, love, Mum got knocked up by either our kind of enemy who your grandda contracted me to marry or a total stranger. And I didn't find out until the day your aunt Keira blew up a church so I could escape the other wedding I was contracted to be in.

I huff out a breath. Even my subconscious thinks it sounds ridiculous.

"Alright, shall we get started?" Dr. Clemente asks as he presses some buttons and pulls a box of blue latex gloves from a shelf on the portable ultrasound machine.

Keira pulls a phone from her back pocket once more. The skin around her eyes crinkles as she narrows her gaze on the screen. Almost as if she can sense my worry, she flashes me the screen without looking up. It's a photo of our sister's smiling face.

She swipes to answer it. "Hang on, Rosie." She presses a button and holds the phone to her shoulder as she walks around the exam table.

The paper crinkles underneath my weight as I shift to sit up, and I cringe. The noise isn't as bad as nails on a chalkboard, but it's closer to it than it isn't. "What's going on?"

"I need to talk to Rosie, and unless you want her to find out about this"—she gestures with the phone to my exposed abdomen—"I'm going to take this outside."

I pull my bottom lip between my teeth and let go. "You didn't tell her about . . ."

"I told her you needed medical attention that couldn't wait for our next move. Here, take this." She holds out her favorite gun, the one she hasn't put down since we got in here.

"Is this really necessary?" I slide it from her hand, the cool metal against my clammy palms some kind of sign. Whether it's a good omen or bad remains to be seen.

She pins me with a deadpan stare. "Shoot anyone who walks in here—including your paramour over there." She jerks her head toward the door and pauses, her gaze flicking over my shoulder for a second. "And the good doctor if he moves wrong."

I roll my eyes and grasp the gun more firmly. "You act like I can't take care of myself."

"Humor me, then." Her words should be teasing, but my sister delivers them with intensity that doesn't feel even remotely amusing.

I sigh and twist my lips to the side. "Fine, fine. I'll shoot Dr. Clemente if he brandishes the doppler wand like a weapon."

She nods twice, the motion swift and harsh. "Good. I'll be right back."

I watch as Keira moves around the exam table, bringing the phone to her ear once more as she leaves. She doesn't close the door all the way, something I'm sure she did intentionally. No doubt so she could hear my cries for help. As if the doctor really is going to hurt me.

"Ready?"

His voice startles me, snapping my focus to him. I side-eye the machine next to me. I can only see an assortment of buttons and knobs, the screen angled away from me.

I settle back, keeping the gun clutched tight in my hand on the side away from him. I roll my head toward him, ignoring the way the scrunching sounds extra loud in my ear.

"Walk me through it first."

"Very well." He inclines his head toward me. "First, I'm going to put some ultrasound gel on your lower abdomen here," he says, pointing a blue-gloved hand at the place between my hip bones. "Then we'll use this to try to pick up a heartbeat."

I blink a few times, my skin feeling prickly all over. "And the screen? Can we see the baby?"

"Let's take a listen first. If it's too early to hear the heartbeat this way, we can try a transvaginal ultrasound and use the screen."

"Fine." I don't bother reminding him that he hasn't earned the level of trust for that.

"Alright, this will be a little cold." He squeezes a dollop of ultrasound gel next to my hip bone.

I flinch at the temperature, despite his warning. That gel feels like it's stored in the refrigerator.

I bounce my gaze between his gloved hand dragging the doppler wand thing across my skin to his face. He doesn't meet my gaze, and my anxiety swells.

"Well?" I snap.

It's a ruse, but he doesn't know that. I'm not angry. Impatient, sure. Scared? Absolutely.

This is it. This is one of those defining moments in my life. This entire day is going to be one of those moments.

There will be a before and an after, and I will be irrevocably changed regardless.

"Just a moment." He presses a few buttons with his free hand, twisting one of the knobs a little. His other hand slows down, pausing on one spot slightly off-center.

Another keystroke, and volume erupts from the machine next to me. A rhythmic sort of sound.

Swoosh-swoosh. Swoosh-swoosh. Swoosh-swoosh.

I hold my breath at the unmistakable sound of a heartbeat.

12

MAEVE

OH MY GOD.

Oh my god.

My eyes flash open, and I have to blink a few times at the sharp white light. I honestly don't even remember closing them. My gaze flies to my abdomen, the spot the doppler wand rests on.

"Could this somehow be my heartbeat?" I work hard to control the tremor in my voice.

"No, this is much too fast and loud to be your heartbeat." His tone is gentle, kind.

I look at him only to find him already staring at me. I swallow around the lump in my throat. "You're sure it's the baby?"

"I'm sure. Congratulations are in order. Baby's heart rate is perfect. While I can't give you an exact date without a more advanced ultrasound and bloodwork, I can say with reasonable certainty that your earlier estimation was probably right."

He slides the wand to the side, and the heartbeat gets quieter. My hand flies out to grasp his wrist before I even remember thinking it.

"I want to listen for a little bit longer. Please."

A small smile plays around the corners of his mouth. "Of course."

Time slips through my fingers like sand as I sit under harsh fluorescent lights in this unfamiliar office. I get lost in the quick, steady thump-thump, thump rhythm. I let myself spiral, just a little bit. Imagining a toddler teetering around a Christmas tree and ripping open presents, imagining laying in the fields of my grandda's backyard with a little girl.

Tears well in the corners of my eyes, and I shut my lids tight. Closing my eyes always heightens my other senses, or maybe it's one of those psychological things. Like when Mum used to tell us to turn the music down in the car so she could see. What she really meant was that she was trying to concentrate.

Thoughts of my mum send a spear of longing straight through my chest. It's an acute agony, like the throbbing of a wound that never healed properly. It's always there, but some days it flares up into something almost unmanageable.

She should be here with me, telling me everything is going to be okay. Reassuring me that I'm not alone.

I can almost feel her hand ghosting along the back of mine. As if the desperate plea from a child for their mother is strong enough to bend the very fabric of space and time.

For a split second, I believe in the supernatural.

The weight of someone grabbing my free hand is startling. My eyes spring open, a smile stretching across my face as I imagine the look on my sister's face.

Only it's not my sister standing next to me, jaw slack and looking worse for wear.

Shock steals my voice as I stare into the familiar dark brown eyes of Santorini—or whatever the hell his name is. I vividly remember the way those eyes of his captured my attention. The intensity in his gaze as he thrusted upward inside of me in these slow, deliberate strokes.

It's the reason I'm sitting in this office today.

Maybe.

It's one of the two possible reasons.

Three butterfly bandages hold the gash on the side of his head together, a thick layer of something smeared across it. His shirt is ripped by the collar and a bruise is already starting to bloom under his left eye.

And still, he takes my breath away.

"Are you alright?"

I don't know who's more surprised by my question: me or him. I don't know what I was going to say, something about who he is or what he was doing at the church. But definitely not something that shows such . . . care like that.

He blinks, those unique hazel starbursts of his dim in this washed-out overhead light. He flips my hand over and presses his palm to mine.

"Am I dead?"

I cock my head to the side. "What? No."

His brows lower over his eyes and his lips twist to the side. "Unless this is part of it, which would make sense." His thumb sweeps across the sensitive skin on my wrist.

I shake my head, the wrinkled paper beneath my head muted somehow. "I don't understand."

"If I'm in hell, then all of this"—he makes a circle in the air with the index finger of his free hand—"makes sense. You were the last thing I remember seeing before waking up here. But that's not surprising. I haven't been able to get you out of my head since the first time we met."

He pauses, his gaze deliberately dropping from my eyes. It cuts an intentional path down my body, stopping on my exposed stomach and abdomen.

"But this." His right hand hovers between my hip bones, a slight tremble. "This is surprising."

Dr. Clemente clears his throat and removes the doppler wand. "I think I better give you two some privacy to—"

Quicker than any viper I've ever seen, he pulls a gun from out of nowhere and points it at Dr. Clemente's head. "We're not done here. Put it back."

"What are you doing?" I lean on my elbows and push to sit up.

"Lay back down, *dolcezza*." His tone is so starkly different with me, softer and smoother. The kind of tenor you reserve for someone precious. I've only ever been spoken to with such reverence one other time from one other man.

The same man I just saw wearing a priest's robes and officiating my arranged marriage.

I lick my lips and try to gather my thoughts, but the idle way he's sweeping his thumb in a pattern across the bottom of my palm is distracting.

Name, we need his name, Maeve. Get it together, I chastise myself.

I clear my throat. "He's right. We have some other things to discuss. Like who you are." I'm proud of how even my voice sounds, considering this verifiable stranger is holding a gun on the doctor next to me. It's not even the gun, not really.

Guns don't scare me, but unpredictable people with guns do.

He looks at me but doesn't pull his aim from Dr. Clemente. His brows sink low over his eyes in stark confusion. "You don't you remember me?"

"Of course I remember you." I want to stuff the earnest words back in my mouth as soon as they leave my lips. I don't know why I'm so eager to appease him. Something about the way his face fell instantly tugged at my heart without any preamble.

"Good," he murmurs, his face settling into something neutral, guarded even. "Because you've been haunting my every waking thought for months."

My breath catches. It's not just his admission but the way he said it. The conviction and unmistakable truth ringing from each syllable that fell from his plush lips.

Focus, Maeve. Fucking focus, I scold myself.

I blink and glance over his shoulder before meeting his gaze again. "Tell me your name."

His lips pull up on the right. "You once told me you knew exactly who I was."

"I thought I did. But maybe I was wrong." I don't know why I'm tiptoeing around the question except that I want him to say it first.

I saw this documentary about leading once. It's this theory that if you ask the right questions, eventually, the person you're talking to will give you the answer you want to hear. Some people subconsciously use context clues or they pick up on the answer from the leading question.

He shakes his head a few times, these small, quick jerks back and forth. "You called out my name when you came all over my cock. I'll never forget that sound."

I roll my lips inward for a moment. It's an unconscious movement, my body is already trying to soothe the mounting anxiety in my gut. Like my very skin and veins and heart are preparing my brain for something. "What's your first name?"

His body freezes then. A stiffening and tightening of every muscle. "Tommaso."

I inhale in a sharp breath as my vision narrows on him, the edges becoming a dark blur.

"What?" The word falls from my lips in a broken whisper. Nervousness flutters in my gut. and I can physically feel my eyes widen past the point of comfort. "I don't understand," I murmur.

I wrack my brain for any information I know about him from Rosie's dossier on the Santorinis. But information on them has always been scarce.

His gaze narrows as it flicks all over my face. "Who did you think I was?"

I feel it then. This rolling, curling fog of danger. It crawls along the floor and climbs up his legs, surrounding us both.

"Nico Santorini."

A muscle in his jaw flutters as he clenches it. "Fucking figures," he mutters. "Now I know I'm dead, because this is fucking hell."

He lets go of my hand, lowers the gun from Dr. Clemente, and steps back all in one coordinated move, like he needs distance from everything—from me.

I should be grateful that he's giving me space. So why aren't I?

Why does it feel like I can't quite get enough air in my lungs?

He scratches the side of his head with the tip of his gun, his gaze firmly fixed on the linoleum floor.

I steal a glance at the doctor, anticipating a barely concealed blubbering mess about to implode. But to my surprise—and relief—he only looks mildly alarmed. He begins to slide the stool he's currently sitting on away from the exam table. It squeaks, the wheels creaking as they roll over a bump.

Tommaso's head whips toward him, aiming the gun in his direction once more. "No, fuck this. If I'm going to be tortured by this fucked-up scenario, then I'm going to steal my moments of peace too. Again, doc. I wanna hear it again."

Dr. Clemente glances at me, and only when I give him a small nod does he roll back to me and resume.

The doctor looks at the screen, Tommaso—god that's going

to take me a minute to get used to calling him that—looks at Dr. Clemente, and I can't take my eyes off of him.

I want to bottle up his expression and pocket it for the rest of my life. I'm not sure if he's the father, and I don't know how I'll ever know until after this baby is here.

We have a mountain of distance between us, peaks of miscommunication and valleys of unfamiliarity.

But this moment is the stuff from movies. I catalog the way his jaw slowly loses tension and his brows unfurl over his eyes. The way his arm lowers until he's no longer holding the doctor at gunpoint.

The fluttering heartbeat floats in the charged space between us. The three of us are quiet as we listen to the tiny life growing inside of me.

My eyes start to burn with unshed tears, the emotion startling in its abruptness. I can't relax exactly, my muscles trembling from too many spikes in adrenaline.

He catches me staring at him, and I don't look away. I'm not ashamed to get caught looking at him. The one and only time I had him was rushed in a dimly lit office. He holds my gaze, looking at me from underneath his lashes.

Surprise jolts my system at the raw vulnerability in his gaze. It's so startlingly different from the resignation and agitation of a few minutes ago. His large hand hovers over me once more, like he's equally desperate and scared to touch me.

"Is it mine?"

13

MAEVE

I LICK MY LIPS, running my tongue over the small split from the fall I took earlier. I don't know how to explain to him that he's not dead, I'm not here to torture him, and he could be the father. But so could a stranger I met at a bar halfway across the country.

"I—"

A loud bang pops the tentative peace between us, stealing whatever was about to tumble from my mouth. I flinch, jumping what feels like a foot off the exam table and dislodging the doppler wand. The gentle whoosh-whoosh cuts off immediately.

I glance over just in time to see Keira use her boot to stop the door from slamming shut in her face. She stands in the doorway with her gun raised and pointed at the man shielding me with his body. Her determined eyes stay on him, almost daring him to make a move. To give her a reason to pull the trigger.

"Get the fuck away from my sister," she snarls.

I sit up with a jolt at the same time Tommaso shifts to his left, placing himself between me and her like a barrier. His body language speaks volumes, and my heart aches a little at the protective gesture. It tugs another string around my heart loose.

I'd wrapped layer after layer of twine around my heart, safeguarding it, after I left Romeo in New York City. It was a calculated move for self-preservation. I knew I wouldn't be able to marry Milano and follow the steps of my carefully laid-out plan if my heart still ached for another.

But then he was at the altar in that church, and for the briefest insane moment, I thought he was there to stop the wedding. To whisk me away because he couldn't bear the thought of me marrying someone who wasn't him.

But that's the private thoughts of a foolish romantic who's watched one too many romcoms recently.

I don't know why Romeo was there, but it wasn't for me.

Just like I still don't know what Tommaso was doing there, but I do know it had nothing to do with me.

And still, my traitorous heart swells when he glares over his shoulder at my sister. My sister would never hurt me, so his protectiveness is misplaced. But he doesn't know that.

He snaps, "You have five seconds to lower your weapon before I make you. Your sister's fucking pregnant."

I rest my hand on his arm, feeling the way he trembles beneath my touch. "It's alright."

"Three seconds," he says, ignoring me.

I change tactics and lean to the side far enough to see Keira. She looks unhinged, eyes wide and face paler than usual. It sounds the alarm bells in my head immediately. "What's wrong?"

"Did you hear me, asshole? I said back the fuck away from my sister."

Okay, so it seems both of them are content to ignore me. I don't know him very well—hell, I don't know him at all outside of the way he feels inside of me—but I understand my sister on a molecular level. So much time spent in high-stakes situations with someone forges an unbreakable connection.

And right now, she's less than a centimeter away from snapping. I don't know what Rosie had to say, but whatever it is freaked her out enough to barge in here with guns blazing.

My heart beats in double time. I tug a couple of soft paper towels from the little box on the ultrasound machine and wipe the gel off with quick movements. "Talk to me, Keira."

Dr. Clemente fades into the background, quite literally crossing the room slowly and pressing his back into the wall to my right.

Her brow furrows as she steals glances at me. Her gaze shifts back to Tommaso too quickly for me to catch her. "No. Not until he moves away from you."

Tommaso shakes his head, a touch of incredulity in his speed. "I'm not going anywhere until you lower your gun."

I exhale quietly, a bone-deep tiredness leeching energy from my body. I wiggle down the exam table, and Tommaso shifts to the left without even looking at me. I roll my eyes even though no one is paying me a second of attention. I slide off the table, and Tommaso takes a step toward me, like he's going to continue to be the barrier between my sister and me.

I arch a brow. "Why don't we all take a step back. No one needs to get hurt."

"You didn't answer me, piccolo seduttrice." He looks across his shoulder at me, murmuring like we're long lovers, "It hasn't been that long since you came into my house—"

"Bullshit." Keira's voice cracks through the air like thunder-snow, loud and icy. "It wasn't your house. You're not Nico Santorini."

Tommaso widens his stance and leans his hip against the corner of the table, close enough that I can feel the heat of his skin against mine. "You're right. I'm Tommaso Santorini, and you're Maeve King's sister."

"What?" I gasp, reeling back.

He turns to face me fully, giving his back to my sister. I hear her swift intake from across the room. In our circles, showing your back to someone is only ever one of two things. An insult because they're not a threat or an act of trust because they wouldn't hurt you.

And I have no idea which of the two he's offering now.

Tommaso shuffles closer until the tips of our boots touch. He smooths my hair behind my ear, his gaze intense and serious. "Did you honestly think I didn't look at the contract before I killed it?"

"I—I don't understand." It's a running theme for me today, and I fucking hate it. I'm usually the one with the answers, the one at the helm of control.

And all I've done is spiral for the last day.

His touch is gentle as he toys with the ends of my hair, weaving the strands through his fingers. "You knew where to find me if you wanted another round."

Another bang sounds in the room, and I flinch for the second time in ten minutes. Tommaso flattens me against the wall in less than a breath, his big body blanketing mine. My palms lie flat against his chest, trapped between the two of us. I have to reason with myself that it's a completely inappropriate time to notice how defined he is or the way his biceps flex as they cage me in.

I crane my neck back as far as possible, but his gaze is over his shoulder.

"What the actual fuck is happening? I swear to god, Clemente, I'm going to fucking ruin you for ratting us out and then I'm going to feed you to my plants."

"Vicious thing, your sister, hm?" There's a hint of pride in his voice that has me pausing. He takes a measured step backward, my hands sliding down his chest. My fingertips dance along the contours of his abs as I pull them away.

I have emotional whiplash from everything already, I'm not

sure I can handle the fallout of my sister turning the doctor into fertilizer.

But fuck it. I'll do what I have to do. I always have.

And when it comes to my sisters, there's nothing I won't do.

Which means I need to stop letting Tommaso shield me from her like she's a threat to me.

I duck around him, and in the next breath, instinct kicks in. I raise my gun, arm steady. I'd forgotten I was still holding it, honestly. But I'm fucking glad I was.

Standing just inside the doorway is a familiar face. One I've only seen once. Even three Long Island Ice Teas in, and I'd still remember a face as perfect as his.

My other one night stand. And the other contender as the father of this baby.

14

MAEVE

"HELLO, BROTHER."

My sexy stranger smirks, the corners of his lips curling up as he cocks his head to the side. He tucks his hands into the pockets of his charcoal trousers and surveys the room. He reminds me of a movie villain, all casual controlled power.

"Brother?" I choke on the word, my vision whiting out for a moment. My brain hurts, sputtering over the snowball of coincidences that smell like duplicity.

The stranger from the bar cocks his head to the side, the smirk slipping from his face. He glances behind me, presumably at his motherfucking brother standing at my back. His gaze narrows, his dark brows creasing over his eyes. "Am I interrupting something." It's not a question.

Tommaso skirts around me, stopping so he's partially blocking me. "Nico. Wasn't expecting to see you here."

My throat tightens and my lips part. It takes me a moment to process what I'm seeing, and I do my best impression of a goldfish for three seconds. My sexy as hell one night stand from

Chicago is the real Nico Santorini. And he just walked into a doctor's office in California.

Tommaso turns his head to the left and glances at me from the corner of his eye. "Are you sure I'm not dead, *dolcezza?*" He says it all so conversationally like we're all just having a casual chat over brunch.

I almost miss the way my sexy stranger—Nico—narrows his eyes into slits.

My mind fractures further when that nickname hits my ears. My breath stutters in my chest as the stupid organ trapped behind my ribs beats harder for it—for him. Betrayal whips against my skin like the sharp blades of grass. At myself. At them. At the fucking fates for all of this.

It's as startling as it is unexpected.

How many surprises and twists can one person take before they simply can't? And what does that look like for me when I reach that point?

Will it be like running into a wall? I'll be left stunned, unable to think of anything other than basic survival.

Or will it be like hurdling off a cliff? And I'll be left a busted, broken version of myself. Until I put everything back together.

"What the fuck is happening?" Keira snarls. Anger drips from her words like poisoned honey, thick and laced with venom.

And a third possibility occurs to me: I might not even hit a proverbial wall or cliff because my sister is going to lose her shit. And one of them will pay the price.

And if I waver for a moment, one single beat of my heart that whispers to just let Keira unleash some of her pent-up rage in this room, then that's a secret I'll take to my grave.

I swallow, shoving all the emotions somewhere in the depths of my consciousness, stuffing them in a closet and locking the door. I can deal with them later. First, I need to get my sister and I out of this room, preferably without her shooting one of them.

Because the fact remains that one of these two strangers in the room fathered this baby.

We're in a draw, the four of us eyeballing one another with varying amounts of distrust. Except for Keira. She's glaring daggers at everyone but me.

And poor Dr. Clemente is muttering something under his breath in Italian, still pressed up against the wall.

Time to go.

"Right, well, as . . . enlightening as this has been. Dr. Clemente, I think it's best if you leave." I jerk my head toward the door, never taking my eye off of Nico.

Danger radiates off of him in waves. It's subtle, like a cheetah lying in wait. But what my sexy stranger doesn't know is that I'm a motherfucking King.

Nico shifts his stance so he's facing the doctor. "Don't you take a fucking step until I tell you, yeah?"

I keep my gun at my side and stalk toward Nico, anger vibrating every inch of my body. I cannot believe this tangled web circumstance we're currently trapped in. "You're not in charge here."

"The fuck I'm not," he snaps at me. His gaze is narrowed and seemingly unflustered as he stares between me and the doctor.

I glance at my feet, the tips of my favorite white boots scuffed from my dance with the church wall earlier today. The absurdity of my entire day catches up to me, and a chuckle bubbles up my throat.

I shake my head a few times and look at Nico from underneath my lashes. I let him view the intent in my eyes. I'm not a malicious person by nature, but I've had enough for one day.

Keira flanks me as soon as she hears my warped laugh. "Oh shit," she mumbles, but her glee belies her words.

"I'm leaving, Nico." I do my best not to sneer his name, but no promises. That closetful of emotions is bursting, my carefully trapped feelings about the situation swelling larger by the second. The wood creaks under the pressure, but still, I power through.

"Wrong," Nico drolls as he steps into my path. His tone suggests he's bored by this whole thing but one glimpse at him, and I know it's all an act. His entire body is thrumming. "You're not going anywhere."

I smile at him then. It's a wild sort of expression, the kind that has to stretch too wide to conceal some of the crazy leaking out. I'm tempted to pull my gun on him and mean it.

"You have no idea who you're talking to, so I'll forgive you. This time. Get out of my way."

He folds his arms across his chest, a smirk tilting up the corner of his mouth. I get a flashback of him sending me that same self-satisfied smug look through the mirror right before he fucked me.

"Cute that you think your little tête-a-tête with my brother has any sway over me."

My mind spins over itself. Curious that he didn't mention how we know each other. More secrets. I tuck that into my back pocket until I need it.

I look over my shoulder at Tommaso. He stands exactly where I left him, his face somehow both blank and pleading. And still so fucking handsome it makes my teeth ache. "Tell your brother to move before my sister embarrasses him."

"Nic," Tommaso hedges.

"Let her go," a new voice commands.

A hand with busted knuckles clamps on Nico's shoulder and tugs him out of the door and to the side.

Romeo's face appears a moment later, just like I knew it would. I'd recognize the sound of his voice anywhere.

Clarity crashes over me with the grace of a rhinoceros. If this were a movie, it'd be a slow-motion flash-reel of previous events.

The Stone Rose Hotel. Nico's office. The coincidental texts

from someone who knew I was the Wren. The canceled marriage contract with Las Vegas. The Red Lion Pub in Chicago. Lainey's surprise party in New York City.

Things I didn't pay enough attention to. Dots I didn't connect.

Fuck me, some of those dots weren't even on my radar as suspicious.

I recall Rosie's initial dossier on the Santorinis, on the three brothers. She couldn't find photos of them, but she did find their names:

Nico, Tommaso, and Romeo Santorini.

Either I've been played or fate has a fucked-up sense of humor.

And I don't believe in coincidences.

I didn't know what my threshold would be, but I've officially reached it. And I lock everything down, wrapping everything in chains and throwing lock after lock to keep it bundled up tight.

I don't waste another second. I need to get the hell out of this room before I scream and do something I'd regret later.

The walls are closing in on me, and I'm two minutes or one more dropped bomb away from my mind splintering in a way that will leave me permanently altered.

I draw my gun up now, pointing it at both of them. "Back up."

Whatever expression is on my face, they don't argue. Romeo pulls back on Nico, and they both take two healthy steps backward, toward the opposite end of the hall.

"Keira." I jerk my chin toward the door, indicating I want her to go first.

"Neither of you deserve her." She pairs her biting opinion with a King glare and rounds the doorway.

"Juliet," Romeo pleads.

I do something stupid then. I've never been the kind of

person who would cut off her nose just to spite her face, but I think if I don't get answers from at least him, I might actually burn the city down on my way out of here.

There's only so much heartbreak and thinly-veiled deception a girl can take.

15

MAEVE

"YOU'RE COMING WITH ME." I curl my fingers in the front of Romeo's black hoodie and tug him toward me, keeping the gun aimed at him and walking backward down the hallway. We both know that I'm not strong enough to physically pull him anywhere, but he comes willingly.

"I don't fucking think—" Nico starts.

"It's fine, Nic," Romeo snaps. He never takes his eyes off of me. Even if I couldn't feel the weight of his concern on the side of my face, I see it out of the corner of my eye as I make sure Nico doesn't bull-rush us.

"I can explain," he says.

"No," I snap.

"I know what you must be thinking."

"No, you don't." I don't even know what I was thinking. Mostly I was doing everything I could not to think right now.

"I didn't know," he says quickly. "Not that you were going to be there or that you'd be here—well, I had hoped you would be here once I figured out Tommy was here. But I—"

"Stop—just stop talking." I rock onto my toes as I abruptly come to a halt in the reception area.

Keira hovers by the side door, poised to push the metal bar and release us from this purgatory. How can one small building—one room—hold so many things that can change my life?

I tuck my gun in the back of my leggings and haul Romeo around until he's right in front of a pair of teal blue accent chairs. They're circle in shape with a high back and slightly lower armrests, and the color pops in the otherwise neutrally decorated reception area.

I can't unpack all of the emotions swirling inside of me, except for one. I wrap my anger around me like a cloak and hold it tightly with both hands.

And then I shove him.

"That's for leaving me at the altar earlier."

I step forward and press my hands against his chest and push him. He takes a step back, his face falling. "And that's for not telling me who you were."

I step into him and shove him once more. For as angry and hurt and confused as I am, it's a weak attempt. "And that—that's for making me fall in love with you when it was all a lie."

To my absolute horror, tears prick my eyes.

My lips tremble with the admission, my stomach tightening with vulnerability and shock. Love? Love? I don't know when it happened or the moment my feelings changed, but as I look at him now, there's no denying it.

I fell in love with him.

It dumps a bucket of water on my rage instead of lighter fluid. I take a step back, my breaths choppy as they heave out of me. Romeo surges forward, wrapping his arms around my shoulders and tugging me into his chest. "I'm sorry, Juliet. You have to believe me. I had no idea who you were—"

"Stop." I pull back hard, jerking out of his hold.

He lets me go but he doesn't give me much space. I cut him a harsh glare, stopping whatever bullshit excuse he's trying to feed me. It's an effective look, one that I'd perfected years ago. "More lies, Romeo?" I roll my lips inward and shake my head. "If that's even your real name," I mutter.

"Of course, it is. And I never lied to you. Never." A shadow clouds his face, his lips pursed to the side.

"Bullshit," Keira curses.

"I swear it, Maeve. On New York."

"I don't want your carefully worded omissions either. They taste like lies all the same."

My gaze bounces all over his face, trying to find the man I thought I knew somewhere between the familiar shape of his nose and the way the skin around his eyes crinkles with something akin to sincerity.

His eyes are darker under this unforgiving light. The secret romantic inside of me believes it's an omen.

Right now, Romeo's eyes are the color of the deepest parts of the ocean. The bright blues lure you in with the promise of their beauty. And by the time you've lost your fear, it's too late. You've been lured into the darkest depths of the ocean, tangled in weeds and desperate to find a way out.

But you can't see past your face. You're surrounded by darkness only deceit can provide.

And you fucking drown.

I guess it's time I learn how to swim.

I blink, letting the icy mask of a King slip over my face. "You lied to me."

He shakes his head slowly, his dark hair a disheveled mess on his head. "Everything between us was real, Juliet. I swear it."

I waver at the sight of his distress, the sincerity etched into his face. My shoulders sink a little, and I mentally shake myself.

Don't cave so easily. You're not a pushover, you're a mother-fucking King.

I roll my shoulders back and stand up straight. "Your word doesn't hold as much weight as you think."

He flinches, his eyes narrowing. I keep my mask up, blinking away the tears pooling in my eyes. I only allow him and everyone else to see the carefully curated slate of nothingness that I want them to see.

Only I know the truth. His words meant everything.

They were my lifeline, my saving grace, and the best parts of my day for too many days. And to find out it was all . . . what? A lie? A constructed situation to somehow exploit me? I don't know. I don't know what the point or purpose of any of them and me is.

I watch emotions play across his features. Either he's not as skilled as his brothers at concealing them, or he doesn't want to. I spent seventy-two hours memorizing the shape of his eyebrows, the way his hair falls over his forehead in a swoop after I ran my fingers through it for too long. The freckle on the right side of his bottom lip and the faint dimple in his left cheek.

And still, I don't notice the shift until he's already in motion.

"Maeve," Keira snaps.

I know she wants me to pull my gun on him—on anyone who crowds me—to make them give me space. But I . . . I just can't.

Romeo slides his hands on either side of my ribs, spinning us around and backing me against the wall faster than I can blink. He blocks out everything until I can only see him.

It's the same move his brother just pulled on me in the exam room. And I seriously consider finding another doctor to examine my head because a head trauma is the only explanation for why I let Romeo crowd into me.

He leans into me, pressing the full length of his body against mine.

"Back up, asshole," Keira snaps from next to us.

"Calm down. He's not going to hurt her," Nico snaps right back at her.

Ah, so I guess he followed us down the hallway too. Our little stalemate didn't dissolve, we just moved locations. I spare an errant thought for Dr. Clemente, hoping he took the opportunity to get clear of here. I only hope his good sense holds and he doesn't call the cops.

"Fuck you. You're lucky I don't shoot you for causing my sister so much distress in her condition," Keira practically growls.

Romeo lowers his head until his face is just two inches in front of mine, recapturing my attention. "Juliet, *mon chéri,*" he murmurs. A plea just for my ears.

The smell of smoke curls around us, sullying the familiar sandalwood and warm, sandy beaches I associate with him. It further isolates us from the bickering happening around us.

"Don't," I choke out the word, turning my head to the side. Too much emotional attachment to a name that was never mine to begin with.

He cups my face with his right hand, his palm is warm against my cheek. How many times did he do this same thing during our weekend tucked away in New York City?

And how can a simple gesture bring me so much pain?

It's too much. This day—these revelations—it's all too much for one person to shoulder.

He guides my face back toward him, tipping my head back against the wall.

"Forget about them. I don't care about anything else but you right now. Are you hurt?"

"Maybe I care about everything else," I bite out at him. I feel my proverbial hackles rising again. Is it possible to give yourself emotional whiplash? I feel out of control, like I'm going to start crying and do something drastic. Anything to give this emotion an outlet. "Maybe I shouldn't though. Maybe I shouldn't care about any of it."

My gaze ping-pongs between his eyes. I press my fingertips into his chest and push him back. He allows a few steps until I can leave the circle of his arms. I take care not to brush against him as I leave.

The clank of the metal bar punctuates the stifling silence. Cool night air wafts in, enticing me further.

"This isn't over," Nico growls out.

I pause with one foot out the door and look over my shoulder. All three wear different expressions, but their bodies are positioned the same. It's all so obvious to me now. Hindsight is tricky like that.

"You and your brothers might lord over Las Vegas, but I'm a motherfucking King."

16

NICO

"IT'S a good thing you boys let the girls go. You don't want to invite that kind of trouble."

I turn around at the sound of the doctor's voice. He leans against the wall in the hallway, half concealed by shadow. "Do you have any idea who I am? Who we are?"

He stands in the dark recesses of the hallway, his silhouette barely visible. He watches me intently, like he's measuring his words carefully. "I know their reputation stretches wide, and they have friends in . . . interesting places."

I grin at him. He's bold for someone who was trembling being trapped in a room with a loose cannon. I don't mean my brother. Well, just my brother.

I've heard of the Kings before. Five daughters from Joseph King, or as the rest of the criminal underground calls him, the Hammer.

I make it a point to be friendly with the Irish—all of the factions on this continent and theirs. My father's perceived grievances aren't my own.

But more than that, I don't want to live my life with so many enemies that I can't enjoy my limited time on this earth.

Tommy claps me on the shoulder as he heads toward the doctor. "I'm on it. C'mon, Doc, let's have a chat. Make sure I've got a clean bill of health and all that."

"We'll be outside by the car," I tell him.

"Don't take too long, Tommy. I don't want them to get too far ahead of us," Rome calls out to Tommy's retreating back.

Tommy gives a quick nod of his head, and with a few flicks his fingers in the air, he disappears inside one of the rooms.

I tug at my cuff, adjusting the black cotton long-sleeved shirt so it lays perfectly over my watch. I'm not used to dressing so casually, but it was a necessary move. A calculated one. Three men in Tom Ford suits blend in at a wedding, but what if we had to ditch the car and go on foot somewhere? Then we'd be easy to spot—too easy.

Just because we can handle the attention doesn't mean I want to. The less clean-up here, the better. Vito said to keep it quiet, so we don't have our same resources here as we do in Las Vegas.

I take a deep, shuddering breath, feeling the weight of the day pressing down on me like a physical force. My shoulders sag under the burden.

When Rome emerged from the smoking church like some religious phoenix, I was surprised. And when Rome tracked Tommy's location to a practice in a town away, my curiosity grew.

But when I stepped through the door, expecting anything but what I saw, I was speechless.

I've spent countless hours burying myself under work and throwing all my attention behind the plan to take out Dad. Sacrificing so much of my time and brain power to this one singular goal. Not that it helped any, considering we fucked that up.

I didn't allow myself to dwell on thoughts of her or our night together. I was content to let it be a true one-night stand. Something to recall on those particularly lonely nights.

Picking up women has never been hard. But finding a woman who isn't trying to fuck me over is nearly impossible. And the freedom my impromptu visit to Chicago is invaluable.

It just so happens those warm feelings of gratitude and nostalgia are tangled up in wavy dark brown hair and deep brown eyes.

And now, another curve ball.

If I believed in any sort of higher power, I might be inclined to think someone is pulling my strings. How many ways can one woman entangle herself in a family?

I roll my shoulders back, stretching out my neck muscles, and do my best to not let the swirling questions in my head pull me under like quicksand.

"We bought ourselves some time today, Rome, but not an unlimited amount. Keep your head in the game."

He paces a little bit, craning his neck to get a better view of the street. "Whatever, Nic. I don't really give a fuck about the game right now."

"Hey," I bark out, stepping toward him. I place a hand on his chest, only applying enough pressure to get his attention.

He glares at my hand for a moment before he bats it away and steps to the side, looking at the fading red taillights down the road. "What."

I step in front of him, blocking his view. Annoyance prickles along my scalp, a testament to my frayed nerves. "The fuck, Rome? Is she really worth everything we've worked toward? Is she worth our fucking freedom from Vito?"

He rocks back on his heels, finally giving me his attention. He tips his chin, his mouth pursed in a stubborn scowl. "And if I said she was?"

My heart beats in my ear, the thrum getting louder and

louder. Shock steals my words for a moment as the first tendrils of outrage wrap their icy fingers around my throat.

"You're going to throw your life away—the lives of your motherfucking brothers—for some—some—"

"You better fucking watch your words here, brother."

It's a warning I don't take. Fury bubbles in my gut like a fountain, and I'm in his face in a blink. My face twists into a mask of anger and outrage asI step into his space. "You're going to throw everything away for a woman you met on the internet?"

I don't see the wind up, but I sure as fuck feel the effects of my brother's right hook. The force of my brother's punch surprises me, my anger quickly swelling with my eye. I reflexively slam my palm over the throbbing and shuffle back a step.

"Don't you ever talk about her like that again," he seethes, not giving me an inch.

"The fuck was that for?" I yell, my tone pitched in incredulity.

"I fucking warned you, man. I told you not to talk about her like that."

He's the one who steps to me now, shoving me much like she did to him ten minutes ago. We're the same height, but he's fucking stronger than he looks. I rock back on my heels before swaying forward and shoving him back a step.

"Would you chill the fuck out?" I snap at him, my voice rising with mounting frustration. "I didn't even say anything."

"It's in your tone, Nic. The dismissive way you treated her, like she's a fucking pawn to squeeze information out of—"

I throw my arm out to the side and yell, "Because she is. She was the one about to marry that motherfucker back there." I jab the air to my right with my index finger. "So maybe pack away some of your righteous outrage because it's misplaced. And you just let the one lead we had drive away."

He's a seething ball of fury, but I doubt it's all meant for me. He spends too much time wrapped up in his own head, and then he just fucking explodes. And it's my job as his brother, as his fucking best friend, to help him through it. Even if he lashes out.

I've never seen my brother so fucking aggressive before—not toward me or anyone. I've never seen him quite like this, a kettle at its boiling point. It's something I would've expected from Tommy, but not Rome. He's even-tempered and almost obsessive about gathering enough intel before we make a move. But this? This is all act first, think later. It's alarmingly unlike him.

Kind of like the time he found our long-lost sisters and kept it a secret from me for months, my subconscious supplies rather unhelpfully. It only serves to further irritate me.

Rome spins around, lacing his fingers behind his head. He takes this big, heaving breath like he's the one who just got fucking rocked in the face. Fucking dick move.

I press my fingers to the tender skin around my eye, wincing at the sharp lance of pain. "You're fucking lucky I love you," I mutter.

He twists around and snarls, "No, you're fucking lucky I love you. Because I love her."

He stares at me then, though this look is so different from everything else he's sent my way. There's still the frustration and intensity, but there's a persistent, quiet fury in his face. An answer to the question I didn't ask. I'm not sure I even want to.

"C'mon, man," I say, pitching my voice lower, more cajoling. "You don't even know her. Just—just give yourself time to really think everything through before you do something you can't take back."

He shakes his head, disappointment turning the corners of his mouth down. "If you really think that, then you don't know me at all."

He pauses for a moment, then exhales sharply with a shake of his head. He walks to the car without another word or looking back.

Concern eats away at my gut, shooting a bolt of anxiety through my veins. Not for the first time today, I'm worried about my youngest brother. And I don't know how to fucking fix it.

I'll find a way though. I always do.

I hear the shuffle of Tommy's boots on the sidewalk a moment later. He stops next to me, our shoulders nearly brushing.

I arch a brow at him, eyeing the brown paper bag in his hand. "You good?"

He shrugs and lifts the bag a little. "It's just pain killers. I'll be fine. What's up with him?" He jerks his chin toward Rome sitting in the car. The light from his laptop illuminates his face.

"That woman? The dark-haired one? She's Rome's internet girlfriend."

He stills next to me, like his whole body freezes. It's a curious reaction, and I find myself staring at my brother with an uncomfortable amount of paranoia for the second time today. What are the odds that both of my brothers pick today to act out of character?

You know, while we're ferreting around on our father's wishes and committing murder outside a motherfucking church? It's probably only the beginning of a very long list of karmic retribution, to be honest. Church and all.

Tommy's reaction reaffirms my earlier decision to keep my own connection to her quiet. For now, at least. I don't see what good could come from filling my brothers in on that night in Chicago. And a small part of me doesn't trust either of their judgment when it comes to her, not right now.

And that's the worst fucking part of this day. The three of us are supposed to be in this together. But something about her is blowing all of that up.

Or maybe I'm being paranoid again.

I twist to the side and give Tommy my full attention. "You okay?"

"I'm fine. Banged up from the explosion, that's all," he says, but his jaw never unclenches. His shoulders don't lose their tightness either.

"She say anything to you? Anything we can use?" I prod.

He shakes his head and shoves his hands into his pockets. "Nah, we didn't talk much."

I narrow my gaze on him. "You sure? You two seemed awfully familiar when I walked in."

He finally looks over at me, his face a neutral mask. "Is there something you want to ask me, brother?"

I lift my shoulders and let them drop in an exaggerated shrug. "Just curious about her, but I suppose I'll get my chance to ask her questions soon enough."

His brows furrow before they smooth out. "Rome's tracking her. How?"

"Where's your phone?" I ask.

Realization brightens his eyes. "So that's how you found me. I was wondering how you got here, considering I don't even know where we are." He looks around, but there's not anything noteworthy around.

"If they still have your phone, Rome can find them," I say, pushing off the curb and crossing the small parking lot.

"And then what?" He quickens his steps to keep pace.

"Then we'll get back to our plan."

"She was never part of that plan," he grits through his clenched teeth.

My lips twitch. It doesn't really matter if he doesn't want her involved, by being the bride at the Milano wedding and being involved with my brothers means she already is. Whether she likes it or not. Whether any of us like it or not.

"We'll see, Tommy, we'll see."

Rome opens the passenger door and sticks his head out. "Let's go. I know where they're headed."

17

MAEVE

KEIRA'S DRIVING AGAIN. I thank the universe for my sisters often, but I'm going to have to start paying homage daily if they keep this up.

"Do you want to talk about it?" she asks, her voice low.

I close my eyes and lean my head against the headrest. "No."

She exhales and changes the radio station to one of those new age channels on satellite radio. The sound of a single, sustained flute sings through the speakers. It's the kind of music you would expect to hear at a spa, all soothing ringing and long, drawn-out sounds.

It's nice, peaceful.

"Okay. What's next?"

My arms and legs feel heavy but my stomach feels light, like a hundred moths are fluttering around inside. "I—I don't know. I need to get out of here, back to New York for now. Regroup and plan my next steps."

"Who were those guys?"

"I think you already know the answer to that," I answer with a sigh.

"I have guesses, maybe an assumption or two. But I want to hear it from you."

I open my eyes and stare straight ahead. "Well, I don't want to talk about it right now."

I don't have to peek to know that my sister is biting her tongue. I bet she has that wrinkle between her furrowed brows too. She sighs again. "Okay, but I'm here. When you're ready to talk. Or just need someone to listen."

Warmth settles inside my chest, and I reach over and squeeze her bicep softly. "Thank you. For everything."

She offers me a smile quickly before refocusing on the road. "Of course, that's what sisters are for, remember? You taught us that."

Before I can respond, her phone rings. Keira glances at her phone tucked in the cupholder and presses a button on the screen. "Hey, Rosie."

"Keira? Where are you?" Rosie asks, skipping any pleasantries.

"We just left that doctor's office. We ran into some . . . complications," Keira says.

"Complications? What kind of complications?" Rosie asks, a note of alarm making her voice sort of shrill by the last word. "Where's Maeve?"

"I'm here, Rosie." I do my best to keep my voice even.

"Oh thank god. Listen, there's been an update on that thing I called about earlier."

"Fuck," Keira curses under her breath.

I shift in my seat, my hip smarting from sitting too close to the center console. "What thing? What's going on?"

"You didn't tell her?" Rosie's incredulous.

"We didn't exactly have time. Complications, remember?" Keira raises her brows as she emphasizes the last word.

Rosie sighs, the noise loud in the speaker. "Fine, but you owe me. Besides, Maeve told me I was her favorite sister two months ago, so I guess that's partial payment." She sounds smug even through the phone line.

I roll my eyes. "I did no such thing."

Keira huffs, her lips pursing for a moment before she opens her mouth. "Whatever. I'm not going to stoop to your level and tell you that Maeve told me I'm the best sister ever last month."

Before they really dissolve into an argument, I interrupt. "As much as I enjoy watching you two make up stories, someone better tell me what's really going on."

Rosie clears her throat. "Right. Well. Keira filled me in on an abridged version of today's events and told me to find you an exit strategy."

I frown at Keira, and she catches my expression before she refocuses on the road.

"What?" she says, lifting a shoulder. "We needed something more concrete than you going back to New York City. That's the first place they'll look for you."

"No one knows where our vacation house is, Keira. I'll be fine," I argue.

"Not exactly," Rosie interjects.

I shift my gaze to the phone as if she can even see me. "What do you mean?"

Rosie sighs, this long-winded exhale like she's gearing up for a big speech. "Well, remember when you were contacted by someone out of the blue? Someone who was so good that I had to ask Rush for help, and even he——"

"I remember," I interrupt her. I don't like cutting anyone off, but I don't think I can take another reminder of Romeo right now. Not when everything is still so fresh.

I cringe thinking about how I blurted out that I loved him like some teenager with her first boyfriend. Whatever, it's fine. I'm about to go underground—as underground as someone who's going to have a baby in seven months can.

"Right. Well, after that, I wiped some forums with any mention of us and put some extra security measures into place."

"Rosie, we're almost to the airfield. We're fleeing a multi-level crime scene, remember? Skip to the important part," Keira says when Rosie pauses.

"I'm getting to that," Rosie snaps. "What I was trying to tell you is that those extra precautions work like an alarm system. I get pinged every time someone mentions any of us—real names or monikers. And I just got one. It's bad, Maeve. Really bad."

My gut churns like I might throw up. "Tell me."

"Ten million," she says, her voice quiet. "Twenty million alive."

"What?" Keira says.

I lean in closer, as if eliminating those few inches of space between me and the phone will do anything. "Who? Who's it for, Rosie?"

She replies softly, "You. It's for you."

My stomach drops, and I suck in a sharp breath. "What the fuck?" My voice is barely audible.

"Can you trace it? Who posted it and who's backing it?" Keira asks.

"It's set up in a new dark web marketplace, The Bricks. It's one that we've never had any cause to pay attention to. It's normally petty shit like stolen art and pirated jewels. And none of our usual types frequent there, so I didn't have the proper eyes on it. Not like that would matter much, anyway." She mumbles the last part.

"You didn't shut it down?" Keira shouts, her anger a mask for her fear.

"Don't yell at me, Keira. I'm not omniscient, and I'm not fucking god, I don't run the marketplaces—I don't even know who does. No one knows shit about any of the dark web market-places. They're specifically built so no one knows how they operate." Frustration bleeds from her voice, and I can't help the knee-jerk response to soothe her.

"It's alright, Rosie. You did good, yeah? We'll figure something out." I keep my voice even, despite the quaking inside my body. Fuck, this isn't good. "Wait. Who does it say specifically? The Wren? Because we can work with that, no one knows who—"

"No. It's posted for Maeve King. Firstborn daughter to Joseph King," Rosie says.

"Motherfucking fuck." Keira slams her palms on the steering wheel, the thwack loud enough that I feel it in my own palms. She exhales through her nose. "Sorry, I didn't mean to lash out. I'm just—I don't know what to do. How can we take it down?"

"It's fine. I'm upset too, I've just had a few minutes head start to process. And I'm not sure if we can. It's already been verified."

"Goddammit," Keira bites the curse out.

"So the money is already there," I murmur.

"Exactly. Follow the money, find the guy. That's what I always say," Rosie says, injecting some pep into her voice. Bless my optimistic sister.

I've heard the same phrase and philosophy from Rush Fitzgerald for fifteen years now. He wasn't wrong then, and she's not wrong now. Usually, you can trace anything back if you follow the money long enough.

But these dark markets exist solely in a gray area. A sort of limbo for the anonymous. It's like one of those freelance websites where people post job listings for graphic design and foreign translations. But instead of innocent, honest livings, the dark market is a cesspool for the criminal and the depraved.

"But here's where it gets . . . interesting," Rosie says. "Ready?"

Keira's shoulders are closer to her ears now, wrought with tension. "Aye, tell us."

"Vito Santorini publicly claimed the hit on the church, boasted about his boys taking the Milano crime family off the map. Made some bold, sweeping comments about taking all the women and having his first stable." Rosie spits the word with as much distaste as I feel.

I make a mental note to add Vito Santorini to our list. Perhaps he won't be as vocal after the Fairy Godmothers pay him a visit.

Maybe I will poison a Santorini after all.

"And seventeen seconds after your job was posted, one for Nico, Tommaso, and Romeo Santorini was posted. Five million each, dead or alive."

"Verified?" Keira asks.

"Yes. But there's more," Rosie says.

"How could there be more?" I murmur.

"I just saw that Il Diavoli publicly called it."

My skin feels itchy, and I'm flushed from head to toe. I crack the window to let some cool fresh air in, hoping it'll wipe away the urge to vomit. I can't catch my breath, anxiety and adrenaline pumping in tandem in my veins.

Il Diavoli are a group of Italian highly trained assassins known for their gruesome scenes. They're shells of humans, plucked from their homes—or in a lot of cases, orphanages—and placed into a secret academy no later than age six. The stories from that place are enough to give you nightmares for years.

They're messy and unpredictable and always, always down for the money. You don't negotiate with them, and they never show mercy.

They're evil masquerading as humans.

My mind is filled with haunting visions of Tommaso and Romeo—and even that cold bastard, Nico—with permanent smiles carved into their faces. They paralyze me, locking my muscles in their icy grip.

My vision blurs as the road in front of us melts into a watercolor painting. "Who?"

My sisters don't hear me, too busy lost in their argument over something neither one of them have control over.

I pitch my voice louder and say, "Who, Rosie?"

They stop mid-sentence. "What? I told you, Il Diavoli called dibs."

"No, I know. But who's hit did they pick up? Mine or theirs?"

"Theirs. They called first rights on the hit, but it's more for posturing than claiming. This job posted in The Bricks isn't like the others. Whoever posted it made it auction-style."

I can't breathe, the air around me thinning. I lower the window further, desperate to get more air into the car.

"It's going to be a bloodbath," I murmur.

18

MAEVE

"THEY'LL BE lucky to make it out of California," I mumble to myself, my mind spinning.

"How many people are we talking about, Rosie? Five? Ten?" Keira asks.

"I-I don't know. With an auction this size and Il Diavoli throwing their weight behind it," she trails off.

But she doesn't need to say it, we're all thinking the same thing. Every assassin will flock to the bet like vultures. It's not only for the money either. The prospect of getting one-up on Il Diavoli is too irresistible to ignore. It's a once-in-a-lifetime chance at glory. An instant status booster.

And in an environment where the only thing with more value than money is reputation.

"So, what? Twenty? Thirty?" Keira asks.

"Fifty minimum," Rosie says.

Keira rears back. "Fifty? Jesus fucking Christ."

"This didn't have a disclaimer or any caveats. They essentially rang the dinner bell for every assassin—amateur and professional—and told them to get fucking messy," Rosie says.

I rake my front teeth over my bottom lip as a long-forgotten memory rises to the surface. I try to remember something I heard in Da's office a long time ago. "No. It won't be fifty." I look across my shoulder and stare at my sister's face. "It'll be everyone."

She steals a glance at me before stepping on the gas pedal. "What do you mean? How many is everyone?"

"I once overheard Da talking to his generals. It was maybe three or four years after Mum left. It was late, and we'd had a sister sleepover that night, but I couldn't fall asleep."

"You always were a night owl," Keira muses.

I incline my head. "Well, that night I went looking for a snack, but before I hit the stairs, I heard voices coming from the kitchen. So I stayed in the shadows, hovering on the landing of the staircase. They were talking about an auction. At the time I didn't understand. I thought Da was going to donate to a fundraiser, you know how he liked to keep up pretenses and all that."

"Aye, I remember," Keira says.

"He said an auction for Mum. Make it messy."

You know that sort of weighted silence that comes in a conversation when someone is reevaluating everything? It's not heavy necessarily, more like it holds space for everyone to dismantle the bomb that was placed at our feet. It gives the emotional reckoning time to breathe and adjust, gives your brain time to reconsider things with new information.

The three of us hold space together as we silently contemplate the idea that our da ordered a manhunt on the people responsible for Mum's death.

It shouldn't be surprising, not really. I mean, the man's called The Hammer, and it's not because he's a handyman. He's a fucking assassin, only he's not in the shadows about it.

Everyone knows what's about to go down if The Hammer shows up on their doorstep. He doesn't really do house calls like that anymore, having passed that particular baton off years ago. But you don't forget the violence and pain and fear someone inflicts on you simply because they no longer have that job.

I'll never forget the way families of other Syndicate members cowered out of the way for Da. Like he was going to take out someone's uncle in the cereal aisle at the grocery.

"Holy shit," Rosie whispers.

"I mean, I'm not surprised, not really. We all know what Da is capable of—just look at the contract that got us in this mess in the first place," Keira says.

"A marriage contract isn't exactly the same thing as an auction-style hit on the dark marketplace," Rosie says.

Keira scoffs. "Isn't it? They're both death sentences."

"Maeve's not dead!" Rosie shouts. "So, just take it down a little, aye, Keira? Not everything has to be life-or-death."

"This is literally life-or-death, Roisin!" Exasperation oozes from Keira's voice.

"Turn around," I interrupt them.

Keira jerks her head to the side, staring at me like I started speaking a foreign language. "What?"

"Turn the car around, Keira. We have to go back."

Her eyebrows hit her hairline. "Go back? Are you insane?"

"We have to warn them," I argue.

"We barely got out of there without a goddamn gun fight or did you forget that while you were making moon eyes at all of them?"

"Excuse me?" I snap, shifting so my shoulder hits the passenger window while staring at my sister's profile with narrowed eyes. "What the fuck are moon eyes, anyway?"

She waves her right hand in the air, like she's wafting away my words. "You know exactly what I mean."

My scalp prickles with irritation, and I glare at her. "I don't appreciate the insinuation that I can't make level-headed decisions."

She snaps her mouth shut, the skin around her eyes tight. "C'mon, Maeve, you know that's not what I meant. It's obvious there's some tension there with at least two of those Santorini boys."

I fold my arms across my chest, unmoved by her weak backpedaling. "And?"

"And—and—and nothing!" Her voice rises with each word. She grips the steering wheel, the leather creaking under her fists. "We're not turning around, Maeve. We need to get out of here, hole up somewhere and figure out how to get you off the fucking docket!"

I know she's protecting me, that she thinks she's doing the right thing, and I love her all the more for it.

I uncross my arms, my shoulders softening in their stiffness. Snapping back at her never works. She's a constant spark, always ready for the tinder to strike so she can explode. She thrives in chaos and she never backs down in arguments. Going toe-to-toe with her while she's speeding down the highway isn't the time to try and out-snap at her, even if I had the energy to.

Which I definitely don't. It's taken everything in me right now not to paint the upholstery with my paltry breakfast. Despite my deep breaths through my nose, a blind sort of panic smothers me, wrapping me up tight like Fiona's weighted blanket. It squeezes tighter and tighter, and with each second that my sister flies down the road in the opposite direction, I feel like I'm losing air.

Annoyance bubbles up at me like carbonation in a can. As if fate itself is shaking me up over and over and over again, daring me to explode. Well fate just might get its wish tonight, because I'm getting closer and closer to losing it.

"If you don't turn this car around right now, I swear to god, Keira, I'm going to jump out and start walking myself."

"Please," she scoffs. "We're doing sixty on the highway. You're not going to jump out of the car."

"What's going on?" Rosie's voice rises three octaves in three words.

"I'm not fucking around, Keira." Bile creeps up my throat. I can't shake the feeling that if I get on the plane without warning them, then I'll never see any of them again. I curl my fingers around the door handle. "Stop the car."

She reels back, looking at me like she's never seen me before. As if I'm prone to outlandish outbursts or have a flair for the dramatic like one of our other sisters. "What the hell, Maeve? We're almost to the airfield, just chill out, will you?"

Frustration sinks its claws into my words, drawing them back down my throat and stuffing them into my gut. I sigh, this noisy, caustic sound. The tiniest barrier exists between me and the simmering rage spilling out all over the car—all over my sister.

Keira doesn't deserve that. None of my sisters do. it's only because I know my sister doesn't deserve my ire and terror-induced panic that I keep it bottled up, reinforcing that barrier.

"No, I will not chill out. We're not just talking about something as mundane as the weather. This—this is bigger than us, then all of us. This is more than casual conversations we have around our roundtable about looking into possible men before taking them out. We've never had to deal with them before—"

"Do you honestly think that I don't know Il Diavoli's reputation?"

"No, I know you do but—but this isn't your decision, Keira."

"The hell it's not! You're my sister!" she yells.

"Aye, and I love you. But a child needs both parents. We know that better than anyone."

"Aye, we do. Which is why I know this child needs you. Outside of the biological reasons, you're the best thing to happen to that baby. You'd never forgive yourself if something happened, and I won't let you put yourself in a position to risk that. I'd rather you hate me forever than hate yourself for running back into a pit of violence."

I stare at my sister, my eyes wide and watering. Underneath her heated words were mountains of love. It's quiet, any rebuttal dying on my tongue.

"Holy shit, you're pregnant?" Rosie says with a gasp.

19

MAEVE

"SURPRISE," I say, my voice weak.

We're quiet as the car slows down as she turns right, the large gates of the private airfield looming directly in front of us. Bright spotlights illuminate the road leading up to the terminal. My mind races, unable to latch onto one thought securely. I'm thankful for the silence, even though I'm sure Rosie is properly freaking out on the inside. Hell, maybe she put us on mute. I wouldn't be surprised.

I'll answer her million questions, just not right now.

I look over at my sister, watching the way the streetlights cast shadows all over her beautiful face. A face that looks so different from mine, and yet, is so achingly familiar.

"Please, Keira. I have to warn them."

She slows down, her foot easing on the brake until we come to a complete stop in front of a small building. She throws the car in park and shifts in her seat until she's facing me. "Look, I get it, okay? It's just . . . I'm trying to do the best thing for you." She reaches over and grabs my hand, untangling my fingers from their knotted grip in the hem of my tee. "Everything will be fine. Okay?" Her eyebrows rise, not in surprise but a gentle cajoling.

I'm shaking my head before she even finishes talking. "No, Keira. I don't think anything is ever going to be okay again." I gesture to my stomach. "This changes everything."

She looks at me for a long moment before bracing one hand on the center console between us and arching her butt off the seat. She snags a phone out of her back pocket and tosses it into my lap. "Here. Call them."

"Is this Santorini's? I mean, Tommaso's?" I correct myself immediately.

I called him one thing in my head for months, and despite my best efforts to not think of him, thoughts . . . and visions found their way into my consciousness more times than I care to admit. It's going to take some time for me to adjust to his new name—his real name.

Keira lifts a shoulder in a halfhearted shrug, unapologetic in her theft. "There was a lot going on. Besides, I kinda thought there might be something useful on it for Rosie to take. But I'm glad I took it. Now you can call and warn him at least."

"Thanks." I grip the black phone in my hand, my fingers aching with how tightly I squeeze the edges. It's not the same as driving back to the doctor's office where we left them, but it's better than nothing.

And in the quiet recess of my soul, I can admit that my actions weren't entirely altruistic. I want to see them again, as fucked-up as it is. But it's a thought I plan to keep to myself.

"Um, did you guys forget about me?" Rosie's voice startles me.

I looked toward Keira's phone in the cupholder, surprised to see the call still connected. I suppose I sort of did forget, distractedly wading through knee-deep panic.

"Damn," Keira whistles under her breath. "I didn't know you were physically capable of being that quiet."

Keira's quip pierces the thick bubble of tension in the car, and the three of us chuckle. It's halfhearted at best, but given the circumstances, I'll take it.

"I'm going to pretend that that wasn't an insult simply because we don't have the time for me to school you on how, in fact, I am very quiet," Rosie says.

I imagine the way my sister's face looks when she delivers that little line. Chin tilted upward, her nose reaching for the sky, and her eyebrows arched into haughty curves over her dark brown eyes.

Keira cocks her head to the side, her lips twisting, and stares at the phone. "Is that some kind of reference to sex?"

More tension eases from the car, like a balloon losing air. The only response from Rosie is laughter. The kind that froths up out of nowhere, it's all startled shock, with a touch of hysteria. Honestly, given the information overload in the last few hours, I'm not surprised. I'd be more concerned if we all weren't on the edge right now.

"First of all, we don't have time to discuss my sex life," Rosie says through a laugh.

"Oh, so there is one to discuss? Do I need to come to Chicago?" Keira interrupts her. She slides into the big sister role so effortlessly. I have complete confidence in her ability to handle everything when I'm gone.

Because that's what's going to happen. The beginning threads of a plan start to take shape in my mind.

"Oh my god, Keira. You're worse than Fiona," Rosie says with a groan.

"Yeah, yeah, yeah. I'm mostly kidding, but I have to go now. We just got to the private airstrip, and I need to adjust our flight plan."

"And Maeve has a phone call to make," Rosie says. "It's fine. I need to make a few phone calls and inquiries myself. Call me once you're in the air, okay? Don't forget to take your go-bags with you. That way I can track you if I have to."

"Okay." My voice comes out a squeak, and I have to clear my throat and try again. "Okay, got it. And Rosie? I'll talk to you soon, aye? Love you."

"Love you more. Bye," she sings the words.

The call disconnects, and I stare at the phone in my hand once more.

"I'll be right back," Keira says. "Make your call, Maeve. We don't have a lot of time."

She said we don't have a lot of time, but I can't help but feel that she meant they don't have a lot of time.

I watch my sister as she crosses the small parking lot and enters the terminal. It's a small, single-room building with huge floor-to-ceiling windows along two of the four walls. Luckily, I can see everything clearly from my position in the car. Which is great, because I'm feeling three steps past paranoid at this point.

Once I'm satisfied that she's not in danger, I unlock Tommaso's phone. I'm sure Rosie would have a few choice things to say about the lack of passcode. And while normally, I would agree with her, I only find myself feeling profoundly thankful. It's either careless or confident, but either way, it means I can use it to warn them.

I go to his contacts, my thumb hovering over Romeo's name. He's in Tommaso's phone as Rome, so I guess he was telling the truth about that much.

I shake my head, scattering those thoughts away for now. They don't dissolve or die, they just take up space elsewhere for now.

I press his name quickly, putting the call on speakerphone. It connects on the first ring.

"Juliet?"

I clear my throat, unsure if I'm comforted by the sound of his voice or more anxious because it's so familiar.

How do you tell someone that they have an entire community of underground assassins gunning for them at this very moment?

"Romeo, hi. I—I don't know how to say this."

"Whatever it is, you can tell me, okay? Where are you? I'll come to you right now," he says quickly.

"No, don't." I shake my head, stopping myself. I exhale, blowing out a breath and finding my courage hiding behind my exhaustion. "There's no easy way to say this, so I'm just going to say it. I just got confirmation that somebody put out a hit on you. And your brothers."

I anxiously wait for a response, holding my breath as the silence stretches. Finally, faint rustling fills the air, followed by a harsh exhale.

"Romeo? Are you there?" I pitch my voice louder, watching my sister talk to the man behind the counter in the terminal building.

"Yeah, sorry. I'm here. I put you on speakerphone, okay? I just think this is something all three of us should hear."

"Of course," I say with a nod. "My sister just informed me that a job went up for the three of you. Plus, a separate one for me. All within the last hour."

"Where?" Nico's voice is harsh, and I try my best not to take it personally.

"It's a dark web marketplace called The Bricks. We have security measures in place to monitor the dark web for our names. And while we found it, The Bricks really isn't on our radar."

"Why?" Nico asks.

"They primarily deal in art and jewels. It's a marketplace more suited for thieves of stolen goods but not skin," Romeo answers, but he sounds almost distracted. The soft clicking of keyboard keys filter through the speaker, and I realize someone's typing on a computer.

Dots connect in my mind on a subconscious level, the realization that Romeo likely has computer tech skills beyond even Rosie's dawns. And considering Rosie's rivals Rush's, I'm impressed.

I'm sure once I have ten minutes to myself to decompress, there are going to be many, many more dots that now connect about Rome.

"Right, well, I don't know what happened at the church. Or why you were there. Or why there was a courtyard full of bodies, but it seems like this might be a revenge hit. But that's not really the worst of it."

"What's worse than an ordered hit posted on the dark marketplace?" Nico asks.

"When it's auction-style, and Il Diavoli publicly challenged everyone," I deadpan.

"Motherfucking cunts," Tommaso seethes.

It's the first time he's spoken, and I can't deny the tiny part of me that's relieved to hear his voice. I don't think I'll be able to get the image of his prone body out of my head anytime soon.

"Oh fuck. Where are you, Maeve? Right now, where are you?" Romeo asks, urgency quickening his words.

"I'm at a private airstrip," I answer automatically. I wince as soon as the words are out of my mouth. I probably shouldn't have offered that up so easily. It's a good thing Keira's still inside.

"Don't move. We'll be right there."

20

MAEVE

I LEAN against the passenger door, clutching Tommaso's phone hard enough my knuckles are starting to ache. I watch my sister as she leaves the building, throwing a friendly wave over her shoulder. She's going to be pissed I told them where we are, but I don't regret it.

It's hard to always be the one with all the answers, the fixer in the family. And I'm fucking tired. Maybe I'll wake up tomorrow energized and ready to tackle this chaotic mess with The Bricks and Il Diavoli, but today I'm tired.

I'm exhausted and confused, and I just need to not bear all the weight right now. And heaven help anyone who crosses my sisters, renowned badasses in their own rights.

But this? This is bigger than me and them.

We need to be strategic, and we'll need help. There are favors to cash in and moves to make. It's not impossible, but it won't be easy.

And that's before I factor in a pregnancy. I meant what I said to Keira. This baby changes everything.

And for now, the Santorinis and I share a common enemy and a mutual interest. It makes us allies.

"Good news, Maeve. We're wheels up in forty-five minutes." Keira stops a few feet away from me, her gaze sharp and assessing. "Everything okay? Did you get ahold of them?"

"So I may have let it slip where we are."

I hear the squeal of tires before the last word even leaves my lips. It's the kind of noise a car makes when they take a turn too fast. My adrenaline spikes as the car races toward us. The dark SUV swerves to park to the right of our car, ten feet away.

Romeo throws open the rear passenger door and jumps out before the car is even shut off. Soot streaks across his forehead and there's dirt on his cheek.

He rushes toward me, eyes a little too wide and hair disheveled like he's been running his hands through it since I left the doctor's office.

"Are you okay?" Romeo asks, his voice laced with worry. He gets close to me, close enough that we share the same air. He trembles like he's physically restraining himself from touching me.

"Relax, Romeo. You just saw her an hour ago," Keira says, sneering his name and rolling her eyes.

He ignores her, keeping his attention on me. "Are you okay?"

"I'm fine, Romeo," I assure him softly, feeling a rush of gratitude for his concern. Hope blossoms like a sapling in the spring under his gaze.

Tommaso and Nico climb out of the car, both looking on edge. The sight of all three of them together brings a sense of calm to my racing heart. It reaffirms my decision to tell them where we are. And about Il Diavoli and The Bricks.

I take a step back, my butt bumping against the car. I rest a hand on the side mirror, steadying myself.

"We need to go soon. Keira got us a flight plan," I say finally, my voice barely above a whisper.

"Where are we going?" he asks immediately.

I look at him from underneath my lashes, my breath catching at his use of the word we. "I—I'm not sure. New York first to grab some things, then . . ." I let my voice tail off, unsure how to even finish the sentence.

"Perfect. I love New York." He says it so calmly like we talking about takeout options, not fleeing across the country.

I run my tongue across my bottom lip, unsure what to do with his quiet confidence. Like we don't have a mountain of secrets and truths between us.

He takes a half-step toward me. "I made a mistake."

I shake my head a few times, these small jerk movements. "What mistake?"

"I didn't know, Juliet. I didn't know then what I know now."

My heart seizes inside my chest and my eyes grow wide. Did Tommaso tell him about the baby? I wanted to be the one to break that news to him. It should've been me.

He shuffles closer another step. "I should've given in to the chase. I should've tracked that perfect ass down the moment I woke up in that hotel room alone. I thought it was part of a game, and I was willing to play by your rules. I didn't realize that what you needed was for me to continue our game."

My head tips to the side, my hair falling over my shoulder. "Our game?"

"Aye," he murmurs, stepping close enough to feel the heat of him against me. He plants his left hand against the doorframe of the car, effectively blocking out everything else. "The one I created for us."

My head tips back against the car as. I maintain eye contact with him. His blue eyes normally so expressive look like twin pools of midnight water. Dark and endless.

"I let you walk away from me twice, and I won't do it again. I learn from my mistakes, *mon chéri.* So wherever you go, I go too."

I feel a shiver run down my spine at his words, his voice low and rumbling. It's like he knows exactly what to say to make my heart race and my knees weak. I want to be angry with him, to push him away and tell him that he can't just waltz back into my life like this. But I can't. Not when my world is crumbling around me and I need someone to lean on.

"It's not that easy. Il Diavoli—"

"We should go inside," Nico interrupts me. His tone is harsh but not unkind. "If someone catches wind we're in this godforsaken city, this is the first place they'll look. And we're vulnerable here."

Romeo exhales sharply and closes his eyes. He rests his forehead against mine and murmurs, "He's right. Let's take this conversation inside."

"I saw a waiting area to the right of the information desk. I'll make sure it's clear," Keira says.

"I'll go with you," Nico offers.

"I don't need your help," she snaps.

"We'll all go inside." I pitch my voice loud enough for everyone to hear before they get into it. I don't need Keira pulling out her gun again. With the way our day is going, someone inside would call the police on us, and we'd have a whole new set of problems.

I press my fingertips softly against Romeo's chest, applying a little pressure. He takes my wordless cue and takes a step back. I duck underneath his arm and walk between Keira and Nico's silent standoff, heading straight toward the building Keira came out of ten minutes ago.

I don't bother looking back, I know my sister will follow me. And the shuffle of shoes on pavement tells me the men are too.

The waiting area is small and clean. There are only three

chairs, a small coffee table with a stack of magazines, a little credenza along the wall with a coffeepot and mugs. The room is lit by the glow of the fluorescent lights hanging from the ceiling, casting the walls in a soft yellow.

The five of us circle around the coffee table, an awkward silence settling between us like a heavy fog. The tension is nearly tangible as it crackles between us.

"So, we're going to New York?" Tommaso asks.

"Nah, we're"—Keira gestures between me and her with her thumb and pinky finger in the shaka hand—"going to New York. I don't know what you three are doing. I don't even know why you're here." She folds her arms across her chest, giving the three men across the coffee table an impressive glare.

Romeo squares his jaw and takes a step closer, his shirt straining against his chest. His gaze stays glued to me as he answers Keira. "I go where she goes."

"And my brothers and I stay together," Nico says.

Keira's phone buzzes, the low hum interrupting whatever the hell is happening between everyone. She slips it from her back pocket and answers it without looking. "I'm a little busy, Roisin. What is it?"

21

MAEVE

"SO THE WAY I see it, your best option is to go underground." Rosie's on speakerphone, Keira's phone propped up on the credenza.

The five of us are crowded around it on the other side of the room. The three Santorini brothers form a semicircle to my right, Keira and I on the left.

It feels surreal to be standing here with them for a multitude of reasons. But maybe the most important one, or the biggest elephant in the room, is the fact that I've slept with all three of them.

Recently.

Two in the same weekend.

The deeply ingrained misogynistic narrative that the Syndicate—and in subsequent years, Da—shoved down our throats threatens to rise back up and douse me in shame. I thought I'd eradicated that sort of brainwashing years ago, but I suppose some trace evidence is still there.

Or maybe I'm tripped up by the fact that I'm being confronted by all three of them—in an emotional sense—on an already incredibly bad day. No, a bad day is when you acciden-tally drop your favorite iced latte. A bad day is when you get into a disagreement with your sister.

But attending your arranged marriage ceremony under threat of harm against your sisters and then getting thrown from the inside of said church is so much more than a bad day. And this is coming from a woman who routinely does dangerous shit.

There was a bright, shining spot of joy today. And it's bright enough to chase the shadows away, at least for today.

I bite the inside of my cheek to hide the smile. Hearing that soft, steady heartbeat echo around that doctor office was nothing short of magical.

I steal a glance at Tommaso, letting my gaze roam over him for a moment before switching my perusal to Nico. I don't know what I'm hoping to find. It's not like Tinker Bell is going to suddenly pop into existence and sprinkle fairy dust on whoever really is this baby's da.

I give myself a little shake and refocus on the conversation happening around me. I thought it was bad earlier, the tension in the doctor's office thick and oppressive. But it's nothing compared to right now.

The weight of my admissions press down on me like a twelve-foot yellow Burmese python wrapped around my shoulders. Gazes are shifty, never settling too long on one person or place.

As I lock eyes with Tommaso, I realize that I was wrong. It's me who's acting uncomfortable in her own skin, shifting from foot to foot every few seconds and never letting my gaze settle. Everything is heightened, and I realize with stark, shocking clarity that I'm nervous. Apprehensive and scared in a way that I haven't quite experienced before.

For all my talk of being a badass King, I feel out of my depth in this situation. And it's fucking uncomfortable.

Tommaso never breaks our connection, his intensity a

tangible thing stretching between us. The fine tremors in my veins settle the longer he offers me his undivided attention.

"I'm sorry, am I boring you two?" Nico snaps, his pitch louder than it was a moment ago.

My head whips to face him, my shoulders reaching toward my ears. My cheeks feel hot and my shoulders hitch toward my ears, like I've been caught doing something.

Which isn't that far off, not really. I zoned out somewhere around the time Keira challenged Nico for the fifth time.

Tommaso doesn't have the same response, taking his time to peel his gaze from me and swing it toward Nico.

Tommaso gives Nico a hard look, lips tipped into the hint of a smirk. Like he has a secret. "Something to say, brother?"

"Don't you have something to say? We're discussing the safety of your—" he pauses, his lips flattening into a thin line. "I thought we agreed we want what's best for everyone. Unless that's changed?" Nico raises a single brow, a silent challenge.

"I already told you I was in for the island," Tommaso says, shrugging his shoulders.

Nico cuts his gaze to me. It's not accusatory but it's something like that. "Aye, but since we're apparently all in this together, then we all have to agree."

"It has to be unanimous," Romeo murmurs.

I clear my throat, my cheeks heating further. "I'm sorry. It's been a long day. Can you tell me again?"

Nico's gaze scans my face for a moment before it softens, his brows relaxing from their slashed position. "Alright. I was saying it's a private island, big enough for the estate and some beach acreage. A small sister island is a short boat ride across the lagoon. That's where my trusted staff of many years lives full-time. They've been maintaining the villa since I haven't used it yet."

"If you haven't used it yet, then how do you know it'll be a good safe house now?" Keira asks.

A muscle in Nico's jaw pulses as he stares at her for a beat. "It was constructed as my final safe house. A place for my brothers and I to escape to in the direst of situations. I'm not a coward, and we've never run from a fight in our lives. This isn't a casual vacation home. I've gone to extreme lengths to get this island and keep it a secret."

"But this isn't running. It's surviving to see another day." I shake my head, my lips turning down into a frown. "You have no idea how bad it will get when the entirety of the assassins on the dark marketplace find you. It's smart to go underground until we have a better plan."

"It means we don't leave the island unless it's an emergency," Romeo says, looking right at me.

My gaze darts to Tommaso. His imperceptible nod eases me instantly. He knows why I'll have to leave the island. Not that I think it'll come to that. I'm sure they'll find a way to get us out long before then.

"Are we sure the opossum strategy is the best one?" Keira asks, her body tilted toward the phone.

"Nope," Roisin says, popping the p. "But it's our best one, and it's the most conceivable. The church went down with many, many casualties. I'm sure I could hack the hospital and police records to show her listed."

Nico shuffles from foot to foot, the scuff of his shoes loud against the linoleum floor.

I squint at her photo on the screen. "And how will I come back someday if I'm dead?"

Rosie sighs. "That's a problem for later. This is a solution for now."

"And them? Can we edit the records for the Santorinis too?" I turn to face Tommaso. "You could be there too, right? That might work."

"Theoretically," Romeo starts.

"But?" I prompt when he doesn't explain right away.

Romeo scratches the side of his face with his index finger. "Who would sell it?"

"Don't worry about that. Rosie can work her magic, can't you?"

"Of course. If Maeve wants me to, then it's good enough for me," Rosie says. She's so confident, it borders on cheery.

"All this talk of safe houses and editing police records, and yet, I'm still waiting to hear the answer," Keira says, looking at Nico.

Nico arches a brow, his mouth pinched into a frown. "What answer?"

"Who wants you dead?" Keira asks, her tone firm and unyielding.

"Hey." I cut her a glare, my cheeks flushing at her bluntness. But my sister is unapologetic. "It's a good option."

Keira folds her arms across her chest, ignoring me. "You're asking me to trust you with my sister. The least you can do is tell me who the possible enemies are."

"The list is endless," Tommaso says.

"Fuck this, Maeve. We can go on our own, leave right now. It'll be safer that this island."

I shake my head, my temples starting to throb with the beginning of a headache. "No, I'm not doing that to you. I already told you that."

"My island is off the grid. It's only accessibly via boat, a strategic defense," Nico says.

Keira rolls her eyes. "Fucking great. If you're trying to reassure me, you're doing a shitty job. That also leaves you vulnerable in case you have to leave suddenly."

Tommaso shrugs. "Maybe but those are the facts, and I thought that's what you wanted."

"You know, you might want to look at your business plan when you get out of this mess. Favors keep a helluva lot better than grudges," Keira mumbles.

"What? Like you're so perfect? If that were true, then Maeve wouldn't be in the same predicament as us," Nico snaps.

Nico and Keira glare at one another. I decide it's time to wade in before they really get into it.

"Look, it doesn't really matter why or how or even who, not really. We don't have many options and this, this is our best one." I turn to my sister. "This is my best one. I'm in."

22

MAEVE

I COULD DO IT ALONE. I've done it before but those were short—a week, max. We have no idea how long I'll have to stay hidden. But I need to err on the side of caution.

There's a beat of silence.

"It could be months, right, Roisin?" I ask.

She clears her throat. "I don't know, Maeve. I hope not, but I . . . it's too soon to say."

I nod, biting the inside of my cheek to quell my rising anxiety. "I don't want to be alone for months, Keira. I can't." I stress the last word, arching my brows like that move will somehow convey the words I'm not saying.

But I didn't need to worry, she's my sister in every sense of the word. She knows exactly what I mean.

"You won't be alone," Tommaso says.

Keira scoffs. "Yeah, because I'll be with her."

I reach over and grab her hand to get her attention. Before I even open my mouth, her shoulders slump.

Keira's lips twist to the side and she shakes her head. "We'll find somewhere else for you, Maeve. Somewhere that has everything you need. Just give us a little time."

Nico scoffs. "My island has everything you could ever need, but hey, if it's not up to your standards, feel free to not go."

"If she doesn't come, then neither do I," Romeo interjects.

Tommy makes this low noise in the back of his throat, a grunting sort of scoff. I can only assume that's some sort of agreement. Or maybe my imagination is running away from me again.

I keep my gaze on my sister right now. She needs my undivided attention and I don't know if I can look at any of them without letting the wide array of emotions play across my face.

And I would rather die than let them see what they're doing to me. Not when I'm so unprepared.

"We don't have it. And it's a good plan, Keira," I remind her.

"Bullshit. It's held together by a shoestring—"

"It's a private island. That I own. And is only attended by same two employees for the last ten years. If they were going to betray me, they would've done it by now," Nico says, though he's not nearly as patient as me.

Keira glares over my shoulder, presumably at Nico. "People will do a lot of things for money. And thirty-five million dollars is a lot of fucking money."

"Thirty-five? I thought you said the bounty was five a piece," Tommaso says.

"It was. But I'm working with a laptop here, so if there are backdoors and stipulations built in, I can't access it without my computer," Romeo says.

"And how will you be able to do that on some unheard of island?" Keira pops her hip to the side and folds her arms across her chest. It's a challenging stance, confidence that she's caught them in a lie.

"Rome has a whole kit at the island house. Private, rerouted server with satellite service," Nico says.

Keira bristles, but I tuck that piece of information away for later. Like when I need to reach out to my sisters.

"I hate to rush you, but the longer we wait, the higher the chance we'll lose our pilot," Romeo says.

I sigh, hating that I know he's right. Hating the fact that I have to leave my sisters for an undetermined amount of time. And even hating my da for being the catalyst for this whole thing.

I swivel to face the men, locking gazes with Nico. "Alright. I'm in, but this—"

"Maeve, no," Keira interrupts me.

I continue as if she didn't. "Doesn't touch them."

Nico inclines his head.

I look him in the eye. "I want your words."

It's the same thing he said to me at The Red Lion all those weeks ago. A subtle reminder of our history, no matter how brief.

His nostrils flare, and his eyes narrow. Good, I guess he remembers then. "You have my word. No blowback on your sisters."

"We don't need their fucking protection, Maeve. We've got our own ways of protecting you." She glances pointedly to my stomach.

Nico quirks a brow but doesn't comment.

I don't exactly trust him but I distrust the men and women fighting for thirty-five million dollars more. As much as I'm loathe to admit it, I trust Romeo. And I trust Tommaso's instinct. When he stepped in front of me in the doctor's office, it wasn't a calculated move, It was a knee-jerk reaction.

I look between the three men, trying to discern if Tommaso told them about what he heard. That precious sound.

They look varying shades of frustrated, confused, and

anxious. It's impossible to tell who knows what secrets. But my gut . . . my gut tells me I can trust them.

I bite the inside of my cheek and admit to myself that there's a yearning sort of desperation inside of me. For them. It belongs to the hopeless romantic, I'm sure.

And maybe a tiny bit to me. I owe it to myself and to this baby to give them a shot to step up, to become . . . I don't want to say family like this is some romcom movie. And calling it co-parenting doesn't feel right either.

Maybe that's the point.

I don't know what the future will hold, but until I can say definitively that our lives would be better or worse with them in it, I'm going to make fucking lemonade with my bagful of lemons.

I clasp her hands in mine and pull her in for a tight hug. "It's safer for everyone if we're not together. And it's better if Da doesn't think you were involved. Promise me you'll stay out of Ireland until this is all sorted."

"Aye," she grumbles.

"Don't make me pull the sister card, Keira."

"Fine. I promise."

Her reluctant acquiescence isn't unnoticed. But I don't have the mental fortitude to field it right now.

"Good enough." I pull back, stepping away. I bend down and scoop up a go-bag I put together for her. "Here, take this. I had extras from mine."

"Where are you going to go?" Nico asks.

She cuts him a look that's made many men crumble. "Like I'm telling you anything."

I waggle the backpack in front of her, the nylon fabric softly crinkling. "Tell me then."

She pushes my hand toward my chest. "I have my own in the car. In fact, I want you to take my extras. C'mon, let's go grab them together."

I arch a brow at her deflection and follow her back outside. The guys stay in the terminal, but all three of them come to the window, standing vigil.

We stop at the back of the SUV, and Keira glances at them before looking back at me. She opens the trunk and rummages around for a moment. "Here," she says, handing me a black puffy-quilted duffle bag. "Take this."

"Keira, I'm not going to take your actual bags. I'm fine with my go-bag." I hold up my favorite black backpack by the strap.

She pushes it against my chest firmly. "Yes, you are. You don't know where you're going, and I doubt you'll have much access to clothes and toiletries that we use. So, please, take it. I'll be fine without it. I can walk freely, remember?"

I know she means it to soothe me, but it doesn't work. It only serves to remind me that my sisters can be used against me. Or worse, get caught up and become collateral.

I nod and take the duffle bag from her and set it at my feet, next to the two backpacks.

"Do me a favor, yeah? Go find Ava. She's in Monaco still, but I don't trust Da not to follow through on that backup clause in the contract. The one where it outlines if I don't hold the contract, then they'll take Ava."

She rolls her bottom lip inward for a moment. "About that, I was thinking I would come with you, stay close by at least. Ava will be safe with her friends, and then I can run interference here, in case you need me to."

"And what about the remaining members of the Milano family? They'll be out for revenge, and the first place they're going to look is at us. And Da gave them free reign when it comes to us with that contract. She'll need the backup, Keira."

She arches a brow and purses her lips. "And you don't?"

"They need it more," I murmur.

I shake my head as the loving warmth that only a sister can provide fills my chest. I've been the oldest in every facet of that phrase. First child, oldest sister, rightful heir to my da's Syndicate.

"You're too selfless, Maeve. Let me help you. Let us help you," Keira says.

Being first isn't a position in our family that I created or demanded; it was born out of necessity. Having five children will create a natural order of things, and then when Mum died, it only amplified it exponentially.

I became a shield for my sisters—and I did it happily. I was the captain of our ragtag girl gang, making sure we were trained in all the things we were told we couldn't do. Not in the Syndicate life, at least. That was when I thought Da would treat us as equals. Treat me with the respect he taught me to demand from people.

I can't say exactly when it became a habit, but the five of us crossed over the invisible line where they didn't need me to be their captain any longer.

And yet, I still was.

By choice.

Theirs and mine.

A decision born out of love and respect and understanding of our own strengths and weaknesses. I know I would choose them every time, and I have. But in the last two months, they've chosen me first. And that understanding brings an acute sort of pride that I can't explain. It's a soft swell of pride and love with the sharp pang of vulnerability.

I was threatened under sister code to put myself first, to revel in my temporary freedom the last few months. And so I was selfish, and I did.

I don't often indulge in the what-ifs of life, not if I can help it at least. It's dangerous and usually takes me down a rabbit hole I have a hard time getting out of. There are a lot of variables lately, a lot of different ways the events could have unfolded differently.

But the biggest one I keep coming back to is: what if I never met any of them? I know for a fact the outcome would ensure this little miracle wouldn't be here.

"Please, Keira. For this little sunray." I run my palm over my lower abdomen. There's no outward sign of a baby yet, but I feel irreversibly changed inside. And even with everything that transpired, including the series of truly insane coincidences, I wouldn't change it if it meant I wouldn't get this baby.

"Sunray?"

23

MAEVE

A WATERY SORT of laugh bubbles out before I can stop it. "I don't know what to call it. Ugh *it* feels weird, and *baby* doesn't feel right either. And this baby feels like a bright spot in my life. A beam of sunlight."

She chuckles. "I like it." She's quiet for. a moment. "Damn, I can't believe you're having a baby. I thought for sure it'd be Ava first. Sure she'd finally wake up to the fact that her best friends have been in love with her for years."

Amusement lightens my mood as I think about my sister. We've all been waiting for her to wake up to her best friends' feelings.

"But this makes perfect sense, too."

I look from my abdomen to her, arching a single brow. "You think having a baby with our enemies somehow makes sense?"

The side of her mouth hooks into a grin. "They were never our enemies, Maeve. Not really. Those allegiances belong to old men who don't give a fuck about us or anyone else. And anyway, I meant because you're the most maternal person I've ever known. You've been mothering us for a decade." She pauses, her voice lowering. "You're going to be a fantastic mum."

I've never felt so protected in my life and I know my sisters love me in their own way, that is never a question that enters my mind. But for Keira to step up for me like this, to help me even when I have a harebrained plan that *definitely* went awry, to literally step between me in danger. My eyes well, the emotion it brings forth this so all-consuming, so visceral that I can't even find a word for it.

On impulse, I reach for her, a quick snap of my arms, curling around her shoulders, and I pull her into my chest. She reciprocates the hug with the same ferocity as she had earlier.

I hate the pessimistic thoughts that crowd my brain, the doubt that has infiltrated my subconsciousness and now settles in my consciousness.

An alarming amount of emotion swells inside of me, like a tidal wave quickly eroding parts of my identity until they're left in broken fragments at my feet.

If I'm not there, who will watch over them?

Watch over your sisters, take care of them, protect them.

They're words my mum said to me so often that they've somehow embedded themselves into the very fabric of my being.

I'd like to think that I'd always have grown to be a kind, protective older sister, especially in the life we lead. But the truth is, I've had this role—this *identity*—for so long. I'd convinced myself that my purpose I was simply to guide them, to protect and watch over them.

I used to entertain these grand thoughts of what I would do if I didn't have four younger sisters to look after. All the places I would go or the person I would become.

But I never left them, not really. I was convinced that I couldn't take a single day—a week—to myself, because what if they needed me and I wasn't there for them? I'd convinced myself that something terrible would happen.

But what I didn't realize until right this very second is that it was *me* who needed *them* too. I've spent the last couple months away from them, and while it was alright, I didn't revel in it like I once thought I might.

I'll never know how different our life could have been if Mum were still alive, but I know with absolute certainty that I never would've lasted this long without my sisters.

Regret and resignation make excellent bedfellows inside of me. I know I'm doing the right thing—the only thing—by leaving Keira here, but that doesn't mean that it's easy. Or that I like it.

It feels like wet cotton expanding inside of me, bloating me and stuffing every available inch. The sludgy wet clumps weigh me down, slowing my body as if my emotion can physically stop what's happening.

"Promise me you'll take care of them," I murmur against my sister's shoulder.

Keira nods, this jerky, fast movement as she sniffs. "You know I will, Maeve. Just until you're back though, okay. Then you can take the reins again."

"You have to check in with Rosie. She's going to say she's fine, but you need to visit her. And you have to check in with O'Boyle first."

"I will."

"And don't let Fi brush you off, because she will. Those elitist pricks are worse than some of the Syndicate's soldiers. I'm worried she's too stubborn to bail on that school even if that's the right call."

"I know, Maeve."

"And make sure Ava is okay. Those friends of hers are reckless, and if she spends too much time with them without one of us to anchor her, she's impulsive. Too impulsive."

"I know," she murmurs.

Her reassuring tone doesn't ease my worries, my thoughts tumbling too fast to stop them from spiraling. "And don't forget to keep tabs on Da. I hate what he did, and I don't trust him not to do something else stupid. Don't give him the opportunity, okay? Maybe Rosie can put one of those sneaky spyware things on his computer? No one goes on vacation alone anymore, not when it isn't safe, okay?"

Some of her best qualities are also the most dangerous. She's headstrong and determined. Impulsive and fiercely loyal. And terrifyingly lethal.

"We'd never green-light something without you," she says, squeezing me tighter.

My sister and I are no strangers to goodbyes. The five of us routinely say farewell to one another when we split up and go on vacations. Sometimes we went weeks without seeing one another if our schedules conflicted. But we could talk, and there was an end date, even if it was abstract.

This is an open-ended farewell, like a one-way ticket to a private, surprise destination. I don't even know where we're going, and intellectually, I understand it's safer that way. But emotionally—it feels like goodbye.

"This isn't goodbye," I rasp. It's a reminder for me as much as her. My nose stings, and I blink away the tears that fill my eyes

"Of course not," she grumbles as she sniffs again, her face tucked in close. Her chin just resting on top of my shoulder.

"I'll see you soon." I smooth my hand along her back in wide arcs.

"Not soon enough," she whispers, her voice cracking a little. "The next time I see you, you could have a baby with you. This tiny little thing that will exist wholly of you—and none of those assholes back there."

A laugh catches me off-guard, her feelings on the Santorinis clear. "We'll fix it, aye? Rosie will pull in Rush, I'm sure. And get Rush to pull in the Five Families. Barter a favor if you have to. I'll see you soon, long before I have this baby."

She pulls away with a sniff, setting her hands on my shoulders. Her eyes are glassy, tear tracks down the apples of her cheeks. "Promise?"

Like a Pavlovian response, the sight of her tears sets off my own. It's a quirk I've always had. If one of my sisters cries, it's like my soul reaches out and shares their sorrow.

"Aye, I promise."

At this point what else is there to say? My sister and I are just sharing space, neither one of us quick to leave each other. Not when there's so much unknown left.

A throat clears from behind me. "I don't want to rush you, but we need to move. The plane is ready, and the fewer eyes that see us, the better," Romeo says.

Keira and I both straighten, startled by our audience. She glares at Romeo behind me.

"I thought you said this was safe." There's accusation in her tone, more than even she would normally throw at someone. A defensive mechanism, one to soothe her own anxieties and to cover up the fact that she's terrified, I'm sure.

"It is safe. We've already been through this. You know I wouldn't put Maeve in danger," Romeo says.

"I don't know anything about you." Some of Keira's aggression has simmered, leaving only a sort of resigned frustration.

"He's right. We should go, and so should you." I do mu best to keep my voice even, placating even. I reach down and haul the backpack and duffle bag up, throwing one strap from each over my shoulder. "The more distance between you and me, the better."

Keira bites her bottom lip, shifting from foot to foot before slipping the duffle bag from my shoulder and anchoring it on hers. I can see the refusal written all over her face, but it never leaves he mouth. "Aye, alright. I'll walk you over."

Romeo hols my gaze for a moment, scanning me from head to toe before he nods and turns around. I hold my breath, waiting for him to say something—anything. About him, me us— the baby. I keep waiting for one of them to bring up the baby, but so far, it's only been about the plan.

I should be relieved, shouldn't I? Then why do I feel dread pooling in my gut?

The two of us follow Romeo across the small parking lot, around the corner to the little row of private planes. Tommaso and Nico are twenty feet ahead of us, both of them carrying overnight bags on their shoulders.

"There's a satellite phone in the front pocket of my bag, plus a backup one in the duffle," Keira says quietly. "Call me."

"In one week, I know," I interrupt her. We've already had this conversation.

"You should call me when you get there," she grumbles.

"It's not safe," she says at the same time I do. Only her tone is more begrudgingly.

I arch a brow and look over my shoulder at her. She's scowling, throwing glares at the men ahead of us, not that they're paying much attention to her.

I bump her shoulder with mine to get her attention. "Tell Ava and Fi, about me, I mean." I tilt my head toward my stomach. "I, uh, don't know when I'll be able to talk to them, and I don't want them to feel left out."

Her shoulders settle back down and she looks at me, her gaze bouncing around. "Of course."

Her gaze scatters around, never resting on anything and skirting right over me. It's one of her only tells. She's nervous.

I rest my fingers on her forearm, hoping to settle her nerves. "Hey, whatever it is, you can tell me."

She blows out a breath, her cheeks puffing up. "Right, so I just wanted to tell you that it's okay."

"What's okay?"

She tips her head toward the men walking in front of us, out of earshot thankfully. "If you happen to find yourself in a literal paradise like Santorini claims, maybe indulge in some *self care*." Her brows rise toward her hairline with the last two words. "Take some me time. And then maybe some Tommaso time, and Romeo time, and even that asshole Nico."

My brows bunch over my eyes, my feet slowing as we approach the stairs to the plane. My mouth drops open, but no words come out right away. I'm actually speechless. "Are you— are you telling me to sleep with them while I'm hiding out?"

She flashes a caricature of a grin at me. "Hell yes I am. The damage is done, Maeve. You're already knocked up, so you should ride those trains often."

"Oh my god," I say around a laugh. "That's the kind of thing I'd expect Rosie to say, not you."

Her grin widens. "Well, I'm channeling our sister, so I guess I did good. But seriously, if you did jump back into bed with them, I wouldn't judge you. Feelings free, of course, because those guys are dicks. But they sure are pretty. I bet they fuck like—"

"Okay, okay," I say with a laugh, pulling her in for a final hug. "Love you. We'll talk soon."

She pulls back first, hands me the duffle bag, and nudges me toward the stairs. "I better hear from you in one week, Maeve. Or I'm going to track you down myself."

I situate the bag on my shoulder and start toward the stairs. "I'll talk to you in a week."

"And try not to stress so much. It's bad for the baby," she calls when I'm at the top.

I shake my head with a smile, waving over my shoulder at her as I step inside the plane.

"Did she just say *baby*?" Romeo asks with wide eyes.

24

TOMMASO

I PLANT my hand in Romeo's chest and shove him back into one of the flight attendant's alcoves in the front of the plane. "Not now, Rome."

I step into the space he was just in, blocking his view of her. If he chooses to see it as a metaphor for something else, well, that's on him. I'm simply helping my girl onto the plane.

I'm still shocked she's fucking here. And *pregnant*. I wished I had the foresight to record the sound of the little miracle's heart beating. I've been replaying the gentle whoosh-whoosh in my head since. It's been playing in the background of everything, like some sort of soundtrack.

When she called Rome and told him about the hit on us, I wasn't surprised. Not really. I always figured my card would get punched early. I didn't know how, but I knew it would happen sooner than later. You don't live the way I have, do the things I've done, and not expect to get taken out of the game early.

A hit out on both of my brothers though? That *is* unexpected. But that's not even what's fucking me up the most. It's the

177

job on her, and the fact that they would pay double for her alive that has me nearly feral.

I'm excellent at masking my emotions, a necessity born from childhood that morphed into a stillness that's proven quite useful for me. It's given me the freedom to slip into the background of almost any situation, to wipe my face clean into a true neutral.

On the outside, I'm unruffled, and inside, it feels like every cell in my body is rioting. The fiber of my being brays for violence, to end everyone who dares come for her.

Because that means they're coming for my baby, too. And I'll kill every single person on this earth who dares to breathe on her if that's what it takes to keep them both safe.

But until I get the opportunity to rid the world of the evil, depraved assassins trying to catch a pay day on us, I'm going to fucking woo my girl. Luckily for the both of us, I recently binged some cult classic 80s movies.

She's the princess, Rome's the brain, Nic's the athlete, and I'm the crazy one, of course. And all four of us are criminals.

I remember all the times Rome boasted about *the Wren* and all the jobs she pulled off, with the help of her sisters, I bet. I plan to use the next few hours on this flight to get to know her as much as I can. I feel like a sponge, desperate for information on her, ready to soak it up.

And I'm not going to let my little brother ruin my time with her by running his mouth. I don't know the extent of their relationship yet, but nothing changes the fact that we were together a couple of months ago.

I fucking knew she was life-changing.

"Here." I reach out and slide the straps of one backpack and duffle bag off of her shoulder. "Let me help you."

"Oh, um, okay, I guess."

I walk down the narrow aisle, the dark patterned runner

surprisingly soft under my steps. I stow her packs under a compartment that doubles as a table in front of a pair of seats.

"How's this?"

She looks around, her gaze pausing on Nico in the last row, his phone glued to his ear. I'm not sure who he's talking to. I honestly don't remember what they said the next steps are, because I was too busy thinking about her. Besides, I'm not the brains of this operation, I'm just the muscle.

"It's great. Whose plane is this?" she asks as she scoots in to the window seat.

It's objectively a nice private jet. Everything is done in shades of cream and dark charcoal. The seats are cream-colored leather with black stitching, a theme that's kept throughout the entire cabin and all the trimming.

I plop into the window seat next to her, feeling the heat of her immediately. "Honestly, I'm not sure. But Nic wouldn't have us on it if he didn't trust the owner."

She tucks her other backpack underneath the table in front of us. "You, maybe, but he doesn't care about me."

There's something off about the way she says that, a slight uptilt in inflection that piques my interest. I turn to look at her. "Should he?"

She stills, bent over and fussing with the bags. She straightens up slowly and looks at me. "Yes."

Rome shuffles down the aisle, pausing in front of our seats. "Juliet, can we talk?"

I grit my teeth, trying to temper my annoyance. I'm not feeling very generous right now. I want her all to myself, which is what he's probably thinking too. But he can fucking get in line.

She looks at him, her lips parting and her cheeks flushing the prettiest shade of pink. I wonder if she's replaying the moment she dropped the l-word bomb on him.

I wonder what she would do if she knew I was jealous. I hold my breath, warring between the urge to tell him to get lost and the need to see what decision she makes.

"Ladies and gentlemen, this is your captain speaking. Since we have a skeleton crew aboard today, at your request, please help yourself to anything the flight attendants stocked before they deplaned. If you could please take your seats as my copilot, Jerry, and I get ready for takeoff. I'll let you know when it's safe to move about the cabin," the captain says over the intercom system.

"Later, Romeo," Maeve murmurs. Her lips say one thing, but her eyes say something else entirely.

Damn. I suck in a breath. What I would give to have her look at me like that, like I hung the moon or some shit.

Rome raps his knuckles on the table in front of us twice. "Yeah, sure."

He sits in one of the three rows behind us. I don't have to turn around to know his gaze is already lasered-in on us. Or more accurately—her. I can't even fault him for it.

She's like this exotic creature. Her energy feels the same as it did that fateful night, but seeing her again feels different—*more*.

She buckles herself without another word, pulling the belt taut against her abdomen. I have a moment of panic, remembering exactly where that wand thing was on her stomach when we heard our baby.

But pregnant people fly all the time, right? Fuck, I really need to get one of those baby books. I've never really been into reading non-fiction. If I'm going to read anything, it's those classic murder mystery novels. But for her—for this baby—I'm willing to try.

I fasten my seatbelt, watching her the entire time. Her head is turned away from me, her gaze firmly outside. She can't see much, the sky darkening to the deepest shade of blue before it turns black.

We're taxiing down the runway now, just a minute from take-off. My throat gets dry the longer she looks out the window and not at me.

"You're not afraid of flying, are you?"

As far as small talk goes, it could've been worse. But it's definitely not my strong suit. Shit, is it hot in here? I tug at my collar, giving my neck a brief reprieve from the restrictive cotton of my black tee.

She looks over her shoulder at me, her brows low over her eyes. The rattling in my chest settles when her eyes are on me. "And if I was?"

"Are you?" I counter.

A smirk flits across her lips. "No. I'm no stranger to flying."

Good. This is good, right? I slide my hands along my thighs, grounding myself as I search for something else to talk about. Some common ground.

Why the fuck am I so nervous right now?

"Nic said there were bodies behind the church, where we last were."

She stills as she looks at me, and I want to shove the words back in my mouth. Fuck.

I roll my head from side to side, craning my neck. "Uh, shit. I don't know why I said that. I meant to ask what happened at the church."

She wiggles a little, adjusting herself so she's partially tilted toward me, her shoulders pressing against the seatback. She doesn't lose the calculated gaze. "You don't remember?"

I shake my head, willing my heart to stop racing inside my chest like I'm a fucking thirteen-year-old talking to a chick. "Nah, I thought I was dead for the first part. Remember?"

She nods and wets her lips with the tip of her tongue. "Aye, I remember. We should, uh, probably talk about . . ." She trails off, her gaze flitting around the cabin.

I couldn't have planned the timing more perfectly if I orchestrated it myself. I reach under my seat and grab the paper bag I took from the doctor's office. I set it on the table in front of her. "Here. I thought you might need these."

"What's this?" She eyes the paper bag like it holds a snake, all furrowed brows and pursed lips.

I nod my chin toward it. "Open it."

She gently unrolls the top of the bag, the noise swallowed up by the roaring of the engine as we start our ascent into the air. A soft gasp leaves her lips, and even though all the background noise, I hear it.

I decide it's going to be another sound I replay over and over again.

Can someone be addicted to sounds? Is that a thing? I should ask Rome to look that shit up, because in the span of a few hours, I've collected two sounds that I want to hear over and over again for the rest of my life.

"Where did you get these? He didn't offer them to me," she says, pulling out bottles of prenatal vitamins.

I lift a shoulder. "He didn't exactly offer them to me, either. I strongly suggested he give me whatever he had in his office that you might need." I jerk my chin toward the bag once more. "There's anti-nausea stuff in there too. A bracelet and some low-dose meds that he had a ton of samples for. He said there are instructions on all of it, but we should probably have Rome look that shit up and double-check." I look to the right and grumble, "I don't trust that doctor."

I startle when I feel her arms wrap around me as best she can from this angle.

"Thank you," she murmurs against my shoulder.

"Of course," I murmur. "I'm going to take care of you, Maeve." I run my lips over the top of her head.

She pulls back, her teeth sinking into her bottom lip. "About that." Her gaze darts to the side for a moment before settling on mine. "You should know that there's a chance it's not . . . yours."

25

TOMMASO

MY HEART STOPS FOR A MOMENT, panic squeezing its fist so tightly around it that I forget how to breathe. Adrenaline slushes through my veins, not nearly as quick as usual. Like the events from the day tapped me.

I shake my head a little, dislodging the anxiety wrapped around what's left of my heart. Nah, I don't believe it. I remember when we were together, the date clearly etched into my consciousness.

She left a permanent brand on me that night. She was a surprise beacon of hope on a particularly rough day of *chatting* with traitors. She was unexpected in the best of ways, confident and demanding. She took her pleasure from me, and I genuinely thought she would follow me into the shower for another round.

The crushing disappointment I felt when I realized she bailed without a word is nothing compared to the feeling coursing through my veins right now.

"I—I'm sorry. This is all so much, on top of the church, and I . . . . I didn't know I was pregnant until today. And your brother—"

I tip my head back against the headrest, squeezing my eyes tight as realization rolls over me in a slow wave.

I'm not known for my puzzle-solving skills, but even I can put these pieces together. Maeve is Rome's Wren. He's been obsessed with her for months, long before we really started razzing him about it.

Did she come to the house for him? As quickly as that thought comes, I dismiss it. No, she came because she wanted to get out of the contract.

Self-loathing curdles like spoiled milk in my gut. Her and I fucked one night—when she thought I was someone else. There's no way I can compete with the likes of my little brother, the man she's been spending time with for who the fuck knows how long.

Her hand lands on my forearm, pulling me out of my spiral.

"Hey, are you okay? I know it's . . . a lot to process. And I—I don't know what to say," she murmurs.

I consciously relax my fingers, releasing the death grip on the armrests. I meet her gaze, noting the way the skin crinkles around her eyes. "Rome?"

Her lips part but no sound comes out. She closes her mouth and clears her throat. Her cheeks pinken and she shakes her head. "Not exactly."

My eyes widen as my own lips part in shock. "*Nic?*"

She rolls her shoulders back and straightens her spine. "I won't apologize if that's what you're looking for. We didn't owe each other anything that night, and I don't expect that to change just because this"—she places her palm on her stomach—"changed."

Her words should soothe me, bring me comfort in the knowledge that she doesn't have expectations of me. But ironically, it does the opposite. I don't have the mental capacity to unpack that little revelation tonight, my body aching in places I'll feel for days.

But I can't rest until she knows where I stand. In the few seconds it took for her to let me off the hook, my desires crystallized.

"That's where you're wrong, *dolcezza*. Now that you're here, everything changes. And this"—I ghost my palm above hers, not quite touching her skin—"means everything."

"But what if it's not yours? I don't want to get your hopes up." She's not being unkind. She's trying to temper my expectations. But she doesn't know me well enough to recognize my determination and conviction.

"You don't believe me yet. That's alright. I'm going to prove it to you, *dolcezza*," I murmur softly. "This is mine, and so are you."

Her pupils dilate, her mouth parting on a small exhale. "We had one night, Tommaso. You don't even know me."

"We're going to be on an island together for the foreseeable future, I'm not worried."

"With your brothers," she deadpans.

I arch a brow, offering her a cocky little smirk. "Like I said, I'm not worried."

MAEVE FALLS asleep with her head leaning against the window after another half hour of comfortable silence. I unbuckle my seatbelt quietly, unwilling to wake her up. I don't like the purple smudges of exhaustion underneath her eyes.

I plan on making sure her stay at Nic's island is stress-free and luxurious—as much as it can be when you're hiding out from a mob of assassins with varying skill levels.

That's why I need to get this *conversation* out of the way.

I snag a plush throw from a cabinet behind our seats and drape it over Maeve, careful not to jostle her. Once I'm satisfied with the steady rise and fall of her chest, I prowl toward my brothers in the back.

Nic's been fielding calls, no doubt from our guys back home. I can only imagine how many people have heard the news—both that Vito claimed the hit and put targets on our backs and the fact that we have some sizable hits on us.

The sound of Rome's keys depressing with every keystroke hasn't stopped since we got in the air. I'm sure he's trying to find more information—on her hit and ours. He said he was limited with this current equipment, so I hope whatever shit Nic got for the safe house is adequate.

Nic tips his chin up in greeting, but he doesn't pull his gaze from his phone. "Hey."

I flutter my fingers a little, my hands hanging loosely at my sides. "Everything okay?"

Nic drops his phone on the table to his right, it's smaller than the one at our seats, more like a side table than anything. He pushes to his feet, stretching his neck from side to side. "Yeah. Just issuing orders to the soldiers I know are loyal to us. I'm not going to let Vito burn our shit to the ground with his greed and incompetence while we're gone."

I nod, biting the inside of my cheek and waiting for the perfect moment. "Good, good."

"And her? Did you get more information from her?"

I cock my head to the side, pulling my arm back and launching it at my brother's face. He rocks backward with a shout.

"What the fuck, Tommy!"

I barely have to shake my hand out. "Fuck off. I pulled my punch and you know it."

He glares at me, the skin around his eye flushing an angry red. "What the fuck was that for? And why the fuck do you two think you can just fucking punch me like that?"

I stare at him, garnering his attention. Once I have it, I offer him one of my famous smiles. It's too wide and a touch crazy. I happen to think I look approachable, friendly even.

Nic scowls at me. "Knock that shit off. You don't fucking scare me, man."

I shrug both shoulders. "When it comes to her, maybe I should."

"What does that mean?" Rome asks, his tone sharp.

I point my finger at him. "Yours is coming, brother."

Rome throws his hands up. "What the fuck did I do?"

"You made her upset, back at the doctor's office," I explain like it's the most logical thing in the world. Isn't it though?

"And?" Nic snaps. "Are you her protector now or something?"

I narrow my gaze at my brother. "Does she need one from you?"

He grits his teeth, a muscle in his jaw twitching. "Don't be absurd."

I lift my brows and grin at him. "If you say so, brother."

"Are you two done? I found something that might be useful," Rome says.

I hold Nic's gaze, determined to stay right where I am until he understands how serious I am. I can see it written all over his stiff posture, the way his lips thin the longer he looks at me.

He's fucking furious with me right now. I let his anger roll off of me like a dewdrop on a blade of grass. I love him—Rome too—but I'm not budging on this. I can't explain it to them any better than I can understand it myself.

He breaks first, looking at Rome and snapping, "What?"

Rome arches a brow at him before focusing on his laptop. "I can't get behind the layers of protection around The Bricks, not even with my set up back in Vegas. But what I did find was Vito's statement. It originated from somewhere in Italy."

"You think he's there?" Nic asks.

Rome runs his hand through his hair, letting the strands stick up in a way that suggests he's been doing this for a while already. "It's possible. I don't think he's capable of rerouting the information so it looks like he's in Italy. So either he's there—"

"Or he paid someone in Italy to share it," Nic finishes his thought.

"Or he's in contact with Il Diavoli." Both of my brothers look at me. I flush a little, the tacky feeling of doubt smacking against my face. "What?"

"Nothing," Rome says quickly. "It's just that I didn't think of that, but it actually makes the most sense."

"What would Vito stand to gain by eliminating us?" Nic grips his chin, his gaze unfocused as looks across the cabin.

I run my hand over my jaw, scratching at my stubble. "I think the better question is: why is he willing to dump fifteen million dollars to take us out when he could've done it for a fraction of that at home?"

"And why would he issue a hit on Maeve? He doesn't even know about her," Rome asks.

"Doesn't he though? She was contracted to marry Nic before I killed it."

That gets their attention. Both of my brothers look at me like they've never seen me before.

"You never did tell us how you ended that contract," Nic says.

And I don't ever plan on telling him. "Some things are better left a mystery." I sit down in one of the two seats across from them, ready to watch them both like a hawk when I drop this little information bomb on them. "There is one thing you should know though. Maeve's pregnant. And it's mine."

26

MAEVE

I FEEL like I've been traveling for days. I'm exhausted, both mentally and physically. Every inch of me aches from the travel, my body in desperate need of rest.

The flight from California to Texas wasn't long. But coupled with the drive to Georgia, where we switched cars, and then backtracking to Mississippi to switch cars again, I'm exhausted. After an eternity of travel time, we finally made it to the marina where we boarded Nico's yacht.

I'm not necessarily a boat person, but even I can admit it's a thing of beauty. The black paint glistens in the moonlight, and the gold trim shines brightly against the night sky.

Nico gives us the barest tour of the amenities before he retreats to get everything ready. Apparently, there's a small storage facility by the marina's office where he keeps things we'll need for our last leg of the trip.

In addition to the main cabin, there are two wide cabins below deck with three beds total: a central cabin with single beds, a VIP cabin with a huge walk-in wardrobe, and a bow master cabin in a raised position with en suite bathroom. There's also an elegant salon lounge area and dining room adorned with plush gray couches, mahogany tables and cabinets, and wooden floors covered in Persian-style carpets. On top of all that there is an open air flybridge deck where you can sit under the stars while looking out onto breathtaking views of nature's beauty.

It's where I find myself now. My heart flutters as blackness envelops the shore, swallowing it whole. There is nothing but black and blue as far as the eye can see.

How is it that things taste when your heart flutters? Adventure dances along the back of my tongue as we sail into the night.

The deck is made of a smooth, wooden material with a cherry finish. The colors blend with the night sky, making the yacht seem to disappear into the air around it. Small lights sparkle on the railings and on the deck, creating a faint golden hue of the outline of the entire yacht.

I sink into one end of the plush beige loveseats facing the front of the boat. The salty breeze swirls around me in a comforting embrace.

My head is pounding and my eyes are drooping heavily as I fight against the urge to doze off. But I know that if I give in now, exhaustion will sink into my bones and make it hard for me not only to continue standing but also comprehend what's going on around me.

Suddenly, I feel something. Not a sound or a smell, but an energy. It's soft, but I can feel it pulsing through me like an electric shock.

I look up just in time to see a figure slowly making his way towards me. The light of the stars dances off his shoulders and the moonlight catches his face as he draws closer.

Romeo.

He looks almost like a dream, emerging from the dark like I conjured him myself.

His expression is soft, yet intense as he all but prowls toward me. His eyes are dark as they meet mine. He stops a few feet away from me, as if uncertain if he should come any closer or not. His body is tense and his posture guarded as though he is expecting some kind of reaction from me that might break our fragile connection in two pieces forever.

My mind spins with all the memories that come flooding back in this moment: all those late night texts and our weekend in New York City.

"Hey," he says softly, his voice a low, husky tenor that sends shivers down my spine.

"Hey." My own voice is barely above a whisper.

We stare at each other for a moment, the tension between us palpable. I tilt my head to the right, to the cushion next to me. Romeo accepts my wordless invitation and sits next to me. Our legs brush against one another, sending sparks of awareness down my spine.

"Do you want to talk about it?" he murmurs.

The fact that there are so many different topics he could be referencing is too much for me tackle.

"I don't want to talk about anything right now. I think . . . I think I need a little space from the situation," I reply, my voice low. I brace myself, anticipating push-back, but I should've known better.

"Okay."

Four letter have never sounded so comforting before. I exhale, my shoulders releasing tension I didn't realize I was harboring until now.

He takes my hand in his, his strong fingers interlacing with mine. The silence is comforting, a balm to my frayed nerves.

The stars above twinkle like diamonds on a midnight sky. The soft lapping of the waves against the boat is a soothing lullaby as we bask in each other's company. We stare out at the horizon, lost in our own thoughts until finally my stomach growls.

A granola bar lands on my lap. But not just any granola bar. It's the kind with chocolate chips and oats and pieces of dried fruit and nuts.

And one of my favorite snacks.

I look at Romeo, my eyes widening in surprise. "What's this?"

"You should eat. It's been a long day, and I have vivid memories of you when you're hangry." He smiles, a small, knowing grin that's a touch smug to be entirely altruistic.

"I don't get hangry," I reply with a sniff, tearing the package open with one hand.

"Okay," he says easily.

The same word—the same four letters—but this one is said playfully. It's alarming how easy it feels with him, despite everything unsaid between us.

Still, my mind is too heavy to dive into such things right now.

I break off a piece and pop it in my mouth, instantly grateful. I didn't realize how hungry I was until this moment. I can't actually remember the last time I ate, but judging by how ravenous I feel, I'd guess it's been too long.

"Thank you," I whisper.

He runs his thumb across the delicate bones in my wrist. "Of course."

"Tell me something, Romeo."

He looks at me, his expression open. "What do you want to know?"

I lift a shoulder and pop another bite of chocolatey goodness in my mouth. "Tell me a story."

His eyes practically twinkle like they're plucked from the sky above. A half-smile unfurls on his lips, and I can sense a lightness in him that wasn't there before.

And suddenly, it feels like we're one under the same blanketed night, connected by something much greater than we ever could've imagined.

And then he tells me Shakespearean stories of faraway places and talks about fictional characters and their adventures.

His voice is mesmerizing, calming, and enchanting. He weaves it so effortlessly, like he's quilting me a blanket.

I slowly lean into him, resting my head against his shoulder, listening as he continues speaking softly into night air. His hands continue to hold mine as we cruise through the water like thieves in the night.

I DON'T KNOW how long I was asleep for, but it's deep enough that I don't rouse from sleep right away. Consciousness comes slowly, and when I crack open my eyelids, I come face to face with a white tee.

"I can walk," I croak.

Arms tighten around my back and under my knees, bringing me even closer to his chest.

"Don't be ridiculous."

It takes me a moment to match the voice. I was expecting Romeo, maybe Tommaso. But what I didn't anticipate was to wake up in Nico's arms of all people.

My eyes widen, and my heart skips a beat before it pounds against my ribcage. I look closely at him, an unobstructed view of the man I haven't been able to stop thinking about for so long.

Wind swirls through his hair, sliding it across his forehead. Yellow bollard lights illuminate half of his face, highlighting his lips. He looks like someone who walked off the pages of a romance novel. A dark knight, carrying me from danger bridal-style.

If he asks me about in the morning, I'm going to blame it on being half-awake. But the need is too strong.

I reach up and trace my index fingertip across his bottom lip. It's plumper than his top lip, bordering on pouty.

"What are you doing, Maeve?" he says, his voice barely above a whisper.

I drop my hand from his mouth, curling my fingers into fist against my chest. "What are you doing? Why are you carrying me?"

The wood planks creak under our combined weight. The bright yard spotlights grow closer with every step, and I feel like this fragile moment between us is about to end.

"Because you were asleep," he replies matter-of-factly, his voice still low.

I don't want to admit how much I find the whole gesture romantic, even if he doesn't wrap me in pretty words.

"I could've walked," I protest weakly, knowing full well that I won't try too much harder than this.

"I know," Nico says with a smirk.

The words send shivers down my spine.

He carries me inside the house without turning on any lights. For someone who claims to not spend much time here, he certainly has the route memorized. He carries me through the kitchen and down a hallway, through a bedroom door and placing me down on the edge of a bed. A soft pool of light from a lamp at the bedside table offers enough light that I can see his face clearly. Not that it helps me much, he's still virtually expressionless. If I didn't know any better, he looks almost angry.

His hands linger, slow to leave my skin. "This is your room while we're here."

I glance toward the open door. "Where's Romeo? Tommaso?"

Nico takes a step back, away from me. "They're bringing some things off the boat." He pauses, gritting his teeth. "Do you want me to get one of them?"

"No," I say, shaking my head and scooting back on the bed. "I just want to sleep."

He nods in understanding as he walks backward toward the door. "I'll be around if you need anything, but help yourself to anything here."

I look at him for a moment, torn between asking him to stay and letting him leave so I can go back to sleep.

27

MAEVE

"SIXTY SECONDS, MAEVE," Keira says, her voice is tinny and small in my ear. This satellite phone muffles her voice so strangely, I almost didn't recognize it when she called.

"I hate everything about this situation," I murmur.

"Use it as a gift."

"A gift? You think being without all of you is a gift for me?"

"No," she says with a sigh. "Being with them is. Use it as an opportunity."

I feel like a petulant child, sulking and moody. Those words, though said clearly in her voice, don't *feel* like her. "God, you sound like—"

"You?" she interrupts with a laugh. "Good. Then it means I'm doing my job filling in your impressive shoes."

I laugh, the familiarity now making sense. "It does sound like something I would say."

"You *have* said it. To all of us at several different points," she deadpans.

My laughter tapers off and I sigh. "I miss you guys. How are the girls?"

"We miss you too. And we're all fine. It's crickets from Da, and no one has made any moves toward any of us. We're all protected."

"Good. That's good." I glance at the clock. "Five minutes isn't enough time."

"Aye, but we agreed anything longer, and we'd be inviting trouble. We don't want anyone to piggy-back on our call and find you."

"I know, I know. You're sure you're safe? Ava's with you?" It was the first thing I asked, but I can't shake my anxiety, and if we had more time, I'd *triple*-check.

"Aye, we're all safe. I promise I'll break our schedule if it's an emergency. But you're okay, right? You and the baby? And the guys? How are they treating you?" Her words run together quickly, rushing to get out before our timer goes off.

"It's fine. Everything is fine." I waft my hand in the air, waving her questions away.

"I was half-sure I wouldn't even reach you because you'd be dick-deep in your own personal harem."

I practically choke on air at the casual way she drops that bomb.

"You okay?" she asks.

I clear my throat a little. "Yeah, sorry. You took me by surprise. I wasn't expecting you to say that."

"So, are you?"

"Nah, I've been busy." I keep my voice low.

She's quiet for a moment. "Okay. Tell me what you've been up to? Hows the house and is it as nice as Nico said it would be? Because I gotta be honest, I was half-hoping he was full of shit. But then I realized that would mean you would be trapped in a shitty place, so I changed my mind. I hope for everyone's sake that it's as amazing as he claimed."

"It is really nice. And it's beautiful here. He wasn't exaggerating that part."

I'm not lying. It is beautiful here, but it's a bullshit answer. I'm evading all her tough questions like a pro, and she's gracious enough not to call me on it.

Guilt burns in the back of my throat regardless. I'm not proud of the way I've been hiding out in my room since we got here, but I can't make myself snap out of it.

I feel . . . off.

Restless and without purpose.

I feel fucking sad.

I've never been one who had to schedule out every minute of every day, but I did have control over my days. I had purpose. Even if it was something small, I had *things* to do.

And here, there is nothing but endless water all around me.

I feel like this island, floating adrift in the middle of the water. And I don't know how to fix it.

"What about you seeing a doctor?" Keira asks, breaking me from my spiral.

"The staff, Margaret and Edward, both have some medical training. Tommaso said he'd figure something out if we're here longer than a few weeks. Though we'd have to go back to—"

"Uh, uh, uh. Don't tell me where you are. Or what city you're closest to. I don't want to know," she interrupts.

"Plausible deniability, aye, I know." Beeping sounds in the background, a frenetic chirping sound. My heart sinks further, the ache of missing them so sharp it pierces my soul.

"Two weeks. I'll call you again, aye?"

"Yes, two weeks. Love to you all," I quicken my words.

"Love you more," she says before the call abruptly cuts off.

I roll over and set the satellite phone on the nightstand. I thought I would feel better after talking to her, calmer. But if anything, I feel worse now.

It's like I'm trapped in a dream, unable to wake myself up. I'm in this glass cage, watching my sisters live their lives without me.

I stare out the window, fiddling with the hem of my borrowed sweatshirt and feeling generally sorry for myself.

I'm not particularly used to pity parties, usually preferring action to stillness. But I can't do that here, where I'm forced to be still. Maybe Keira's right though. Maybe I should take this situation as an opportunity.

For what exactly? I'm not sure yet. But I know I won't figure it out if I stay inside this room forever.

I mean, I could. It's a big open floor plan.

The cove ceiling is made up entirely of reclaimed weathered wood in shades of gray and blonde wood. Recessed lighting dots the wide ceiling, with two three-blade fans.

The platform bed is bigger than a California king, floating on an extended platform dais and with a mini headboard hidden behind the mountain of fluffy pillows. All the fabric in the room is varying shades of cream and gray, giving it a calming neutral vibe.

A TV is mounted to the wall across from the bed, and there's a little reading nook in the opposite corner. The floors are reclaimed wood in a slightly richer color than the ceiling, and a plush cream circle rug grounds the whole room.

Matching accordion doors that span almost the length of the wall separate the luxurious private bathroom from the bedroom. There's an entire wall of floor-to-ceiling windows that opens up, folding to the right in an accordion style.

There's a stamped concrete patio off the wall of windows with an oversized outdoor loveseat and little table. It connects to several other small patios outside what I assume are bedrooms. And they all feed into the larger outdoor space in the backyard.

An outdoor kitchen, a hot tub, an impressive zero-gravity

pool with a slide and grotto on one end, beach loungers and several different patio sets.

It's paradise. A fairytale out of a movie or a dream. White sandy beaches that I imagine feel like powdered sugar underneath your feet. The gentle hum of the ocean should be the perfect soundtrack for an afternoon spent lazing on one of the hammocks between two trees. The clear turquoise color of the water that I just know it warm and inviting.

And yet, I stay inside this borrowed room in a temporary safe house with a perpetual cloud of melancholy hanging over my head.

My hands are tied here, and the feeling of helplessness is as foreign as it is unwelcome.

Goddammit. Keira's right. I can practically hear her gloating right now.

I sigh as I look around the room. If I had to stay somewhere for an undetermined amount of time, there are worse places to be.

Someone knocks on my door, and I look over to see my bedroom door ajar and Tommaso filling it.

I eye him with suspicion. "Were you listening to my conversation?"

He stuffs his hands in his pockets and leans his shoulder against the doorframe. "Nah, it's a small house."

His answer is so absurd I stare at him without blinking for a moment. Then the side of his mouth hooks up into a slow grin. The kind that makes smart girls do stupid things.

I cock my head to the side and let my own smile blossom on my face. "We're on an island."

"A small one." His eyes look playful, actually everything about him seems relaxed today. "C'mon. You've been holed up in your room for a week. Let's go explore the house."

I look at Tommaso, give him a proper once over. I haven't

seen him or the other two much since we got here. I demanded space, and surprisingly, they didn't push.

Tommaso's dressed in a pair of low-slung black board shorts and an ocean blue graphic tee. His cheeks look sun-kissed like he has spent our time here outside.

"Yeah, alright."

His face brightens, his smile widening and his eyes shining with delight. "Yeah? Damn, okay. I thought you'd take some more convincing. I had Margaret make chocolate doughnuts to bribe you and everything, but I guess we don't need them."

My heart skips a beat. Maybe it's a coincidence, but chocolate doughnuts just happen to be my favorite. I swing my legs over the side of my bed and slide to the floor.

"It'd be a shame to let perfectly good doughnuts go to waste. Maybe we should start our tour in the kitchen."

He laughs and steps into the hallway as I cross the threshold. "Of course. Who am I to refuse my girl?"

I know it's ridiculous, but I swear my heart thumps extra hard at the casual way he said *my girl*. Like it's a fact or a forgone conclusion. Or maybe he's manifesting.

I don't correct him—I wouldn't even know what to say. And there's a small part of me that doesn't *want* to correct him. It's the same wanton woman who revels in his possessiveness.

Maybe this island will be my blessing in disguise after all.

28

MAEVE

TOMMASO LEADS ME OUTSIDE, to the back patio overlooking the pool and the ocean beyond it. I take a seat at the rectangular ten-chair patio table underneath the large umbrella. My eyes widen at the sheer beauty of everything around me. The sun is a bright ball of light toward the horizon, shining from the place where the water meets the air. It paints streaks of golden light onto the surface of the water, creating an almost magical effect that takes my breath away.

The sound of waves cresting fills in the silence between us as Tommaso takes a seat beside me. I can feel him watching me as I take it all in, but he doesn't speak. His presence is enough.

The salty sea air swirls around us and causes a tingling sensation on my senses as I relax into my chair. It feels good to be outside, to feel the ocean air on my skin.

After a moment, Tommaso speaks up. "Did you know Margaret trained to be a pastry chef?"

I turn to him, and he's already standing up and lifting the clear dome-shaped cover off the platter of doughnuts. The smell of chocolate frosting and a hint of cinnamon wafts toward me, making my mouth water.

"No, I didn't know that." I pluck one of the doughnuts off of the platter and take a bite. The rich chocolate melts against my tastebuds, and I groan.

"Good, right?" he asks, setting the platter down and grabbing his own.

I swipe my tongue in the corner of my mouth, clearing the chocolate frosting from my top lip. "They remind me of the ones my mum made."

He tilts his head to the side. "Did you do that a lot? Bake with your mom?"

Like anytime I think of her or those fond memories, my chest gets warm and fuzzy. I lift my shoulder up. "Aye, when she was alive, she taught my sisters and I all sorts of things. Like most mums do, I guess."

"Nah, not all moms."

I look at him, waiting for a beat to see if he says anything else. When he doesn't say anything, I swallow and look out into the water.

"My mum died when I was twelve," I say quietly.

"I'm sorry, Maeve." His voice is equally low.

I exhale and look at him. "It was a long time ago. So then I taught my sisters what I knew."

He's quiet, content to listen and enjoy these truly delicious doughnuts.

"And god were we bad at it for a while," I say around a laugh.

"But you kept doing it."

"Aye, we kept practicing. Until finally, we were all decent. And then we were good. Some of us were better than others, but I like to think Mum would've been proud."

He smiles. "I'm sure she would be. What was your favorite thing to bake?"

I think for a moment. "My favorite was always the chocolate chip cookies. It's deceptively simple, but I love them spruced up with walnuts and peanut butter chips."

"Me too." He flashes me a lopsided grin, and I feel my cheeks warm. He leans closer, and I can feel his warmth against my side. His laughter sounds like honey as it fills the air around us, thick and sweet.

"What about you? Do you have a sweet tooth, Tommaso?"

His dark brown eyes sparkle with mischief, reading an innuendo in my innocent question.

"Oh, *dolcezza*," he practically purrs as he leans in closer to brush his lips against the shell of my ear. "I have an insatiable sweet tooth."

I shiver at the sensation, feeling heat pool low in my belly.

"Is that so?" My heart kicks a quick rhythm against my ribs as I meet his gaze. His eyes are already trained on me, their intensity making desire roll over me in a wave.

We are definitely not talking about dessert anymore.

I don't know what he reads in my expression, but he brushes his lips across my cheek and sits back in his chair without another word. There's a small part of me that's disappointed he didn't take it further. But a bigger part recognizes that this is good too.

We talk until the sun soars across the sky. Tommaso bringing different things to snack on every few hours. We talk about our families, sharing stories and laughing until we know each other well enough that it feels like we've been together for far longer than just one day.

Tommaso looks at me with admiration in his eyes, something that sparks a warmth within me that grows with every passing moment we spend together.

FOR THE PAST FOUR MORNINGS, Tommaso has knocked on my door and asked if I wanted to eat breakfast with him.

Chocolate doughnuts, maple bacon scones, peanut butter and banana pancakes, Belgian waffles. I've eaten more decadent breakfast foods in the last week than I have in the last year. If he's trying to win me over with delicious food, it's definitely working.

One cinnamon roll later, Tommaso and I are sitting on the edge of the pool. Our legs bump against one another in the water, the temperature warm but still refreshing.

I'm wearing a pair of short cotton black sleep shorts and a loose fitting racerback tank top. It's an outfit better suited for sleeping or lounging, but I don't exactly have a ton of options here.

"Favorite ice cream flavor?" I ask. We've been playing a loose version of twenty questions, only we're just asking one another silly, little things. It's surprising what you can learn about a person by just asking what their favorite foods and movies and songs are.

It's been nice to spend this time with him. No, better than nice. It's been great. If I closed my eyes, I could almost pretend that we were on a date. To be honest, every day has felt like a date.

"Mint chip, hands down," he answers without question. "You?"

"I'm more of a salted caramel or butter pecan girl myself."

He grins at me, this flirty appreciative look that has me heating up. We're propped up on the side of the pool with an umbrella blocking out the hot sun.

I side-eye him, playfully bracing for his answer to my next question. "Musicals?"

He smiles, bumping his shoulder against mine. "Have you been talking to one of my brothers, *dolcezza?*"

I roll my lips inward to smother my smile. "Should I have?"

"Nah, I'm not ashamed to say that I love musicals. Plays, I could do without. But musicals are a must."

I nod a few times. "Yeah, I like them too. I don't get to see them enough though."

"Once we can leave, I'll take you to one."

"Really?" My brows rise, my smile stretching wider across my face. "I'd like that."

"Anything for you, *dolcezza*. Favorite color?" He says it so easily like the notion isn't new or grand, like it just *is*. Like he really would do anything for me and not even blink at it.

I blink a few times to focus on his question. A picture of my grandda's land and the surrounding green meadows pops into my brain. "The color of freshly cut grass in the peak of summer. You?"

"Black. But not just any regular ol' black. Nah, my favorite color is a sneaky black. The kind that looks solid from a distance, but when you get up close, you can see that it's a deep shade of brown that almost sparkles in the sunlight."

His fingers toy with the end of my hair. I'd gathered it in a twist and tossed it over one shoulder to let the gentle breeze sweep across my neck.

I study him as he looks at the way his fingers twirl in and out of a lock of my hair with the same kind of intensity I have when I'm formulating a plan.

To be the object of such attentiveness is . . . addicting, heady. From another man, it might be a line. But I have a sneaking suspicion that Tommaso doesn't do anything like other men.

I recognize the same swell of recklessness I felt in Las Vegas and Chicago and New York City as it rolls up my body.

"Tommaso," I whisper, tilting my head toward him.

"Hm?" he answers, his gaze still on his hand.

I twist to the side, clasping his hand in mine. His gaze flies to mine a second before I close the distance between us. I press my lips against his. In the five seconds it takes him to respond, I swear my stomach drops twice.

But then Tommaso surges forward, palms my cheek, and claims my mouth in such a primal way that I forget about everything except the way his lips and tongue feel against mine.

29

MAEVE

TOMMASO FRAMES my face with his big palm, angling my head to deepen our kiss. It goes from innocent to explicit in less time than I thought was possible.

I twist further into him, but the angle is all wrong. I'm not close enough. A noise of frustration hits the back of my throat.

He pulls back long enough to anchor his hands around my waist and pull me into his lap. I straddle his thighs, my head a second behind my body on the feeling of weightlessness.

He pulls me down firmly on him, and I wiggle closer, so we're lined up perfectly. I'm not sly or seductive when I sink down on his cock.

My eyes close on contact, reveling in the way his cock bumps against my aching pussy. I didn't realize I was this turned on. I feel like a powder keg, dangerous in my desire for him.

The suddenness pulls me up short. I tip my head toward the sky, and he uses it as an invitation to drag his lips down my neck.

Should I be grinding on Tommaso when I'm pretty sure I'm in love with Romeo? On paper it feels like it should be wrong. But if it's wrong, then why does it feel so, so . . . right?

Being here with Tommaso feels *right*.

"Hey, where'd you go?" He guides my face toward his once more.

His eyes have darkened to almost completely black, the slivers of hazel starburst swallowed by lust. His brows are low over his eyes, his kiss-swollen lips turned down.

I sink my hand into the hair at the back of his head, shifting closer to him. "I'm here."

"We go at your pace, remember?" he murmurs against my lips.

I swipe my tongue across my bottom lip, accidentally flicking his lip in the process. He groans, the sound reverberating through my chest.

"Talk to me, *piccola seduttrice*. What's wrong?"

"It's just—" I stop, my gaze flicking to his right, toward the house.

"If you're worried about my brothers, then don't. The three of us came to an . . . agreement of sorts."

My head jerks back, my mouth falling open.

He shakes his head and coaxes me back toward him. "Whatever you're thinking, it's not that."

I settle over him once more, willing to hear what he has to say. "Tell me then."

"I told them the truth: you're mine."

Ice floods my veins in an instant, freezing my arousal. I narrow my gaze at him. "You know I'm not, right?"

He looks up at me from underneath his lashes. "Aren't you though?"

"We barely know each other, Tommaso," I say, exasperation dripping from every word.

"I've had enough bad in my life to recognize the good when I see it." He slides his hands up my ribs, settling them just underneath my breasts. "To wrap my palms around it and hold onto it."

My gaze ping-pongs between his eyes. Confusion and wariness settle around my shoulders like a cloak. "And if I wasn't pregnant? Would you still feel like this is a *good decision*? Like I'm yours?"

He ghosts his lips across my jar, murmuring, "Every night I closed my eyes and thought of you. I would remember the perfect way you rode my cock in my brother's office. I would see your eyes in the color of the clouds right before the sun set. I would hear your voice in the wind, whispering cries of pleasure like I was trapped in the best kind of dream.

"I've never felt such a connection with someone before. I thought you were some kind of karmic gift, an apology for all the bullshit the universe or god or whoever's there put me through. Like you were *made* for me."

I want to let his words land on my skin, seep into my pores, and infuse themselves into my bloodstream. But I can't, not yet. Not until he understands where I'm coming from.

"If we're going to do this—whatever this is—then you should know I have feelings for Romeo. Real feelings." I hold my breath, bracing for his reaction.

He doesn't skip a beat. "And Nic?"

"I don't know Nico like I know Romeo—like I thought I *knew* Romeo."

"I already knew about Rome. And if you develop feelings for Nic, then we'll talk about it."

My eyes widen, not that he can see it. He's too busy dragging his nose up along the sensitive spot on my neck. "And you don't care?"

"I'm not worried about my brothers, *piccola seduttrice*. If one of them wants you, they're going to have to go through me." His tongue flicks out, trailing along a particularly sensitive spot behind my ear.

Goosebumps skitter down my spine. "I won't choose, Tommaso," I say around a low exhale.

"I'm not asking you to, Maeve."

I slowly release a breath with a low laugh. "You're either incredibly cocky or confident."

"I prefer optimistic, *dolcezza*."

I can't resist teasing him. "I hope you enjoy sharing."

He captures my lips with a little growl. There's no hesitation as he resumes our kiss. My iced-over arousal thaws the moment he starts fucking me with his tongue.

I imagine the way it would feel to have his tongue on my pussy, swirling around my clit, teasing and taunting me. The way he would grip my inner thighs, hold them open so he could take his fill of my pussy.

My chest flushes with desire, my fantasies spurred on by the way Tommaso claims my mouth. I rock my hips forward, searching for that delicious friction. His cock hardens underneath me, his board shorts doing little to conceal his arousal. I roll my hips again, this time his cock hitting the perfect spot to send a flash of tingles through my fingertips.

Pleasure rolls over me, a slow-motion wave that has my toes curling. I want more.

I throw my arms around his neck, bringing us impossibly closer once more. Still, it's not close enough. I whimper, and he drags his mouth from mine.

"Tell me what you need."

"You," I murmur.

He shudders, this little ripple that winds down his whole body. He slides his grip down to settle just above my hips. And in one move too smooth to even prepare for, he lifts me up at the same time that he leans back.

An embarrassing squeak flies from my mouth, and I brace my hands against his chest. The corners of his mouth curl up into a self-satisfied grin. I'd call it smug if I wasn't so interested to see where this is going.

I'm on my knees, hovering just above his waist. He runs his palms over my hips, reverence in their touch. He pauses around the tops of my thighs, his thumbs brushing that tender skin right at the crease of my hip.

His fingers apply a little pressure, and it takes me a moment to realize it's his subtle way of telling me to scoot up.

I shuffle forward, thankful for the smooth tile around the pool and not the stamped concrete of the patio area.

"What about . . ." I jerk my head toward the house.

"Don't worry about my brothers. Agreement, remember?" he murmurs, his gaze already zeroing in on the apex of my thighs.

Tommaso settles me right above his face. The heat of his breath against my most sensitive flesh sends goosebumps cascading down my back. He hooks a finger around the small seam of my booty shorts, and with one hard yank, the unmistakable sound of stitches splitting hits my ears.

It's such a primal, sexually dominant move that my pussy clenches in delight.

"What was that for?" I try to sound stern, but it mostly comes out as dreamy.

"They were in my way." His lips brush against my skin, and it's only his grip on my hips that holds me off of his face. "Don't worry. I'll buy you new ones."

"We're on an island," I remind him, lowering myself the barest centimeter toward his mouth.

He shrugs his shoulders, his eyes alight with mischief and hazy lust. "Then you can wear my clothes. Problem solved."

He doesn't give me a chance to respond, instead pulling me onto his mouth. He devours me like I'm his last meal, licking and sucking and fucking until I'm a delirious mess of nerve endings.

Pleasure sparks from every inch of my skin, electrifying me from the inside out. He slides two fingers inside of me, pressing against that magical spot that has me seeing stars as if he commanded it himself.

A kaleidoscope of color splashes behind my closed lids, an extraordinary light show to usher me back to earth.

I blink my eyes open, the dopey post-orgasmic grin already plastered on my face.

"Holy shit," I mutter, easing off of his face.

He licks his lips, his eyes darkening. "Fucking delicious. I changed my mind. *You're* my favorite dessert. Best I've ever had."

30

MAEVE

IT'S LATE, and I can't sleep.

I've never struggled with insomnia, but I'm no stranger to long nights on a *vacation*. This couldn't be more different. Instead of having all the responsibility and prepping for a job, I have virtually none here. The only person I'm responsible for is me.

And this baby, I amend, running a palm over my lower stomach.

A baby book mysteriously showed up on my nightstand when I came back from dinner with Tommaso. We stuffed our faces with pizza made in the brick oven on the patio. He walked me back to my room and gave me the kiss of a lifetime outside my bedroom door.

I thought about dragging him inside and letting myself explore him more, but I resisted. It's been nearly a week of dates. Daily day-long dates. Time and meals spent together that feels suspiciously like dating. As much as you can date while hiding out on a remote island.

The hopeless romantic in me is desperate for more. More

time spent getting to know him, more time discovering the island, more time kissing him.

Okay, so the last one admittedly outshines the rest, but it's hardly my fault. The man puts his whole body and soul into each kiss. I can't be held liable for the way it ignites this spark inside of me. I thought that sort of romantic glimmer was a myth, something that fizzles out quickly.

I know it's early, and unconventional given my current pregnancy status, but I'm quietly starry-eyed about Tommaso. Hopeful and excited. And drenched in lust.

I've gone years without dating much. Sure, I hooked up with guys when the need arose. But I felt more in one afternoon with Tommaso than I have with anyone else.

Except for one.

Romeo.

Is it possible to miss someone who's only down the hall?

I want to face-palm myself when I realize that I'm actively living one of those cliché situations. I told them I wanted space, and they gave it to me. For seven days, none of them wandered over to my room or tried to coax me out. And then like some sort of magical hourglass was up, Tommaso knocked on my door, and he hasn't stopped since.

So I guess it's only Romeo and Nico giving me space now. The latter I'm not even remotely surprised about. There seems to be a wedge there, an unknown obstacle that I don't know how to conquer yet.

I thought that's what I wanted—what I *needed*. But I didn't realize my mistake until now. They were respecting my wishes and I . . . I was wallowing and wishing they wouldn't.

I squeeze my eyes shut, shame coursing through me like a swift, cold river.

The truth lies plainly in front of me. I was waiting on Romeo. I wanted him to barge into my room, demand I listen to him, refuse to leave until he . . . I don't know, made everything better.

Shit.

I'm not that person. I don't say one thing when I mean something else entirely. I try to never place expectations on someone else unless they're mutually agreed to.

It'd be easy to write it all off as processing everything from that fateful day at the church. But that feels somehow cowardly even if it has threads of truth to it.

I did need to process everything. Honestly, I'm *still* working though some things. Like the fact that I'm going to have a baby in seven months—*a baby*! That alone blows my mind, forget about the church and the hits and the contract.

But that feels like a cop-out, even if I'm the only one who bears witness to the revelation.

So tomorrow, I'm going to find Romeo. And I'm going to give him a chance. A chance to explain . . . and maybe a chance for more.

My footsteps are quiet as I walk through the halls toward the kitchen. I let myself get a little lost in my thoughts of Romeo.

I wonder if Tommaso is going to show up at my bedroom door tomorrow. Maybe we'll spend the afternoon by the water again.

I'd like to walk on the beach, see if there are any shells or other interesting things that have washed up. When we were little, Mum took us to the coast once. We spent the entire day up and down the beach, collecting shells, pieces of coral, and even sea glass.

Mum carried our little treasures home in an empty grocery bag. Then we all took turns cleaning the shells in our kitchen sink. Once they were dry, Mum carefully put them in one of her favorite vases.

I wonder if I can find an empty vase somewhere in the

kitchen. Maybe in the massive pantry of theirs. It might be kind of nice to have something that's a little bit mine here. Something that reminds me of home, of my mum and sisters.

I barely even walked the beach since I've been here. Only the morning after we arrived so I could get my bearings.

It's quiet on this end of the house. It's a ranch-style villa, designed in a sort of U shape. Four bedrooms are on one end of the villa, and the kitchen is on the other side. A theatre room, a living room, a family room, a dining room, two offices, and a home gym between the two sides.

I draw up short when I see Romeo sitting on a stool in the center of the island in the dark. His head bent low, his dark brown hair falling forward. A half-empty bottle of whiskey sits next to his highball glass.

He swirls around the two fingers of whiskey, around and around and around, staring into it as if it holds all the answers to the world's problems.

"Just say what you came to say, Tommy, and leave me to drink in peace."

He sounds so melancholy, so dejected. It calls to me, a swan song from his soul to mine.

"Romeo," I murmur.

He spins around on his stool and stands up too fast, the stool scrapes against the ceramic tile floor. His eyes are glassy and wide, his lips parted with a sigh. "*Mon chéri*," he breathes.

My heart clenches at the familiar nickname, said in the same breathless cadence. He waivers, rocking forward slightly before catching himself, like he's curbing his instinct to reach out to me.

I stop right in front of him, close enough to see his features in the dim light cast from the strings of Edison bulbs on the patio. The French doors are open, the warm breeze trickling in off the water.

I let my gaze roam over him, noting his general disarray. His navy tee looks stretched out around the collar, like he was fiddling with it all day. Dark smudges underneath his eyes and a scruffy jaw. He looks so unlike himself, which I understand is a strange thing to think about someone you haven't spent that much in-person time with.

"Are you okay?"

"Who gives a fuck about me. I'm sorry, Juliet. Fuck, I'm so sorry. You said space, and I promised myself I'd give you whatever you need, but I can't spend another moment without talking to you. Your absence has left an ache in my chest that won't go away, no matter how many times I assure myself that you're safe here."

His words rush out in an intense wave of emotion, catching me by surprise.

"I swear I didn't know you were going to be at the church." He stares at me, his gaze pleading for understanding. There's an urgency to his words, like he's racing to get them out.

I nod, a few slow tilts of my chin, a swirling chasm of emotion starting to open inside my chest.

I wanted to talk to Romeo, to tell him how I really feel about things. I thought it would be tomorrow, but fate has other plans. I swipe my tongue along my bottom lip, and shift my weight, preparing to bare pieces of myself.

"Why didn't you though?"

He tilts his head to the side, his brows rising toward his hairline. "Why didn't I . . . know you were going to be at the church?"

"Aye, why didn't you know? You wormed yourself into my life, Romeo, carving out a place just for you, and then—"

"Then you left," he interjects, his eyes widening.

I grit my teeth at the accusation in his voice. "Aye, I did. Because I had to fulfill a contract my da signed otherwise they were going to take my little sister instead. I didn't have a choice."

"But I didn't know that." He shakes his head, his gaze imploring me to understand.

And I do. Logically I realize that he couldn't have known everything, but it's my traitorous heart that expected him to know —to do something when I couldn't. But my logic isn't riding shotgun today, hell, it's not even on the same train. Right now, my heart's the one in the driver's seat, and it's barreling toward these messy feelings.

"How could I have known that?" he murmurs.

"How did you find me in the first place?"

He shifts from foot to foot. "Curiosity, interest, fascination, obsession, need."

Our gazes lock. "All of that for me?"

"I've been unmistakably drawn to you for longer than I care to admit. I worked tirelessly to connect the dots of who you were. I developed programs to help me find you—"

"Then you should've found me at the church," I snap. I rear back, my anger taking me by surprise. My eyes water, and my breaths come in quick, choppy inhales. Oh fuck, why did I blurt that out like that?

31

MAEVE

ROMEO'S FACE FALLS, anguish and regret painting his features in broad strokes of sadness. "Maeve, I—"

I take another step back, gripping my hands into fists at my side. I look at anything but him, glancing at the patio and twinkling lights outside. My cheeks burn with shame. I wanted to talk to Romeo, not yell at him and place blame where it doesn't belong.

"No, no. It's fine." My throat feels so tight, I have to work hard to swallow "I shouldn't have said that. I shouldn't have *expected* that from you. You didn't owe me anything."

He surges forward, his hand snaking out to palm the back of my neck, stopping me from retreating. "Bullshit. You should've expected that of me, and I should've delivered." He rests his forehead against mine, lowering his voice. "I should've tracked your ass down the moment I woke up alone in that hotel."

I curl my fingers in the fabric of his shirt, stretching it out further as I hold on to him and try to release the shameful weight I've carried for the last couple of weeks. "I wish you would have."

His free hand settles on my hip. "The outcome might've been

the same. A blown-up church, an entire family wiped out, hits out on all of us."

I cock my head slightly to the right, my heart racing in anticipation. "But we'd be different."

"Fate brought us back together, and you should know that I'm never letting you go."

I bite the inside of my cheek, stuffing the urge to tell him all the reasons he probably should let me go.

"And we don't have to talk about it if you don't want to, but just know that I already know. And it doesn't change anything for me, yeah?" It's almost like he read my mind, plucking my worry out and ironing out the wrinkle.

His palm smooths around my hip and rests gently on the natural swell of my stomach. I'm not far enough along to really start showing, so this is all courtesy of the entire thin-crust cheese pizza I ate at dinner.

If I wasn't already falling in love with him, this might push me over the edge. It's touching and reassuring and so overwhelming, I'm a little lost for words.

"I—I don't know what to say, Romeo," I whisper.

"Just say yes, *mon chéri*." His voice lowers, somehow more intimate.

"To what?"

"To this. Us. Everything."

My heart slams against my ribs, pounding out a rhythm that beats only for him. There are an infinite number of unknowns, and our days might very well be numbered. Questions we can't answer because we don't have the solution or because it's an impossible choice.

But this? This is an easy acceptance. Spending my days with Romeo and Tommaso in literal paradise isn't a hardship.

Keira's right. It's a gift.

So starting now, I'm going to start living on my terms.

"Yes," I say right before I bridge the small gap between our mouths and press my lips to his.

He pulls back, his gaze searching mine and his brows dipping low over his eyes. "Yes?"

"Yes," I say with a nod, grinning at his enthusiasm and relief.

"Oh fuck yes. You won't regret this, I swear it, Maeve." He kisses me every few words, like he can't keep his lips off of mine for longer than two seconds.

"I know," I assure him, sinking into his hold and kissing him with all the passion that's coursing through my veins.

"I'm going to make it up to you, starting right now." He kisses me, a soft ghosting of his lips across mine. It's a tease and a promise.

He backs me up against the wall behind us. It's a built-in cherry oak cabinet system, and the handle digs in between my shoulder blades. He shuffles me to the side, so my back is flush with the door.

Romeo sinks to his knees. He skims his palms up over my bare legs, rounding my knees, and slides them up my thighs. His fingertips dig into my flesh, little pressure points of possession as he stares at me from underneath his dark lashes.

He drags his lips along the same path as his hands, stopping when he reaches the hem of my oversized sleep tee. His fingers curl around the hem and slowly drag it up until nothing stands between Romeo and my lace-covered pussy.

He runs his nose along the edge of my panties. My legs widen without conscious thought, giving him more room.

He makes a low noise of approval in the back of his throat. "Do you have any idea how often I dreamt of this? How many times I have thought of nothing more than eating this perfect pussy? How many mornings I woke up with a craving only you can satisfy?"

I slide my hand into his hair as my lids lower with lust. "Show me."

He flashes me a carnal grin, chuckling against my skin. I can feel the heat of his breath, and my thighs clench in anticipation. "With pleasure, *mon chéri*."

My head tips back, thumping against the cabinet when he peels my underwear down my legs in one swift movement. In the next breath, he feasts.

He uses his thumbs to spread me open enough to seal his lips around my clit. He doesn't waste any time, diving headfirst into my pleasure.

Pinpricks of light dance before my eyes as he uses his tongue and lips to dominate my clit. I curl my fingers in his hair, holding his face against me and rocking my hips into his face.

"That's my girl, take what you need from me," he murmurs against my skin.

He releases his hold on my shirt, and I scramble to grab it with my free hand. I don't want anything between us, the urgency to crest that peak hammering against my skin.

He lifts one of my thighs and places it over his shoulder, smirking at me. "Hold onto me."

He doesn't wait for my nod before he starts tongue-fucking my pussy. My toes curl against the tile floor, the coolness grounding me from my rapidly overheating body.

It's not until he slides his finger inside, and then another, that I start careening toward bliss.

"Oh my god. Oh, fuck. Romeo," I chant, looking down at the top of his head as I grind against his face.

I tip my head back again, opening my eyes and relishing the way pleasure liquifies my bones. Movement to my right catches my attention. I expect it to be a palm tree blowing in the breeze. But it's not.

It's Nico, watching us from the shadows.

Romeo curls his fingers, hitting that magical spot that makes me astral project. My legs seize and my neck arches back, breaking our connection. I freefall into the most exquisite form of bliss I've ever known.

How can these men give me such amazing orgasms every single time? It's a madness I never want to wake up from.

I float back to earth, my pants filling the quiet kitchen. I open my eyes, looking to the right and finding the shadowed alcove empty.

Romeo pushes to his feet. The expression on his face is hunger personified. "That was exquisite—you're exquisite." He kisses me then, and I taste myself on his lips.

He pulls away too soon. "C'mon, let's get you to bed."

"What about you?"

"That was for me as much as it was for you, Maeve." He links our hands together and tugs me out of the kitchen.

Romeo pulls me to a stop in front of my bedroom door. He draws my hand up to his mouth, brushing his lips across my knuckles and murmuring, "'Good night, good night. Parting is such sweet sorrow, that I shall say good night till it be morrow.'"

I didn't know what moon eyes meant when Keira flung it at me, but I think I finally understand. My heart swells and a light airy sort of tingle floats through my body.

I don't bother hiding my smile. "You're too charming for your own good, you know."

We say goodnight, and it's not until I'm underneath the covers that I remember that Nico watched Romeo and I tonight.

And Romeo never gave back my panties.

32

TOMMASO

"HEY," Nic says from my doorway.

I adjust my black tee and turn to face him. "What's up?"

He tips his chin toward me. "I just got confirmation that The Carnival is shut down."

"And we're sure that's the right choice? There's no one else who can run it for us while we're MIA? Because I gotta tell ya, brother, going dark unexpectedly will not be good for us long-term."

"We run the risk of not having a long term anything if we don't play this smart."

I nod, trying to focus on what he's saying. But it's hard to concentrate on shit happening hundreds of miles and an ocean away when I have a date with my girl. I didn't realize what we've been doing—what *I've* been doing—until now. And with that realization came a wave of uncertainty.

I wanted to do something extra nice for her. Partly to make up for all the dirty ways I defiled her in my mind last night. Mostly just because I want to be around her.

It's an intoxicating feeling, one that I've been given the

chance to sink into. I've never even gone on a fucking date before, too busy running shit for Nic or Vito. Too busy doing everything I can to scrub the images of my life in the Outfit out of my brain.

My brothers give me shit for always watching movies, but it's the best way to empty my mind and replace the shit no one should have to see with something else. It's more effective than drugs and alcohol, and believe me, I've fucking tried it all over the years.

I've leaned into this ritual with movies for long enough that I'm sure my brothers don't really remember those days where I'd lose myself in the bottom of a bottle. Those were some of my darkest days, and I'm never going to go back there. Not if I can help it.

So, yeah, I watch a lot of television to soothe my battered and broken soul.

Except for last night.

Last night I came back to my room and watched the ocean from my patio for a couple hours. It was the calmest my mind has been in months. And it's all because of her.

She makes me feel alive again. She brings me hope, and fuck me because I feel like an idiot for even thinking it, but *joy*. Two things so foreign that I didn't recognize them at first.

I know she thinks it's all because of the baby, and while she's not wrong, I *am* thinking about the baby. She's not entirely right either. It's her. It's always been her. *She's* the one who's plagued my waking thoughts for months.

My stomach twinges as visions of a little gray-eyed, black-haired toddler running around come unbidden.

It was never a future I envisioned for myself. Never one I thought I deserved. I'm sure I still don't fucking deserve it, but I'm an opportunist.

And I'm fucking greedy for her.

"Hey, are you even fucking listening to me?" Nic steps in front of me, his brows angry slashes across his forehead.

I rock back on my heels, a chuckle slipping free. "Not really."

He takes another step toward me. "What the fuck, man? Is this a joke to you? It's our future—"

I place a palm on his chest, extending my elbow straight to put more space between us. "Nah, man. That's where you've got it twisted. That shit back in Vegas? It doesn't fucking matter."

He rears back like I punched him again, looking at me like he's never seen me before. He's not wrong. He doesn't know this version of me. Fuck, I don't even know who this is—who I am when I'm with her.

"Of course it fucking matters. That's our life, Tommy."

"Have you talked to her yet?" I arch a brow.

His lips flatten into a line. "What?"

"Have you talked to Maeve yet?"

He folds his arm across his chest and widens his legs a little.

"Yeah, that's what I thought," I murmur with a grin. "Damn, Nic. I never pegged you for a coward."

His eyes flash with warning, narrowing on me. But his intimidation tactics don't fucking work on me. One of the only perks of having Vito as your father.

He looks at me for a moment, tension vibrating his body like his muscles are taut. "I'm not a fucking coward, and you know it. I don't even know why the fuck you would want me to talk to her if you want her so bad."

I don't know why either, except that I have a sneaking suspicion that my girl has a thing for him too. And I don't know, there's an intense need inside my gut that urges me to do everything I can to make her happy.

How can I even entertain the idea of sharing her while still feeling so possessive?

I shrug and look at my brother, really looking at him. He

looks different since we've been here. Aged in a way that doesn't reflect physically, more like he's *mentally* aged. Like his aura is dim and bent or something.

I head toward the door. "Who knows why we do anything we do. Look, I'm late for a date with my girl. But I wanted to let you know that I know." I pause next to him, looking over my shoulder at his profile. "I *know*, Nic. And still, I've claimed her . . . and the baby."

I walk out of my room, whistling a tune from *Rent*, content to let my brother ruminate on that little truth bomb. Honestly, I was fucking gentle. If I didn't love him so much, I wouldn't have even said anything.

Now he has the facts, it's on him to make his next move.

"Knock, knock." I rap my knuckles on the door frame of Maeve's bedroom. Her door is open halfway, like she left it open just for me.

"In daylight, in sunsets, in cups of coffee," I mumble, caught up in the song and arrested by the sight of Maeve in nothing but an oversize tee. She's a fucking goddess, temptation in human form.

I feel like a fucking tool the moment the lyrics are out of my mouth, but whatever. I'm committed now. And if it makes her smile, I'll be here every morning with another one.

She turns her head toward me, offering a sleepy sort of smile. "Is that . . . *Rent?*"

"How would you measure a year, *dolcezza?*"

She shakes her head, her black hair fanning all around her, and her smile turns wicked. "In inches?"

Ah, so my girl is feeling flirty this morning.

I give her another once-over, taking my time to let my gaze caress every inch of skin I can see—and the ones I hidden behind cotton.

I was robbed of this version of her in our brief time together.

I got the barest taste of it in our time here, and I find that I'm fucking desperate for more.

I want her sleepy and her soft in the morning, and I want her hungry and her satisfied at night. I want *everything*.

"Why are you looking at me like that?" She grins, scooting up the bed and leaning against the headboard. She runs a hand down her hair and flicks her gaze to the side for a moment before coming back to me.

My chest feels warm. I like that she can't keep her eyes off of me.

I shrug, feeling the corners of my mouth book up into a grin. "No reason." I lean against her doorway. "Wanna get breakfast with me?"

"With us," my brother says from next to me.

She frowns, this adorable little line between her brows, as she looks between the two of us.

My grin grows wide, a giddy sort of anticipation singing in my veins. I knew Romeo would step in at some point, but I didn't expect it to be right now. I never minded a little competition.

"Sure, with us. On the terrace."

She rolls her eyes. "Who names things like that on a house?"

"Who buys an island?" I quip.

She cocks her head to the side, a soft smile pulling at the edges of her delectable lips as she glances between the two of us. I dream about her lips and what they can do—what they have done.

"Yeah, I can do breakfast. Let me change quick."

I grin and lean against the door frame at the same time Romeo says, "Of course."

She arches both brows at us, looking pointedly at where we stand in the doorway. "Alone."

I slip both hands from my pockets and hold them up, palms facing her. "Now, where's the fun in that, *dolcezza*?"

33

MAEVE

FOR FIVE DAYS, Tommaso and Romeo knock on my door in the morning. Early enough to catch me before breakfast but not too early that they ever wake me up. If I didn't search every inch of this room for a camera when I first got here, I would be tempted to think they were spying on me. Their timing is uncanny.

Nico only joined us for the first morning. It was surprisingly nice. A little awkward at first, but as soon as we tucked into the food, it settled into something much more comfortable.

I stretch, enjoying the way my muscles bunch and flex as I wake up. The slumbering butterflies in my stomach start to flutter around, eager to see who will once again be outside my door first: Tommaso or Romeo?

Like someone is reading my mind, there's a soft knock on the door a moment later. I scoot up in my bed, adjusting my over-sized tee so it doesn't drape too far down my shoulder. I found it neatly folded on my nightstand two days ago. I'm just waiting to see which man claims it because it's definitely one of theirs. My bet's on Tommaso. He's sneaky in his possessiveness. "Come in."

The door opens soundlessly, Tommaso's broad shoulders filling the doorframe. I don't know if I'll ever get used to the way he looks—the way all of them look.

Sun-kissed from our time outside, wind-swept hair, and so many goddamn muscles it makes my pussy clench just thinking about them manhandling me.

We haven't done more than makeout. I would assume they harbored some kind of regret except for the fact that they stills show up every morning, attentive and caring. We spend our days getting to know one another and exploring the island.

I've only seen Nico a couple of times, including the breakfast with Tommaso and Romeo.

I've taken Keira's advice to heart. And so far, it's been the best decision since I've been here.

"Ready for breakfast, *dolcezza*? We had Margaret make those pumpkin pancakes you loved so much."

My stomach growls, and my cheeks heat. "I guess there's your answer."

He taps on the door frame twice. "Perfect, and after breakfast, we have a surprise for you."

My heart skips a beat. "A surprise?"

He grins, his eyes sparkling with excitement. "We're going to have a movie marathon. All of us."

WE'RE on our third Marvel movie when I run out of popcorn. The four of us are laid out on one of their plush dove gray U-shaped couches. The cushions are extra long, so you can practically lay down when you sit back.

Well, I can. I guess there's one benefit of being short.

"Damn," I whisper when my fingertips meet the bottom of the cool metal bowl.

"Here, you can have mine, Juliet," Romeo offers from next to me.

I wrinkle my nose at the smell of parmesan cheese sprinkled on top of his.

"Oh, that's okay. I'll just go grab some more. I left half the batch in the kitchen."

Tommaso brought out one of those Whirly-Pop air poppers that you stir on the stove. All of us got our own giant bowls and topped it with whatever we wanted.

I stuck with butter and salt, Romeo went with parmesan cheese sprinkled on top, Tommaso tossed his with chocolate candy, and Nico doused his in hot sauce.

Romeo leans toward the coffee table and snatches the remote. "I'll pause it."

"Thank you." I lean forward and brush my lips across the corner of his mouth on instinct. These small moments of connection are increasing between us, and I don't hate it. I don't hate it at all. I pull back before it can turn into anything and stand up with my bowl clutched to my stomach. "I'll be right back."

"Take your time, *dolcezza*," Tommaso murmurs.

Nico, per usual, is silent. I don't let his quietness bother me. I don't want to get egotistical and think it has anything to do with me. For all I know, he dislikes Marvel movies. Or it could be something else entirely.

I'm having too good of a time to try to figure out what the hell Nico's problem is.

I make quick work of fixing another bowl of popcorn and walk back to the theatre room. I slow down when I hear their murmured voices, the temptation to overhear what they're saying is too great. I haven't really had many opportunities to witness the three of them interact, and curiosity has me in its clutches.

I slow down right outside the corner that opens into the

spacious theatre room. I peek around the wall in time to see Tommaso toss a handful of popcorn at Romeo.

It hits him in the face, bounces off his chest, and lands on the couch. I pause with my own popcorn halfway to my mouth, my feet stilling. I'm half-hidden in the hallway, right before it opens up to the spacious living room.

"The fuck was that for?" Romeo grumbles.

"That"—Tommaso points a finger at him—"is for hogging her."

The three of them are exactly where I left them: spread out on the couch. Romeo sits on the side closest to the floor-to-ceiling sliding glass doors. They're cracked open a few inches to let the warm ocean breeze in. Tommaso lies sprawled out in the crease of the couch, decidedly closer to where I was sitting before I got up.

Nico sits on the opposite side. I didn't realize it until now, but he's almost directly facing my spot on the couch.

Nico Santorini strikes me as the kind of man who never puts his back to possible danger. I'm choosing to take it as a compliment.

I *am* fucking dangerous. Pregnant or not. The sooner they remember that, the better.

Romeo plucks some kernels from the couch and pops them in his mouth. "You jealous, brother?" he taunts with a grin.

Tommaso leans his head back against the cushion. "Nah. Nothing to be jealous about, but you should know your fucking nicknames are elementary level, bro."

"Bullshit," Romeo says with a laugh.

I roll my lips inward to curb a chuckle. I could step in and squash this but the opportunity to see how it plays out is too enticing. To see how they act and what they say when I'm not watching.

You can tell a lot about a person by how they behave with those closest to them.

For all my talk to Keira, I don't really know them. Do I think they'll hurt me? No. For more than one reason. The least of which is they'd be idiots to try anything. And if there's one thing I can say for certain, it's that the Santorini brothers are no fools.

"Enough," Nico snaps. "The two of you are fighting over her like dogs to scraps."

Tommaso whips his head toward Nico. Tension lines his shoulders in an instant. "Watch it."

"Fuck off, Tommy, it's true, and you know it." Nico runs his hands down his face and blows out a breath. "You two are acting like we're on some fucking vacation together, like we didn't leave a fucking shitstorm the size of Nevada back home."

Romeo shakes his head at Nico. "You don't have to be here, man." He switches his gaze to Tommaso. "Neither do you. I'm fine here with Maeve until it's safe."

Tommaso scoffs. "Don't insult me again, brother. That's my woman—and that's *my* fucking baby. I'm not going anywhere."

I ignore the way my body responds to Tommaso's heated words. Now isn't the time to let those pesky feelings get in the way of some award-worthy eavesdropping.

Nico started shaking his head halfway through Tommaso's declaration.

"You don't know that, man," Romeo mutters.

But I can't take my eyes off of Nico. The way he tenses like he's shutting every single part of his body down.

Tommaso sits forward, resting his forearms on his knees. "The fuck I don't. You didn't hear it, Rome." He whips his gaze to Nico. "Neither of you did."

Nico steeples his fingers in front of his face, the sides of his index fingers tapping against his bottom lip. "I don't need to hear shit. You have no idea who she is or if that doctor was even real. For all you know, this could be an elaborate scheme to fuck us over."

"Look around you, brother. The four of us are in the middle of the ocean with only your staff on the sister island behind us! What could she possibly have to gain here?" Romeo asks, his tone bordering on exasperated, like this is a long-had conversation.

Nico straightens back, letting his hands drop between his knees. "I don't know. Why do women ever claim paternity? Money? Power?"

Romeo laughs, but it lacks any real warmth. "Come on, man. Do you even know who she is? Their wealth and power and prestige could wipe the floor with ours ten times over."

Nico shrugs. "Maybe, but I'll remain skeptical of her until she proves otherwise."

"Nah, you're not skeptical, brother. You're fucking delusional, grasping at straws because you can't fucking stand it," Tommaso says, a grin flirting across his lips.

Nico's shoulders hike toward his ears. "Stand what?"

"The fact that you want her. Just as much as we do," Tommaso says, flicking his fingers between him and Romeo. "And for maybe the first time in your life, you have to fucking work for it."

I pause with a kernel halfway to my mouth, my brows straining toward my hairline.

"Fuck you, Tommy. Like I don't work hard?" Nico growls.

Tommaso inclines his head, his lips pursed to the side. "Nah, not when it comes to people. People are easy for you, man. They always have been. And I'm not judging you, I'm just saying that *she* isn't."

"Because she's not like everyone else," Romeo says quietly.

"Exactly," Tommaso says, snapping his fingers and pointing

at Romeo. That grin comes back in an instant. "She's a fucking unicorn, bro."

"And you're a fucking idiot if you don't get your head out of your ass and see it," Romeo finishes.

34

MAEVE

I SIT down on the zero-gravity slope of the pool, letting the warm water lap up around my waist as I decompress after my conversation with Keira.

We used up every second of our five-minute allotment. Somehow, my heart doesn't feel as heavy as it did last time. The fact that it's been quiet for all of my sisters helps.

But Rosie is no closer to figuring out any information on who posted the hits. And even if she does find it, I have no idea how we'll be able to stop it.

That's part of the cruel beauty of the dark marketplaces. Once the job is posted and the funds are secured, it takes on a life of its own. As hard as it's been not being able to talk to my sisters whenever I get the urge, playing dead seems to be working.

Still, the fact that Keira is watching over all our sisters settles my anxiety immensely.

I brace my hands behind me, palms flat, and tip my head back toward the sky, letting the stars' light shine down on me in my new bikini.

Like some sort of magical spell, I find a little present on my nightstand every night. The baby book, a chocolate frosted doughnut, lemon drop candies, a miniature vase with a single peony. And a black string, triangle bikini.

At first, I thought it might've been from the staff. Nico said they prefer to work at their own schedule, but adjusted it around when they know we're not using those parts of the villa. Apparently, he's only been here a few times since he purchased this island, but this is the only time he's stayed here for longer than seventy-two hours.

But I doubt Margaret really cares if I have a bikini to wear instead of short shorts and a tank top. So now it's just a matter of *who* is leaving me little treats. Or maybe they're doing it together?

Excitement flutters inside my lower belly at the prospect of getting them to do other things together.

It's been two days since the movie marathon. Two days spent with Romeo and Tommaso.

And two days without so much as a glimpse of Nico. I had harbored these sort of romanticized notions of him boldly declaring his intent like some hero in a regency romance novel. But that might be wishful thinking. And these goddamn hormones.

At least that's what I'm blaming it on. In one of the chapters of the baby book, they talk about the increased libido a lot of women have late in their first trimester. Apparently, it could last through the second trimester.

I'm on a remote island with three of the hottest men I've ever laid eyes on, so it's not exactly a hardship. But still, I'm in uncharted waters in more ways than one.

It's quiet out here, the ocean's waves a soundtrack to my wandering thoughts. I'm accustomed to a certain amount of alone time every day, and not that the guys were smothering me by any means, but I didn't realize how much I needed it until now.

It affords me the opportunity to recharge my mental batteries, helps me come back to center.

I stay that way, eyes closed and in the water for another hour before I'm ready to come out. I bid the stars farewell, vowing to bring one of my men out here tomorrow night, and wrap myself in a fluffy blue-and-white-striped beach towel.

I pause next to the lounger by the patio door, looking into the darkened kitchen as I rub the towel over my legs. I don't want to track water into the house. Margaret made some chocolate chip cookies this morning, and I've been salivating for them for at least ten minutes.

NICO

I watch her like a starving man looks at a steak. I stand in the shadows of the kitchen for over an hour, watching Maeve lounge in the pool like she doesn't have a care in the world. Like she isn't the catalyst for all this fucked-up shit we're caught in the middle of.

They're uncharitable thoughts, and I'm not even sure if they're true. But I can't stop the bitter thoughts as they sprout up.

Thou doth protest too much, a voice in my head murmurs. It sounds suspiciously like both of my brothers. Which is fucking weird.

I shake it off and watch her as she walks toward the kitchen, taking the time to run the towel over her delectable curves. My mouth waters at the sight of her. Her tits barely fit in that bikini, and her ass hangs out of the back, those little strings doing the absolute bare minimum at holding those scraps of fabric together.

My gaze zeroes in on the small swell of her stomach. Is that new? Is it too early for her to start showing? I make a mental note to look that up later.

Just the thought of her carrying my child is enough to incite a possessiveness so severe, I'm not sure either one of us are ready for it.

I don't move from my spot against the wall as I watch her beeline for the cookie jar. Her back is to me, her long hair pulled into one of those messy ponytails. It shouldn't make her look so sexy, but it does. Small tendrils of hair fall around her neck and face, damp and slightly waving.

It's all I seem to be doing lately: watching her.

It's fucking annoying and distracting. And if I was honest with myself, I could admit that I don't like the way she makes me feel.

She takes a bite of the cookie, and the sweetest moan fills the room. My cock swells at the sound, a vivid flashback of us in Chicago playing before my eyes.

And something inside of me snaps, fractures from the rest of me and floats into oblivion. I stalk toward her, not stopping until her back is flush with my front. I curl my hands into fists to stop myself from reaching out and touching her.

"Maeve," I curse her name against the curve of her neck.

She freezes for a moment, but that's all it lasts. She exhales, her ass pressing against my cock.

"Nico," she breathes my name like a prayer, like she was hoping for me to crowd her against the island. "Were you watching me again?"

"And if I was?" I challenge, running my nose from her ear to her shoulder.

She tilts her head to the side to give me better access. "I like your eyes on me, even when I'm with your brothers."

"You may have them fooled, but I'm onto you," I murmur

against her hair. The reminder of her and them sends a lick of rage up my spine.

She tips her head back onto my shoulder, tilting her face toward mine. My breath hitches in my throat when I catch the scent of sugared lemons.

"Is that right?" She pitches her voice low to match mine.

I bury my nose in her hair, inhaling a deep breath of her scent. I crowd her further against the island, bracing my hands on either side of her. My cock nestles perfectly in between her ass cheeks, hard already. I'm always fucking hard around her. And if I could just stop thinking about the way her pussy feels squeezing the life out of me, I would be irritated by the fact that I'm *always fucking hard around her.*

She's a goddamn sorceress, I'm sure of it.

"I see you, watch the way you are with them." I snake my hand between her and the island, smoothing my palm up between her tits and pausing at the hollow of her throat. "The way you let them touch you. Like they have a right."

Her breath hitches and she shifts her weight from foot to foot. All it does is wiggle her ass against my cock. My fingers twitch on her skin, never hard enough to hurt her. Just a touch of pressure, the kind that I know makes her feel alive.

"I like it when they touch me," she breathes.

It's a tease and a taunt. Much like her, really.

My hand skates up the front of her throat, stopping underneath her chin and tipping her head back. The small light above the stove casts her face in yellowed shadows, but it could be pitch black in here, and I'd still be taken aback by her.

"That's the problem, baby girl. You're not theirs to touch. You're mine." I crane my neck forward and capture her mouth with my own.

It's greedy and messy and so fucking perfect I could come just from the way her ass rubs against my cock and her tongue fights for dominance with mine.

Her hand clamps around my wrist, holding me to her as she grinds against me. She pulls away, her chest heaving with these gasping sort of breaths.

"I'm not yours."

I drag my teeth down her neck, pulling back when her words register. My vision gets narrow, and this primal part of me explodes. I grip her by the waist and haul her perfect ass onto the counter.

I don't give her any space, gripping her thighs and opening her legs wide enough for me to step between them. I get in her face, our lips barely brushing. "You want to try that again?"

She arches a brow but doesn't pull away. "You don't even talk to me, Nico."

My hands tighten their grip on her thighs. "Is that what you need? My words?"

She slides her hand into the hair at the back of my head, bringing our faces closer together. "Yes. Your words and your presence."

"You want my words, baby girl?" It's a taunt. One I don't give her time to respond to. "I'm plagued by the memory of the way your cunt strangled my cock that night. It's plays on repeat over and over again, and I'm this close to losing my mind over it. Over *you*. And if I don't get inside of you soon, I'm going to fucking explode," I snarl. "How's that for my fucking words?"

She places her palm in the middle of my chest and pushes. It's not forceful, so I take the cue and shuffle back a step. My gaze narrows into slits, watching her every move with a hyper focused sort of predatory intensity.

I track the way she leans forward, scooting her ass to the edge of the counter. The way her hand glides over my chest and settles on top of my traps. I see the moment her lips part and her eyes darken. It's the same moment her hand pushes against my traps.

I swipe my bottom lip with my tongue, her intention clear now. "Ah, my girl wants me to get on my knees? Is that it?"

"Yes," she murmurs, wiggling impossibly closer to the edge.

If she goes any closer, she's going to fall off. Not that I would ever let her fall.

I lean in close, dip my head toward her and murmur against her mouth. "Now I want *your* words. Tell me to get on my knees and eat your pussy."

She slides her fingers in my hair, tugging the strands taut. "Get on your knees, Nico. I want you to make me come."

I knew she wouldn't hesitate. Not my girl. My cock swells in my pants, and I have to shift it for a moment of relief. I surge forward, plunging my tongue in her mouth once more, and she wraps her arms and legs around me, leaving no room between us.

I slide my hands under her ass and shift her to the stool next to me. It's a better height for what we have planned. I untie the strings holding her bikini bottoms together in two flicks of my wrist.

Is it selfish of me to want to ruin her in ways that will have her thinking of me for days? Reminders of me every time she lets Tommy kiss her or Rome touch her.

I drop to my knees, and I don't get up until my girl screams my name.

35

MAEVE

I'M ASTRAL PROJECTING. It's the only explanation for the way I'm hovering above my body right now. Nico doesn't let up, eating my pussy like he'll literally die if he stops.

"It's too much. Too good." I tug on his hair, a conflict to my hips rolling against this face. My nerve endings are frayed, cut wide open. My skin feels like it's covered in goosebumps and stars dance behind my eyes.

The wet noises of Nico absolutely devouring me flood the kitchen, ramping up my desire impossibly further. His broad shoulders wedge my legs open, one hand underneath my ass, tilting my hips toward his face. He fucks with me two fingers, these long, hard thrusts that time perfectly with his tongue on my clit.

One orgasm rolls into two, and I lose all sense of myself for one single perfect moment in time.

I'm still coasting in pleasure when he surges to his feet. He palms my face and smashes his lips against mine in a brutal kiss. I can feel the shape of his cock through the thin material of his athletic shorts, and my lower belly clenches.

I ache to feel him inside of me. To feel the burn and stretch of his cock as he takes his time.

I just came twice, and I'm already lusting for more? I don't recognize myself in this moment, a sensual goddess demanding more and more from her men.

"You didn't scream my name," he rasps against my lips, drawing me out of my thoughts. "You yelled for them. Called their names out while you came all over their faces."

There's accusation in his voice, but I'm stuck on the confirmation that he was watching me both times. Warmth cascades down my shoulders at that knowledge. I decide to play, just a little.

"Maybe they made me come harder." It's a whispered taunt, a lie in contrast to my orgasm still on his face.

"Baby girl, you just soaked my face. Twice. There's no way my brothers made you come harder than I did," he growls, rolling his hips against me.

He sinks his fingers into my hair, tugging on the strands at the back of my neck. "You're a thief and a liar, Maeve King."

My lids sink lower as desire sludges through my veins like molasses. It's heady and addictive. "I've never lied to you."

He takes his teeth over my bottom lip before soothing the sting with his tongue. He shuffles closer still, wedging his cock against my pussy so tight, I can feel every ridge. Any further, and we'd merge into one.

"Didn't you, though? You let my brother think this is his." He palms my pussy. "Because this might be his." He slides his palm upward to rest on the small swell of my stomach. "But you and I know the truth. You're mine in every sense of the word."

The conviction in his voice speaks to my own possessiveness, a quality I didn't realize I even had until these three men.

"And you? Are you mine?"

He stares at me, his eyes in conflict with his body language. I imagine a war going on inside Nico Santorini. I only wonder which side will win.

"As much as I might hate the idea of sharing you, I am. Undeniably."

My lips brush against his as I speak. "And so are they." It's a whispered taunt. Not a revelation but a fact. I know it's going to incite him. And maybe that's what I want—to push him a little.

He grabs me from underneath my ass, picks me up, and stalks across the kitchen. He drops me on the oversized couch in the family room, his body covering mine instantly.

"You make me fucking crazy," he says into my mouth as he tugs my hair. "No one should have this kind of power over me."

My neck arches, and I hold his gaze as I snake my hand between us, sliding it underneath his shorts. I'm not even a little bit surprised that he's not wearing any briefs.

I curl my fingers around his and stroke him hard, enjoying the way he groans under my touch.

He's different from the first night we met. Not just physically either. There's a wildness about him that wasn't present before, either muted or buried.

"You're not theirs like you're mine." He kisses me, swallowing any retort on my tongue. It's a raw explosion of passion, a hard edge roughing up the softness of any feelings he might've just exposed.

He's close to the edge. I can feel it in the almost desperate way he holds me to him and the way his chest rises and falls rapidly, his hips thrusting in time with my hand.

I want to nudge him over the edge. Send him free-falling into utter chaos. There's beauty in the unknown, and I'm selfish enough to want him to join me.

I slide his shorts off his hips, feeling the heavy weight of his cock against my stomach. I position him so the tip of his cock just barely bumps against my pussy, like one thrust and he'd finally be inside of me.

I arch my back further, putting my tits closer to his face. Like the primal beast he is inside, his face drops to my tits barely concealed by the bikini.

He drags his mouth along the swell as I lean back further.

"It feels like I'm his when Tommaso sinks his fucking cock inside of me and fills me up. It feels like I'm his when Romeo recites poetry against my clit like he's auditioning for the next Shakespearan play."

Nic growls against my skin, his palms sliding over my hips as he sits back, balancing on his knees. He bumps the head of his cock against my wet pussy. He drags it through my arousal, nudging my clit and sending sparks of electricity in my veins.

"And this? Does this feel like you're *theirs?*" He thrusts inside of me, his lips finding mine once more. "You can have Romeo's words and Tommy's food, but this"—he trails his fingertips over my abdomen—"this is mine."

He swallows my moan with a groan of his own, and I revel in the feeling of him inside of me. And like the earth psychically shifts beneath us, something clicks into place for me.

36

MAEVE

THINGS CHANGED AFTER THAT NIGHT. We're all finding our footing, but it's easier now. Smoother.

Four weeks, two phone calls with my sister, six movie marathons, and twenty-eight breakfast dates with my men pass in the blink of an eye.

We settle into a new normal. And like I have been most days, I spend some time on my favorite strip of white sandy beach behind the backyard.

It's a picturesque scene, the ocean waves rolling in peacefully in a melody of blues, white, and gray. The clouds streak across the sky, a mix of pastels. The air is salty and somehow sweet, the scent of my coconut sunscreen wafting around.

The sun-kissed sand is hot against my toes, the cool shaded blanket beneath me a sharp contrast. I'm underneath a red and white striped semi-permanent umbrella. A fine layer of sand coats my skin, the delicate grains swirling around on a cool breeze.

A shadow falls over my face, and I squint one eye open to see who it is. My lips curl into a grin when I see Tommaso's silhouette.

"Want some company?" he asks.

"For you? Always." I pat the spot on the blanket next to me.

He smirks as he lays down next to me, angling himself so he's still in the sunshine.

"Here." I wiggle my butt over to make some room on my blanket for him.

He throws his arm over his eyes. "Nah, I'm fine here, *dolcezza*. I like the sunshine."

"Me too," I murmur, looking across the water. "We don't get this kind of sunshine where I grew up. It feels different here."

"I know," he says with a nod. "What was it like where you grew up?"

"Green," I say with a smile. "Lots of green. But mild temperatures, nothing like this."

He reaches over and grabs my hand, lacing our fingers together. "It sounds so different from where I grew up."

I turn my head so I can see his expression. "In Las Vegas?"

"Yeah," he says with a sigh. "I think I'd have liked to have grow up somewhere besides the desert."

"I can understand that." I nod and turn my head back toward the ocean. "It sure is beautiful here though." I squeeze his fingers, feeling the warmth radiating from his skin. The sun is sinking over the water, painting the sky in oranges and purples.

"Yeah, it is."

I don't need to look at him. I can *feel* his gaze on my skin, like he's trying to memorize every single detail.

He takes a deep breath. "It's like something out of a movie," he murmurs.

A soft giggle bubbles up, and I roll onto my side to face him. "Aye, I was just thinking that the other day."

"You were?" He lets go of my hand and props himself on his elbow.

"Aye. We're on a picturesque island in a villa that has every amenity you could think of. It's like a dream. And the company isn't half-bad either," I tease him.

His smile slips into a more serious expression as he brushes my hair off my shoulder. "You know it's real, right? This thing between us. For me, it's real."

I push up off the blanket and scoot closer to him, so our faces are aligned. "For me too, Tommaso."

I brush my mouth along his in a soft kiss, tasting the sea salt on his lips. He palms the back of my neck and presses his lips to mine more firmly. His kiss becomes more passionate, urgent, demanding as our mouths move in a desperate dance for more.

I let out a small gasp when he rolls us over, putting me on the bottom. His hard length is pressed to my stomach, and I'm desperate for more of him.

He kisses me harder, pushing his tongue into my mouth and exploring every inch of me with a passion that takes my breath away. I grip the blanket beneath me, letting out small moans as he moves over me, rolling his hips. His hands slide around my waist and tangle in my hair as his lips move down to my neck.

He pulls back so he can look at me, desire radiating from him like a beacon. I reach up and brush away the sand from his cheeks before leaning in for another kiss. Our tongues dance together, our bodies intertwined in an intimate moment where nothing else matters but us. I wrap one leg around him as his hand slides up my side, making me gasp against his lips.

He breaks away from the kiss with a smirk and begins to trail soft touches over every inch of skin.

He begins by trailing kisses down my neck, before moving to my collarbone and up my sternum. His lips press against my chest, and he bites playfully at the swell of one of my breasts.

"Tommaso," I breathe out softly.

"Maeve," he whispers as his hands travel lower, sliding over the flare of my hips and to my thighs.

"I need you," he whispers with reverence.

"I need you too," I murmur.

"Are you ready for me?"

"Always."

He pulls the strings of my bikini off, tossing them to the side and leaving me completely naked. His hands begin to travel over my legs and hips, his fingers dancing over my skin.

"Beautiful." His eyes are hooded with desire as he looks me over. He drags his fingertips along my thighs, spreading my legs apart.

"So beautiful," he murmurs as his gaze travels up my body. He pushes my legs open wider, settling between them. He lets out a small groan when he sees my pussy glistening for him, my arousal coating my thighs.

He doesn't tease me any further. He leans down and drags his tongue through my folds. I inhale a sharp gasp, the sensation short-circuiting my nerve endings for a moment.

"You taste so good, Maeve," he moans against my skin. He sinks one finger inside of me, making me cry out. He quickly adds another finger, pumping in and out of me.

"I'm so close," I moan the words in surprise.

"I know," he murmurs against my clit. He licks my slit up again and blows softly against my clit as he gently pinches my nipples.

His lips wrap around my clit, his tongue flicking over me with perfect pressure. I reach down and thread my fingers through his hair, pulling him against me as I push my hips up to meet his mouth.

He sinks his fingers deeper inside of me, curving them toward that spot that makes me see stars. My fingers tighten in his hair on impulse. His other hand curves around my hip, holding me in place as I begin to crest over the edge.

"Tommaso," I cry out as the electricity running through my body becomes too much to contain.

"Come on my face, *dolcezza*," he groans against me.

Like he commanded it himself, my muscles tense up around his fingers as he continues to feast, prolonging my orgasm. He doesn't stop until I'm a sweaty, babbling mess.

When I open my eyes, I'm greeted with one of the most arresting sights I've ever seen. Tommaso kneels before me like some sort of god. Shirtless, hair wind-swept, cheeks pink from the sun, and wearing my come on his lips.

He makes a show of licking me from his lips and humming under his breath. "Still the best fucking think I've ever tasted."

I push onto one elbow and reach for him. He meets me half-way, crashing his mouth to mine. Our tongues slip into each other's mouths, and I taste myself.

I break away first, tilting my head back and sucking in mouthfuls of air. "Fuck me, Tommaso."

"With fucking pleasure, *piccola seduttrice*."

37

MAEVE

I LOOK AROUND THE FAIRGROUNDS. The bright splashes of color and blinking lights are almost too much when I'm used to the quiet villa island in the middle of the ocean.

I'm not exactly sure who came up with this carnival idea or what brought it on. I didn't ask too many questions after Romeo broke the good news.

"I'm not sure about this," Nico grumbles, standing close to me.

"C'mon, man. We already agreed we were coming, and we're here now, so let's make the best of it, alright?" Tommaso says, nudging Nico's shoulder.

Nico laces his fingers with mine, tugging me closer to him. "Yeah, well, you distracted me with something magical. I can hardly be held responsible for what I agreed to."

I look at Nico from underneath my lashes, a smile flirting along the edges of my lips. "Did you just call my pussy *magical?*" I stage-whisper.

Teasing Nico still feels so strange. Our relationship a true rollercoaster, one of those ones with dips and whirls, that drags you upside down a few times.

There's nothing conventional about my relationship with any of them, and yet, it's feels so incredibly right and normal.

"He's not wrong, Juliet. It's a thing of beauty and magic. In fact . . ." he trails off, lunging for me like he's going to toss me over his shoulder and steal me away for the day.

"Uh, uh, uh. I don't think so, brother," Tommaso says, placing an arm in front of me to stop Romeo. "We agreed to share her, remember?"

Romeo rolls his eyes, walking on the other side of Tommaso. "Yeah, yeah, yeah. I remember. But I call dibs on paddle boats with Maeve later."

"Still, let's remain vigilant, yeah?" Nico murmurs, his gaze on a constant swivel.

"It's been months, Nic. We haven't heard or seen anything. No one knows we're here, so it's safe."

It's wild to think that months have passed since we took that fateful boat ride to the island. To *our* island.

I don't know the exact moment I started thinking of it as mine—as something we share together—but it feels more like home than anything else has in a long, long time.

Our island feels like the Bermuda Triangle. No time and too much time has passed since we stepped into the shadows of the world. But it doesn't feel like we're in the shadows. It feels like we stepped into the light. Together.

The only people around are families with little kids, a few groups of teenagers, and the carnival workers. It's on the smaller side for a fair, but the concession stands look promising. I can't go on many of the rides at five months pregnant, but there are so many booths with games. I'm going to enjoy beating my men at carnival games all day.

"Oh, look. I love this game," I exclaim, dragging Nico by the arm toward the booth with foam mallets.

NICO

"Jesus fucking Christ. Who made this shit—fucking elves?" Tommy shifts on the orange plastic bench beside me for the fifth time in the last minute.

We've been at this carnival for hours. After we played too many rounds of whatever games Maeve wanted, we bought our weight in carnival food. And then those assholes convinced me to ride the Ferris Wheel.

The car sways back and forth, and I blink against the way my stomach lurches. Exhaling through my nose, I shift closer to the small side, by the poor excuse for a door. There's a higher likelihood of me falling out if I'm pressed up against it like this, but hopefully, my brother stops rocking the car with his incessant whining.

"Why the fuck are we sharing a seat anyway? One of us should be with her. Rome's easily the smallest of the three of us," Tommy says with a huff.

"Let it go, Tommy," I snap, gripping the metal square-shaped bar next to my head.

"Oh shit." Tommy's voice is hushed but not quiet enough.

"What's wrong?" Maeve asks.

I open my eyes, startled to find them already locked on her. Like I sought her out subconsciously. "Nothing."

"Damn, I'm sorry, Nic. I forgot," Rome says.

Maeve looks from Rome to me and back to Rome again. "What am I missing?"

Rome jerks his chin toward me. "Nic doesn't do heights."

Maeve jerks back a few inches before shifting to face me. "Why the hell did you get on then?"

I flex my fingers and tighten my grip on the bar next to me, planting my feet along the metal floor. "I'm fine."

Her brows furrow as she gives me a once-over, and not in the sexy way I like. "You don't look fine."

I roll my shoulders back and fight the urge to look to the left and check our progress. It feels like we've been on this fucking thing for twenty minutes already. A bead of sweat rolls down the back of my neck, sliding into the collar of my sweatshirt. "I said I'm fine, Maeve. It's not a long ride."

"Uh, actually," Rome says, clearing his throat.

I shift my gaze to him. I don't have it in me to even give him my best glare. A lukewarm indifference is the best I can offer right now.

"I slipped the guy twenty to stop the wheel when we're at the top." I want to say he looks sheepish, but I'm not sure he really is. I know exactly why he wanted to stop the ride at the top, and if I didn't feel like I was going to crawl out of my skin any second, I would fucking applaud his ingenuity.

"You're a dick," Tommy mutters with a low laugh.

"What? I didn't remember. I'm sorry, Nic. I just thought Juliet might like to see the view from up here," Rome says.

Tommy folds his arms across his chest, his bicep nudging mine. And the car rocks. *Again.*

I close my eyes and exhale, swallowing down the bile creeping up my esophagus.

"Okay, so there's this vaudeville star, right? She's a total knockout in more ways than one." I can hear the humor in his voice, and I imagine him flashing that smirking grin of his. "One night, she gets home after a late show and finds her husband fucking her sister. So she shoots him."

"As she should," Maeve murmurs.

"Why am I not surprised that's your answer?" Rome says with a small chuckle.

"But then there's another chick, she's got stars in her eyes. So she leaves her husband and fucks some wannabe Hollywood type, and then—"

Maeve laughs, this joyous explosion of delight. It pulls at the tiny scrap of my soul long buried inside my chest. My eyelids open slowly. My breath catches for an entirely different reason.

Backlit by the afternoon sunshine, her dark hair looks like the deepest shade of brown with threads of dark auburn. It cascades down her shoulders, the slight breeze blowing strands across her cheek.

Her head is tipped back in laughter, exposing her throat to me. The sight awakens the beast inside of me. I tip my chin down and look at her from underneath my lashes and my heartbeat pounds loud in my ears.

"How unexpected," Tommy mutters.

"I don't get it," Rome says.

I don't take my eyes off of her as she lowers her head and locks her gaze with mine. The mirth never leaves her eyes, a small smile playing along the corners of her mouth.

"He's explaining the plot to *Chicago*, the musical," she says, the side of her mouth hooking into a full-blown smirk.

Rome chuckles. "Another show, Tommy, really?"

She cocks her head to the side, her voice soft as she says, "Nico and I met in Chicago."

Tommy shrugs, his arm rubbing against mine. "A coincidence. I thought it'd be a good distraction for our big bro to hear about a bunch of women who shoot their men."

Rome makes a tsking noise in the back of his throat. "It seems he's found himself another, less violent distraction."

"You haven't seen her with a blade yet."

Something about Tommy's almost reverent tone grates

against my nerves like a dull butter knife. A persistent, throbbing sort of annoyance. I glare at him, feeling my eyes narrow on his profile.

Not that he even notices me.

No, I'm sure he can feel the weight of my gaze on him. He's too good at his job not to be aware of these sorts of things. Either he's too engrossed in her or he doesn't view me as a threat.

That might be his fatal flaw. Because one way or another, she will be mine.

38

MAEVE

I KEEP my focus on Nico. "I liked your distraction, Tommaso."

"I thought you might, *piccola seduttrice*."

"But Romeo's right. It's not quite the distraction he needs." I cock my head to the other side and study Nico. My hair slides forward, brushing against Romeo's shoulder.

The truth is I don't particularly enjoy heights much either, but so far, I'm okay here. I don't plan to test this theory, so I'm keeping my gaze firmly inside the car and not on the breathtaking view.

These Ferris wheel cars aren't really all that big. They're just spacious enough that we all fit in here, but not comfortably. My legs are thrown over Romeo's lap, but that's mostly because his big palms cover my lower thigh. The heat of his hands scorches his prints through the denim of my jeans and brands themselves against my flesh.

It gives me an idea.

"I'm going to stand up," I murmur quietly, watching the almost aggressive way Nico looks at Tommaso right now.

Romeo pulls my hair back, exposing the side of my neck. He

leans down and runs his nose in the sensitive spot behind my ear. "Do you want to play, *mon chéri?*"

My chest rises with a deep inhale, relishing the feeling of his breath on my skin. "Aye, I'm going to play."

"Switch, Tommy," Romeo commands, his face still buried in my neck.

I push to my feet slowly, Romeo's lips dragging across my skin as if his very touch will keep me tethered to him.

Like I predicted, Nico's gaze zeroes in on me. The car sways ever so slightly, and I brace for his reaction. When he doesn't so much as blink, I exhale a quiet breath.

I stand up straight and grab the bar on the ceiling that runs horizontally between the two benches, perks of being only five-foot-four.

Romeo's magnanimous attitude doesn't fool me for one second. I saw the way he looked at his brothers.

The fact that neither one of them noticed their younger brother's emotional shift is the only thing surprising to me. Romeo's just as possessive and domineering as both of them, but he's sneakier about it. Honestly, they should've realized it already.

I think I'll enjoy watching them squirm a little as their dynamic shifts once again.

But right now, Romeo and Tommaso will be the ones watching. My blood begins to hum in my veins at the thought of the four of us together. There's a tiny part of me, a whisper of a thought really, that balks at the idea. But that's the old Maeve, the one who followed orders blindly, hoping to be seen as an equal.

I outgrew her like an ill-fitting sweater.

Instead, I'm a sleek pair of leather leggings. Bold, dangerous, desirable. I'm sinking into my own wants and needs.

Right now, I *want* to help Nico, and I *need* to feel their eyes on my skin.

"What're you up to, *piccola seduttrice?*" Tommaso asks, his lips brushing against my hair.

A shiver rolls down my back. A premonition or a warning? With these three, it's probably both.

I turn my head an inch toward him and tip my chin up. "Just helping Nico."

He's too tall for the car—all three of them are—so, he has to crouch down, his shoulders rounding over. His broad chest takes up so much more space in the car when he stands.

It's probably why the ride operator gave us a lukewarm glare and issued a blanket *stay seated* warning when we climbed in the car.

Tommaso's grin widens as he takes a tiny hunched step toward. It's more of a shuffle, since I'm in the way.

The car lurches toward Romeo, and it's enough of a swing to snap Nico out of his trance. Tommaso and Romeo both reach out to steady me and the three of us freeze. We're close to the top now.

"I'm fine," I assure them softly.

Nico's gaze flashes to the sides, looking over at the horizon. His Adam's Apple bobs in his throat, and I imagine him desperately swallowing down the panic that must be rapidly rising.

I glance at Tommaso next to me. "Slow. On three." He nods. "One, two, three."

We move at the same time—him to squeeze in next to Romeo and me in Nico's lap.

His hands come around my waist reflexively as my legs settle on either side of his.

I feel the heat of him through the thin material of my panties immediately. I swear these three run hotter than anyone I've ever met, and I mean strictly temperature wise. Though they're so fucking good-looking it hurts sometimes.

283

Nico's fingers spread wide, his thumbs resting just underneath my bra strap. "We never should've gotten on this."

I rest my forearms on his broad shoulders and settle into his lap. His cock lines up perfectly with my pussy in this position, almost like the carnival gods are smiling down on us.

"I'm fine. Besides, it's one of the only rides I can do here."

His grip flexes and tightens briefly. "Then we shouldn't have come here."

I lean in close, the tops of our noses just barely touching. "We needed a bit of fun, don't you think?

"Swimming is fun. Watching movies is fun. Getting propelled two hundred feet in an aluminum boxcar that barely holds our weight is not fun."

I suppress the chuckle but can't contain my smile. "We're perfectly safe and it's about to get a whole lot more fun."

We stop at the top, the car swaying with the sudden halt.

Nico's eyes go wide and his chest starts to quicken with his breath. So I press my lips against his. It only takes him two seconds to respond.

One hand slides to my lower back while the other snakes up between my shoulder blades. He hails me closer to him as he deepens the kiss.

He tastes like summer: powdered sugar from the funnel cake we split earlier and freshly squeezed lemonade.

His lips are soft but demanding,

I pull back and blink a few times to clear the lusty veil from my vision. "I'm going to stand up for a second."

"Don't. It's not safe," he says immediately.

"It's alright. Tommaso and Romeo have me, don't you, boys?"

"Aye we fucking got her," Tommaso says, his voice gravelly and low.

I keep my hands on Nico's shoulders and slide off of his lap.

Planting my feet on the metal floor, I break the connection with him to reach up and hold the ceiling bar once more.

Big hands land on my hips from behind, and I don't need to turn around to know it's Romeo. He smooths his palms around my hips, stopping to push the button snap through the hole and clasp the zipper pull. It feels like an eternity before the zipper is all the way down.

I wiggle my hips in anticipation, and my skirt falls to pool at my feet.

The three of them groan in union. Tommaso leans forward to place gentle kisses along my ass cheek, sending goosebumps down my spine.

And with a precision-like slowness, I sink to my knees in front of Nico. His thumb smudges across my bottom lip, and my tongue flicks out to taste him. He inhales a gasp, and I use it as an opportunity to unzip his pants and tug them lower.

My mouth waters at the sight of his cock. I don't have the time for slow and gentle, so I do what I've been thinking about since the moment I saw him this morning. I slide his cock between my lips and I take him as far down my throat as I can.

His cock bumps the back of my throat, and I breathe through my nose against the sting. Nico groans as he weaves his fingers in my hair. He lets me play, but not long enough. Before I finish, he pulls me off of his dick.

"I want your pussy, baby girl. Are you going to give it to me?" His voice is low, barely above a growl.

I'm on my feet and in his lap faster than I can blink. He turns me around so I face Tommaso and Romeo, and I slowly sink onto his cock.

I toss my head back at the fullness of him at this angle, a groan tearing from my throat. Nico's hands wrap around my thighs, spreading my legs wide for them to see everything.

Tommaso and Romeo both lean forward, sending the car

rocking. I look at Nico out of the corner of my eye, but he's lost in his pleasure.

I exhale, relaxing against Nico's chest and resting my head on his shoulder as I roll my hips. Tommaso shifts forward and circles his fingertip around my clit. Then Nico starts to fuck me from the bottom, and Tommaso increases his tempo, and then I really am flying thirty feet above ground.

39

MAEVE

I BOUNCE on the balls of my feet, excitement making me feel giddy. I've grown to love it here. The slow mornings and the easy afternoons. The family dinners and the time spent with my men.

In a lot of ways, I've found myself on this island.

I thought I'd be here for a few weeks, a month tops. But with every passing day that the threat didn't diminish, our stay extended longer and longer.

My anxiety shifted from unnamed assassins to something far scarier. The reason for my newly formed anxiety throws an elbow into my ribs.

Tommaso promised me I would have this baby surrounded by modern medicine, and I'm going to hold him to it. The only thing I fear more than assassins is delivering a baby on a remote island without the help of a trained medical professional. And pain medicine.

Time slipped from my fingers like the powdered sugar sand on our beach. It feels like just yesterday we arrived on this island, and here we are, leaving for the second time in five months.

Butterflies soar in my belly at the act of leaving the island. It's a weird shift in dynamic. I was once nervous to come here and now I'm scared to leave.

"Oh," I say on a gasp, my hand covering the side of my stomach.

"Baby kicks?" Tommaso asks, a smile on his face.

I grab his hand and place it on my stomach. "Here, just a second."

We're quiet as we walk toward the fairgrounds, Tommaso's large palm warming the side of my stomach. And then baby kicks, right underneath his palm.

"I'll never get tired of feeling that," he murmurs.

"C'mon, you two. We have to stop at the clinic first, remember," Nico hollers from a few feet in front of us.

I roll my eyes at his bossiness. "As if I could forget that I'm gigantic and we need to have the doctor look me over. I'm practically waddling."

Tommaso throws his arm around my shoulder and tugs me close to him, brushing his lips across my head. "You're not gigantic. You're perfect and the most beautiful thing I've ever seen."

My lips twist to the side, and I snark, "You're just saying that because you love me."

"Nah, I'm saying that because it's true. But you're not wrong. I do love you."

Tommaso first told me he loved me three months ago, and I don't think I'll ever get tired of the casual way he expresses it daily.

I nuzzle into him, wrapping my arm around his lower back. "And I love you."

These squishy feelings are new to me. But I've done my best at embracing them *and* these men for who they are. I honestly can't imagine my life without them.

And I don't think I ever want to try.

"C'MON, man. We went last time without a problem," Tommaso says. "Why the second thoughts?"

The four of us are standing just outside the entrance to the carnival on the fairgrounds.

Nic taps his finger on his bottom lip, his gaze darting to me. "I don't know. The doctor said she was fine, but I didn't like the way she looked at us. She didn't seem trustworthy to me."

I lift a shoulder and run my hand over the growing swell of my stomach. "I'm fine. And I had fun last time. I especially liked the Ferris wheel."

A small smile cracks through his tough facade. I just know he's replaying our time thirty feet above ground.

"No Ferris Wheel this time. And before you pout, do I need to remind you that you're seven and a half months pregnant?" He arches a brow.

I pout harder just because he told me not to. My lips twist to the side. "Oh believe me, I haven't forgotten. *Waddling*, remember?"

Tommaso claps his hands together and rubs them. "Perfect. I've got dibs on the ring toss with Maeve."

TOMMASO

I walk next to Nic, my gaze glued to my girl in front of us. Romeo's got his arm around her shoulders and she's laughing at something he said. Jealousy tightens my gut, but I do my best to tamp it down. It's a daily battle for me to not act on my urge to rip her out of my brothers' hands and covet her for myself.

It's only because I know she cares for all of us that I don't.

Two teenage guys walk a little too close to her, and my hackles raise immediately. One of them shoulder-checks Maeve, and she grabs a fistful of his shirt in an instant. She yanks him close just as Nico lunges toward them.

I hold up my arm to block him, content to watch my girl handle herself, confident that she has backup if she needs it.

The guy lowers his head, a dumbass smirk across his face. From this angle, I can't see what her other hand is doing, but I have a pretty fucking good idea.

Nic's body vibrates, and I straighten my arm to stop him from taking a step.

"She can handle herself."

"She shouldn't fucking have to," he hisses. "We're right here."

My brother and I watch the moment the dipshit realizes his mistake. His face blanches and now I know my girl has her favorite knife to his dick. He throws his arms up in the universal surrender gesture.

Maeve looks at us from the corner of her eye, the edges of her smirk barely visible. My own mouth mimics hers without conscious thought.

"What's going on?" Nic grits through clenched teeth.

"Our girl's teaching that punk a lesson."

Maeve yanks him close and maneuvers herself to the side. Underneath the swell of her belly I see the flash of a blade. And fuck yes, right against his dick. I hope she fucking cuts it off for touching her.

"Ah, now I get it. You just wanted to see her pull a blade on someone," Nic muses.

I shrug. "Maybe. It's the hottest fucking thing of my life."

Nic arches a brow. "And if it's against someone else's cock?"

My grin sinks into a frown. "I hadn't thought of it like that."

Nic smirks as Maeve lets go of the asshole. "Exactly."

"Hey Rome," I shout, waiting for him to turn around. I don't take my eyes from the dead man walking as he skirts by us. "Take Maeve to the funnel cakes. Nic and I will be right there."

"You got it, brother," he calls.

I don't wait, trusting Rome to take care of our girl. I smack the back of my hand against Nic's chest. "C'mon, man. Let's teach that asshole a lesson of our own."

Nic grins, it's nothing short of feral. "I'm thinking hands, yeah? That's a good lesson to learn."

My brother and I turn around and stalk after the motherfucker who dared to put his hands on what's ours.

40

MAEVE

ROMEO and I share a funnel cake on a picnic table just off the normal drag of the carnival. It's the same place we ate at last time we were here, so I knew Nico and Tommaso would find us. Though I kind of expected them to be back by now.

"What's taking them so long?"

"I'm sure they're fine, *mon chéri*. They probably got caught up in a vicious game of ring toss," he says with a chuckle.

I remember how competitive they got last time. We were at that booth for almost an hour until I called time and threatened to leave by myself.

I eat the last bit of whipped cream, smoothing my hand over my stomach as the baby moves around. I reach over and grab Romeo's hand and place it on my stomach. "Here, feel this."

His eyes widen and he stares at my stomach as if he can actually see the baby. "I'll never get tired of this, Maeve. Never. It's a gift." He runs his palms reverently over me.

That one word is a running theme for the last year. Time has shaped many things, including my struggles. I'd like to believe that I'm on the other side of things, that I'm able to appreciate the ups and downs for the whole of the journey.

I can't say that I enjoyed being deprived of my sisters, regaled to biweekly satellite phone calls for five to seven minutes. I haven't heard Ava's or Fiona's voices in nearly six months. Keira's kept me updated, and I talked to Roisin a couple times. But it's not the same.

But I can understand that without that chain of events, I wouldn't be here. With the three men I fell in love with. And with a baby on the way.

Like so many things in life, it took time and patience to get here.

And orgasms. Many, many orgasms.

"What do you think? Boy or girl?"

He leans his forehead against mine, effectively creating a little bubble between us. I place my hand over his, and together we feel the force behind our little sunray's kick.

"I don't care. I just want you both healthy."

His answer is perfect, and from any other man in any other situation, I would say it's a line. But from my man who's love language is reciting Shakespeare and poetry, it's genuine.

I tip my chin up and murmur against his lips, "I love you."

"And I love you," he responds instantly. "The universe isn't cruel enough to deny the world a mini Maeve, so I'm betting on a girl."

A chuckle slips past my parted lips, and he captures my mirth with a kiss.

A scream pierces our bubble, and Romeo has his gun in hand faster than I can blink. I pull my own out of my crossbody purse. I didn't have anywhere to tuck it in this flowy maxi dress. It's one of the only things that I can fit into without it pulling too tight across my stomach.

"We need to find the others. *Now*." Adrenaline and anxiety speed through my veins, making my skin feel fluttery.

"No way, Juliet. You know the protocol. We all agreed on it before we left the island, remember?" Romeo steps in front of me, aiming his gun in these semicircles from left to right and back again, constantly swiveling as we cross the fair grounds.

"Aye, I remember. But I don't give a fuck about that right now. I'm not leaving without them," I snap at him, dashing down the little dirt path toward the carnival's main thoroughfare.

Several screams join the first one, sending the hair on my arm toward the sky. They aren't the joyful yells of surprised kids or even the good-natured yelps of friends playing pranks on one another. They're terrified.

A second later, I know why. Gunshots fill the air. One right after the other. Rome wraps himself around me and takes us to the ground immediately. He shifts so his back hits the dirt, rolling to the side so I'm on my back, and bracing himself over my like a human shield.

My heart beats loud in my ears, drowning out everything else. I focus on Rome's face right in front of mine. Everything but his eyes are blurry, our faces too close.

I focus on the way the dark blue color surrounds his pupil, the tiny flecks of light blue. I zone in on the way his dark lashes sweep across his lids. They're entirely too long and that sooty black that women spend good money on in a tube.

He blinks a few times, his gaze bouncing around my face. He rears back, shuffling to the side so he's between me and the possibility of anyone else on this little dirt path. He sets his gun next to us and runs his hands over my bare shoulders and arms before touching every inch of my belly. He spreads his fingers as wide as possible, like he has to be sure we're both okay. He stares at me, his brows furrowing and his lips moving.

I shake my head and blink at him, the sound of his voice piercing through my panic. "What?"

"I asked if you're okay. Are you hurt anywhere?"

I use my free hand to run my palm over my stomach, feeling the baby throw an elbow high up on the left. "No, I don't think so. Here." I grab Romeo's hand, shifting it so it covers where the baby is moving.

He sighs, relief softening his brows instantly. "We're both fine."

He leans down, placing a kiss first on my stomach, right where his palm just was, and then another one on my lips. It's quick and over too soon, but it's an affirmation for him that I'm okay more than anything else.

"We need to go, *mon chéri*. The boys will be at our meeting spot, I'm sure of it." He crouches next to me, balancing on the balls of his feet. He holds a hand out to me, and I grasp it. He pulls me up, settling me on my feet before he laces our fingers together.

Twenty minutes ago, we were holding hands, and yet it felt nothing like it does now. Then it felt like an intimate show of affection, and now it feels like a lifeline.

I cling to Romeo's hand, my other hand clutching the gun so tightly, the metal digs into my fingers. "They could be in trouble, real trouble, Romeo! We can't just leave them."

"We're not going to leave them, Maeve." He pauses at another four-way stop. People are screaming and crying, fleeing in every direction. Even the carnival workers are bailing on their rides and booths, seeking shelter.

I haven't heard any more gunshots, but that doesn't really mean anything. It could be one person or it could be ten, and we'd never hear them coming in a crowd this size.

"This way," he murmurs. "Stay close and shoot anything that comes at you, yeah?"

My stomach tightens, and I wince a little. "Aye, I will."

A group of terrified people run across the path, none of them stopping to pay us any attention. Romeo keeps us off the beaten path, guiding us to our meeting place.

My footsteps quicken when I see the familiar silhouette at our meeting spot by the dock. And my heart drops like a stone into my stomach when there's only one silhouette.

"Nico! Tommaso!" I run the rest of the way, as fast as my stomach will carry me but not fast enough for my fear to settle.

The silhouette turns around and eliminates the space between us in three long strides. "Oh thank fuck, Maeve. I was so worried. Are you hurt?" Nico runs his hands over me, checking for injuries.

"I'm fine." I squeeze his hands. "I'm fine."

"The baby?" he chokes on the words, his eyes wide and fearful. He drops to his knees, eye level with my stomach like he has X-Ray vision.

I bring his hands to cover my stomach. "Baby is fine too. They were just kicking not five minutes ago."

Nico exhales and pulls me into his chest. "Oh thank god."

I look behind him, my gaze darting around for the other piece of my heart. Panic spikes my adrenaline further. "Where's Tommaso?"

41

NICO

MY PHONE VIBRATES in my pocket, and I shift my hold on Maeve to fish it out. I don't recognize the number, but I already know what they're going to say. Call it intuition or fucking bad luck.

"We've got a package that belongs to you." *We have someone from your family.*

My teeth grind together at the sound of Vito's second, Marcus. That slimy fuck just signed his own death. "Yeah, well. I have my own package. More of a present really," he says.

"Is that right? What kind of package?" he asks. It's quiet in the background, and I strain my hearing. All I need is the tiniest noise to give me a clue. Something—anything to help narrow down where Tommy is.

"Let's meet for a swap."

He pauses, and I hear the sound of murmuring voices. It's too muffled to make out anyone familiar, but I'm sure one of them is Vito. He's too fucking proud not to have his entire hand in this mess.

"Nah, it's best if you come here," Marcus says.

I can't agree too quickly, because it'll make me look weak. Plus, we need to give Rome as much time as possible to try to narrow down where the fuck they're really calling from. I have a hard time believing they're still here.

"If you think I'm willingly walking into a trap, then you're fucked-up, Marcus."

"Okay, okay. We'll do an exchange somewhere neutral. The Carnival?"

I try to keep my swift intake of breath quiet. The last thing I need to do is offer them insight in how to further torment and torture. The Carnival isn't exactly neutral, not really. My brothers and I run the entire operation. In fact, I bet Vito doesn't have more than five percent shares left in The Carnival.

I decide in that second that as soon as we get back, I'm going to ask Rome to take everything from him. His wealth, his power, his prestige. And then I'll take his life from him.

I exhale. I'm fucking stuck and we both know it. I can't object to my own club, even though it somehow feels like a trap. For all I know, he replaced the staff at The Carnival and we no longer have allies there.

"Fine. The Carnival, tomorrow night."

"See you there, boy," Marcus says.

"I'm not your fucking boy" I snap and end the call.

"What's going on?" Maeve asks, her voice shrill. "Where's Tommaso, Nico? Where is he?"

I look her in the eye, preparing to break her heart a little. "We're going back to Vegas."

"No," she whispers, backing away from me. Romeo's there, wrapping her up in his arms and offering her comfort.

Vito thinks he has the upper hand. But what they don't know is I have a hidden ace up my sleeve: Maeve King.

She's intelligence and lethal grace in a five foot four package. And more than all of those things: she fucking loves my brother.

Loves him the way he deserves to be loved. She appreciates his quirks and accepts his flaws in stride.

And she threatened to cut my balls off in my sleep if I left her behind. So there's also that. Nothing gets me fucking harder than when she gets fiercely protective like that.

She's the perfect partner for us.

I used to think she was going to be my downfall, but now I realize that she's going to be theirs.

42

NICO

WE'VE BEEN in Las Vegas for only a few hours, having left the island and chartering a private plane as soon as possible. We're all running on fumes and adrenaline.

Rome steps away from Maeve, their fingertips touching until the very last second. Her eyes look glassy, and I imagine what he said to cause such a reaction.

More than likely, she's scared and angry and most of all, vengeful. If it were up to her, she'd march right into Vito's house and take him out point-blank.

But he has too many loyal soldiers, and she'd never walk out alive. It's one of the main reasons Rome and I convinced her to stay behind today.

The only way I'll be able to concentrate on what I need to do is if I know she's safe. What she doesn't know yet is that I asked Keira to come here. Not only to make sure she doesn't run after us, but to help her when I'm gone. I know Tommy and Rome can handle her, but I know she'll want the support from at least one of her sisters.

"Maeve," I murmur, drawing her into my arms.

She tips her chin up, and we reach each other at the same moment. Our lips glide and caress in a kiss that's soft and still urgent. The desire to take it further starts to climb like it always does the moment her lips touch mine.

I pull back and lean my forehead against hers, praying to a god I don't particularly believe in to keep them safe. I rest my hands on either side of her stomach and close my eyes.

"I've thought about it, you know?" My words are low, the persistent fear that if I voice them aloud, they won't come true. "What he or she will look like. Your grey eyes or my light brown ones. Or Tommy's dark eyes."

She inhales, her hands curling around my arm, the place right above my elbow. "I'm sorry, Nico."

She's not apologizing for her time with either of my brothers, and I wouldn't expect her to. She wants the baby to be both mine *and* Tommy's. She won't choose between the three of us, she's said as much on the island.

I once consoled myself with the fact that if this was Tommy's baby, I'd simply whisk her away for however long it took for me to knock her up again. Then I'd know for sure it was mine.

It's not that I wouldn't love it—fuck, I know I'd love any of my brothers' babies with her simply because they're hers.

But those thoughts don't even feel like they belong to me anymore. We're so far removed from the concept of hope it's laughable.

Melancholy floats in, dragging my shoulders down. I'm so fucking sad, but not because this could be Tommy's baby and not mine.

No, I'm fucking devastated that this will be the last time I get to see her, touch her like this.

Vito wants a trade? I'm going to give him the trade of a lifetime. I'm going to hand over the keys to his precious kingdom: me.

"Nothing to be sorry for, baby girl. You've given me a gift. All of us, really. Our time on the island will always be ours, regardless of what happens today." I run my hands over her, loving on her and this baby the best way I know how.

"I should be there with you," she mutters.

I grasp her face, tilting her chin up and threaded my fingers in her soft hair. "You have to stay here. Promise me you will? If you're there, I'll just be worried the entire time."

Her lower lip trembles and her gaze flicks between my eyes. "Promise me you'll be safe."

"You know I will do everything in my power to get us out of there safely." It's not a lie exactly, but still, the half-truth tastes bitter on my tongue.

She pushes onto her tiptoes and whispers against my lips, "Come back to me, aye?"

"I will." And it's not a lie. I will find my way back to her. In the next lifetime. And the one after that. I'll find my way to her in every lifetime.

"Kiss me, baby girl."

The words aren't even out of my mouth before her lips are on mine. I pour everything I have into this kiss, knowing it's going to have to sustain me. I funnel every good emotion I've ever felt.

The first time I felt the baby kick. The first time I tasted her skin. Every single time my heart clenched when I watched her laugh.

Eventually, Rome clears his throat somewhere behind us. We part for the last time, and I finally murmur the words I've been holding onto for too long.

"I love you, Maeve King."

She beams at me, this soft smile. "And I love you, Nico Santorini."

"I brought someone in to keep you company while we're out."

Her brow wrinkles. "Who?"

"Me," Keira says.

Maeve gasps at the sound of her sister's voice, and I know we made the right call bringing her in. The two run toward each other, throwing their arms around one another.

It's the perfect distraction so we can leave. I look at Romeo and jerk my head to the right. He stares longingly at Maeve for a moment longer before he nods.

And together, the two of us leave the hotel and head toward The Carnival.

Fifteen minutes later, we're walking into the warehouse on the backlot of one of our hotels. The Carnival is a converted old warehouse with different *booths* inside.

Karaoke and dancing, a strip club and burlesque show, live music stage, a boxing ring, and a few other areas around the perimeter of the warehouse make up the booths. And in the center is a sizable pub. It's always rowdy but controlled by security easily enough.

The space Rome and I walk into is a skeleton of what it used to be. There's no life, no pulse or atmosphere to the place. It hasn't been used since I gave the order to shut it down. Which should be a good thing, except that Vito brought us here. And he never does anything without intention.

The low lamp lighting from sconces around the perimeter give the space a soft glow. Not that we needed help locating Vito. The man stands in the middle of the dancing area with a wide spotlight beaming directly overhead.

"Boys! You made it," he crows, clapping his hands together. "Come, sit."

Vito pulls out a chair at one of the few tables and sits down. His right hand guys flank him a few feet back.

Rome and I stop in front of the table, and I say, "We'll stand."

"What? No manners for your boss?" Vito runs his hands through his greasy hair, slicking it straight back. The light glints off his thick silver bands on two fingers. It matches the silver chain-link chain around his neck. He tugs the collar of his flashy button-down shirt up, rearranging it like he's about to head out for a night on the town.

"What are we doing here, Vito? Primping or doing business?" I ask, looking to the side with a bored expression plastered on my face.

It's a good ruse to check out who he has stashed around here. So far, I count at least six soldiers hidden in the shadows. Though not all that well if I can casually spot them. I don't immediately recognize any of them, but that's not surprising. I've been gone for months.

Vito smiles. It reminds me of a shark—all teeth. "Ah, Nico. You're usually not so impatient. You must've been spending too much time with your brothers."

"Speaking of my brothers. Where's Tommy?"

Vito tsks. "Not so fast. Where's my trade?"

"Tommy first. For all I know, you don't even have him." I shrug and keep my hands in my pockets. Rome stands stock-still next to me.

Vito sighs and pulls out his phone. He taps something on his screen and holds it to his ear. "It's me. He wants proof it's him." He hangs up without another word.

A second later, screams erupt from the speaker system. My muscles lock with empathy at the sounds of agony filling the air around us. I take a deep breath and shove everything down. I cling to my neutral expression, willing my ears to disassociate.

Vito raises his hand in the air, palm flat, and the speakers cut out. He arches a brow at me, his smug grin pulling wide on his face.

"You expect me to believe that was Tommy? Please," I scoff. "That could've been anyone or some recording off the internet."

Vito's eye twitches as he regards me. Finally, he pulls his phone out of his pocket, bringing it to his ear once more. "My son requires further proof. Bring him out."

I shift onto the balls of my feet, preparing myself for anything.

Two men frog march Tommy out, his head hanging low between his shoulders. His feet shuffle along the floor, so he's not unconscious, at least. I flick my gaze over him briefly, enough to see that he's not hurt too badly but not long enough to give my father another edge.

They slam Tommy into a seat slightly behind and to the right of Vito. He grunts, finally looking at us from underneath his lashes.

Vito holds his hand out toward Tommy like he's fucking Vanna White or something. "Here he is. Now, tell me, son, what would be worth trading for?"

"Me," I say without hesitation.

I feel Rome's surprise, but thankfully, he stays quiet.

I toss my arms out wide. "You can have me, Vito. It's what you always wanted, isn't it, for me to be your faithful little puppet. I'm sure you've noticed how difficult things have been while I was gone."

He rubs his chin, his brows crashing together over his eyes. "See the thing is, son, I don't think I need you."

I tilt my head to the side. "Don't you though? How are you planning on accessing over half our assets and territory and businesses without me?"

Vito drums his fingers on the table before he slams his hand down and pushes to his feet. "See, while you were gone, son, I made some new friends. The kind of friendships that would allow me to grow beyond the confines of Nevada." He walks around the back of his chair, taking slow, measured steps. "But these friends, they require a certain level of commitment. A show of loyalty."

"You were the one who ordered the hits on us," Rome says.

Vito pulls a gun from the back of his pants and taps the end of the gun against his pant leg. He smiles at us. "You have to admit that was genius. But I can't take the credit for it."

Nausea bubbles in my gut, boiling hotter and hotter as Vito's picture becomes clearer.

"Do you remember what I said when I told you what would happen if you didn't follow my rules?"

I clench my hands into fists and try not to look at Tommy. It's not because I don't care, it's because I care too much. And if I allow myself the time to really look at him and see all the damage they did to him, then I'm going to lose my carefully constructed control and fuck this whole thing up.

And the biggest reason why I can't do that is stashed in the hotel, pregnant and waiting for us.

"Enlighten me."

He jerks his head back and his henchmen step out from the shadows and surround him in a loose semicircle directly across from me and Rome.

"It's one of those two birds, one stone thing. See, I needed something to prove my unwavering loyalty, something that they'll use as collateral. And I needed to teach you a lesson about following orders. And I needed the money. Guess it's a three birds, one stone situation." He says the last part with a casual shrug.

I feel like I'm trapped in one of those horror movies. I realize what he's implying a second too late.

Vito's not going to trade Tommy—not for me or anyone else.

"You were always more of a visual learner, son." He raises his arm and fires the gun, right at Tommy.

43

MAEVE

"TOMMASO!" My anguish echoes around the room, bouncing off of the metal exterior walls.

I dash into The Carnival, my stomach cramping and my eyes flooding with tears. Tommaso slumps off the chair, his free hand flying to his chest. Blood pools between his fingers, seeping into his shirt.

"Maeve, no!" Nico yells.

"Juliet!" Romeo lunges for me, but Vito's men step in front of him with their guns drawn. He only stops when the barrels press into his chest.

I draw my own weapon and point it at the back of the soldier's head standing between me and Tommaso. "Get the fuck out of my way right now."

He starts to turn around, raising his right arm, and I don't hesitate. I pull the trigger. I pivot on the ball of my foot and fire round after round at everyone who isn't Nico and Romeo. I take out everyone in my way, aided by my four sisters standing vigil in the rafters above us.

Nico thought I was his ace, his trump card. But in the end, he wasn't willing to risk my safety. And while I respected him, I didn't agree.

There's no way I was going to let my men walk into enemy territory like that without me. Convincing my sisters was easy. All I had to do was pull the sister card and threaten to go without them.

We formulated a plan, and hustled here. My sisters and I are an unmistakable force together. And I knew that if I told Nico and Romeo that I called them in, they would stash me somewhere far away for my safety.

As if I need protecting. As if it isn't everyone else who needs protecting from *me*.

I'm a motherfucking King.

And these men are nothing but dirt beneath my feet. They are the reason Tommaso's on the ground, and they will regret the day they ever decided to back Vito Santorini.

Gunshots split the air, the noise unbelievably loud in here, echoing off the walls. I try to stay as low as possible as I finally land by Tommaso.

I feel a shadow above me, and I raise my gun out of instinct. Vito Santorini's vile face looms above me. My finger depresses the trigger, but his head jerks back before I can pull it.

Vito jerks back and falls to the floor instantly. Nico stands over him, chest slowly rising and falling and face serious. He reminds me of one of those fallen angels.

"Call an ambulance!" I scream, balling up my tee and pressing it to Tommy's chest, halfway to his shoulder. "Shh, stay with me. Please, stay with me."

His eyes are wide as he stares at me. But whatever he's trying to communicate is lost on me, my panic too strong.

My stomach squeezes again, this sharp pain lancing along my abdomen. I exhale and press harder on Tommy's wound.

An eternity passes before the paramedics arrive. I can't tell if it's been two minutes or two hours, everything is a blur.

I blink a few times, trying to clear the hazy film that covers my vision. It doesn't work. My stomach tenses again, this shooting pain ricocheting across my abdomen. I clutch my belly and hunch over a little.

"*Mon chéri*, are you hurt?"

I look up at Romeo standing above me, the paramedics making quick work of getting Tommaso on the gurney.

I lick my dry lips, my hands leaving bloodied prints across my sundress. "I—I think it's the baby."

44

MAEVE

"I CAN'T DO IT. Not without him," I cry. My eyes fill with tears as pain lances across my abdomen again.

We're in the labor and delivery room of the hospital. Once Romeo heard it was the baby, he shuffled me into the back of the ambulance alongside Tommaso. But then they admitted me here, and he's somewhere else. In danger and alone.

"I know, baby, but you have to. Our baby is ready to join us." Romeo smooths my hair back off of my forehead, his voice soft and soothing.

"Not yet. Not until he's here. I promised him. I promised him, Romeo." My voice catches on a sob.

Nico shoulders Romeo out of the way, clasping my head between his big palms. His eyes are a darker shade of brown, his own despair reflected in his pupils. "Look at me."

I hiccup and bring my watery gaze to him. I grit my teeth against another wave of pain tightening my stomach. "We can't leave him alone, unprotected."

He smooths my hair back with his whole palm, his gaze bouncing around my face. "I'll send one of your sisters."

My face crumples when I think of my sisters who flew from all over the world to help me. "They're cleaning up."

"I'll watch over Tommy," Romeo says.

I jerk my head to him. Frenetic energy buzzes underneath my skin, making me feel irrational. "No! You can't leave."

"Shh," Nico says, tilting my face toward him with his thumbs. "Rome will stay here with us. I'll call Fiona, okay? We'll make sure someone's with Tommy."

I shake my head, sending a tear down my cheek. "No, call Keira. And tell her to hurry, okay? I don't want him to be alone."

Nico presses a soft kiss to my sweaty forehead. "Keira then. Now you have to do something for me. Let the nurses check you out, okay?"

I nod again, welcoming the scratch of his stubble against my skin.

"Good girl," he murmurs against my forehead before he presses his lips to mine. He lingers for a moment, applying more pressure before stepping away. "I'm going to make that call in the hallway, get an update on Tommy, and then I'll be right back."

"Aye, right back," I repeat, holding his gaze.

The corner of his mouth twitches as he takes another step back. A nurse steps into the space he vacated and smiles warmly at me. I spare her a brief smile, tilting my head to the side to watch Nico step out of the room.

NICO

I close the door softly behind me, letting the high-pitched click of the door's lock punctuate my mood.

We're in a corner room on the labor and delivery floor, with the rooms on either side of us empty. They'll remain that way for as long as we're here too. I paid enough to buy out the whole fucking floor.

And I'd pay ten times as much for the fucking peace of mind. While Vito isn't an immediate threat anymore—a fact that I haven't even begun to process yet—but he still has men loyal to him. Too fucking many.

I don't relish the task of weeding them out, but that's a problem for another day. One when my brother's out of surgery and my girl is safely at home with our baby.

With our baby.

Goddamn. I don't know if that sentiment will ever get old. I've had months to get used to the idea of bringing a tiny life into this world, and still, the idea terrifies me as much as it electrifies me.

I thought I'd have more time to get used to it, to get the house ready, to get the surprise safe house ready for them.

But now—now everything has gone to shit.

"Fuck," I swear under my breath. I stretch my neck from side to side and loosen the collar on my black button-down shirt. It's stiff with dried blood.

I abandon that train of thought faster than I can blink. I can't fucking think about that right now. I exhale and scan the hallway once more. It's as clear as it's going to get.

I could step into one of the empty rooms, but then no one's watching Maeve's door, and I'm already paranoid as fuck that the security guard's incompetence will fuck us over.

I lean my ass against the wall opposite her room, keeping her in my line of sight. Propping my left foot flat on the wall, I fish my phone out of my pocket and dial Maeve's sister.

Thank fuck she gave us their secure numbers months ago, or we might be fucked.

"Aye," Keira answers on the first ring.

"We've got a situation." Everything I thought I knew turned

out to be bullshit in the last few months, so I'm not going to assume that my line is secure even if hers is. Or fuck, hers could be compromised now too. I drag my hand through my hair, tugging on the ends a little.

I'm confident Maeve's sister will be able to pick up what I'm saying though.

She scoffs. "I'm already taking care of your *situation.*"

I clear my throat. "Thank you for that, by the way."

"Aye. Where's my sister?"

I glance at the window, seeing a glimpse of her between the blinds when the nurse shuffles to the side. I make a mental note to close the blinds completely. "The baby's coming."

"What?" she shrieks. "It's too early."

"That's what she said, but unfortunately, our little one doesn't give a shit about that. They're coming now, and Maeve is . . . struggling."

Several loud thumps are the only things I hear. I pull my phone away from my ear and check my service. One bar still. It's better than most get in a hospital, but it's still not ideal.

"Oi! Maeve needs us. Time to go, babes," Keira hollers.

I jerk the phone away from my ear, but it's too late. My ears ring from the sheer volume. I don't think she even bothered to cover the mouthpiece before she yelled.

I grit my teeth and tamp down my irritation. My nerves are shot, raw and frayed beyond anything I've ever experienced before. But she saved our asses back at The Carnival, and the fact remains: I fucking need her again.

It wasn't all that long ago that I began to trust Maeve. What used to be a trusted triangle turned into a fucked-up rhombus. And here I am, trusting someone else—*again.*

Look how that turned out last time.

It's different, I reason with myself. These are Maeve's sisters. I run my palm down my face, scratching at my beard that's a day or two longer than I usually keep it.

"We'll be there in twenty," Keira says.

The hospital isn't all that far away from The Carnival, but we left a fucking mess. "So soon?"

"I'll forgive the insult, since I know you're stressed. Santorini. My sister may love you, but we're reserving judgment until you fucking earn it. Considering the fucking mess you lot dragged her into, you have a fucking ways to go," she hisses.

I nod several times, not that she can see me. Shame slicks up my back and coils around my neck like a snake. "You're right. I owe you all a debt I'll never be able to repay."

"I'm betting on you, Nic," Rosie hollers in the background. I recognize her voice.

I clear my throat. "I have another favor."

Keira sighs.

"I'll add another favor to my debt," I offer.

"You're racking them up faster than you'll be able to repay them, Santorini. But I'm feeling generous since my niece or nephew is almost here, so out with it."

I roll my lips inward for a moment to gain composure. These King women are fucking lethal with weapons and words.

"We need clothes. Please. Maeve will be in a hospital gown, but Rome and I, we're still covered in blood." I can't bring myself to say Tommy's name right now, not when flashes of my brother bleeding out at my father's feet flash across my vision.

"Fuck. Aye, of course. We'll bring something for all of you," she says, compassion replacing the annoyance in her tone.

"Thank you. Maeve asked for you to be with him until she can."

"You tell my sister not to worry about a thing. We'll handle it, yeah?"

I blow out a breath and drop my head, letting my gaze rest

on my scuffed black shoes. "Yeah. Fourth floor for Maeve. Second for Tommy."

"Twenty minutes, Santorini," she says before the call ends.

I press the button on the side of my phone to send it to standby mode and slip it into my pocket. Pushing off the wall, I search for the nurse who helped me earlier. She seemed agreeable enough, so I'm hopeful she'll be able to update me on Tommy without having to leave this floor.

45

MAEVE

"DID I ever tell you the first moment I saw you?" Nico asks.

My brows dip. "At The Red Lion."

"No. That's the first time *you* saw *me*."

"What?" My lips part in surprise.

"Your hair was longer then. You were wearing this little black jumpsuit, and you walked through the streets of the South Side of Chicago with a swagger I've only ever seen on a grown man carrying more than his weight in firepower."

My nose stings and my sinuses get full. I search his gaze for any sign of deception but all I see is the truth.

"But then I saw you stop outside this little candy shop and help an older woman pick up her bag that ripped open." He uses his thumbs to tilt my chin up, his lips closer to mine. "You're the fiercest woman I've ever known."

"One minute," a nurse says. "Get ready to push soon, Maeve."

I ignore her and the other nurse bustling around the room. I ignore the beeping of the machines and the way the disinfectant smell makes my nose tickle.

Romeo slides his hand in mine. "You've got this, *mon chéri*. And we'll be right here with you the whole time."

I ignore everything except Nico and Romeo. My vision narrows, and I concentrate on breathing.

Time loses all sense of meaning, and the only thing that brings me back to myself is the unmistakable sound of a newborn's cries.

"Congratulations, mom. It's a girl," the nurse says. She whisks her away to the machine in the corner of the room.

I lift a weak hand and push at Nico's chest. "Go with her. Stay with her, okay?"

He pushes my hair off my forehead and skims his lips over the top of my head. "You did so good, baby girl. I'll stay with her. You rest and let them clean you up, okay?"

I nod, my head feeling like a wet noodle. I lean into Romeo's comfort from my other side, letting his familiar tenor soothe me as I try to see what they're doing to her. Our baby.

"Holy fuck. I can't believe we have a daughter," I whisper, my lids feeling heavy.

The last thing I hear is Romeo saying, "She's absolutely beautiful, *mon chéri*."

EPILOGUE

TOMMASO

"Okay, you have to be quick, sweetheart. Just reach out and grab him, okay?"

My four-year-old daughter blinks her big dark brown eyes at me. "Got it, Daddy. Then I get to put it under Mum's pillows, right?"

I wince and shake my head. I hate to deny her anything, but if she sticks another lizard in my wife's bed, I'm never going to be invited back into it.

"No can do, Sienna." Her face falls instantly. "But we can put it in Nic's desk in his office."

"Yes, yes, yes," she says, jumping and clapping her little hands. "I love pulling pranks on Da!"

Our four-year-old calls me Daddy, Nic *Da*, and Rome *Dada*. It's an interesting dynamic, and I often wonder if it's going to shift when the boys start talking.

They're fifteen months old, and we're in the thick of the

exploring stage. The one where they're learning to run, so they go full-speed and often fall down. I can't wait for them to get a little older, so we can rope them in on the pranks.

"You better not be catching lizards and bringing them in my house," Maeve yells.

"Busted," Sienna stage-whispers, her eyes wide.

"C'mon, my little rose, let's go help Mum with the laundry." I scoop her up with an arm around her middle and toss her over my shoulder.

Her little squeals are music to my ears, another sound to tuck away in my ever-growing collection of favorite noises.

A NOTE TO READER

I hope you enjoyed The Wild! This isn't the end for these beloved characters, we'll be seeing them soon! You can expect a novella featuring Maeve and her sisters before the next King sister duet!

This story has been on my mind for over a year, and I am so, so excited that you get to read it now. I hope you enjoyed reading it as much as I loved writing it.

And if you feel so compelled, slide into my DMs or my FB group, Penelope's Black Hearts and tell me your favorite scene or character! Those kinds of messages are like fuel to my little author heart. Plus, I love seeing people's favorites in the harem!

As always, my DMs are always open if you need to slide in there and chat—or proverbially throw your kindle at me! ;)

I would be honored if you had the time to leave a brief review of this book! Reviews are the lifeblood of a book, and I would appreciate it so much.

xoxo

—pen

Stay in the loop!
 Join my newsletter
 Join my Facebook group, Penelope's Black Hearts
 Follow me on Instagram @authorpenelopeblack

ACKNOWLEDGMENTS

Thank you to my readers! Thank you for hanging in there with me on all those cliffs on just about every book I write, sending all of you air hugs for that!

Thank you to my husband who's always the first one to champion me. And I love that you're always shouting, "My wife's a romance author!" with pride to anyone you pass on the street. You're the best, and I love you so much.

To my tiny humans: I love you both more than all the stars in the sky. And you have to wait until you're older to read Mommy's books.

To all the bookstagrammers and bloggers and readers that send me messages and create beautiful edits for my books—I'm still in awe. Thank you so, so much. On my most insecure days, I pull up your edits and kind words and never fails to reignite my spark.

To my wonderful family who's encouraged and supported me —thank you, thank you! And thank you to each and every one of you who read my books.

To my gals Erica + Jen! I'm so grateful to have you both on my team. Thank you for all your help and kindness!

To my beta besties: Tracey, Dorothy, Elaine—I'm so thankful for each of you. Your kindness and support mean the world to me.

To Christine for always being so incredibly kind and helpful.

Thank you to the amazing babes on my ARC team! I'm so grateful to have you in my corner!

To my Songbirds—I'm so lucky to have you all with me on this journey! Thank you for being a safe space!

And finally, I want to thank my author besties! I found y'all this past year, and trust me when I say, I'm never letting you go! I'm forever grateful for the ease in which you fix crowns, champion one another, and become a safe haven for me.

ALSO BY PENELOPE BLACK

THE BROTHERHOOD SERIES

Wolf

Rush

Sully

THE FIVE FAMILIES SERIES

Gilded Princess

Twisted Queen

Vicious Reign

Fractured Dynasty

STANDALONES

When It Ends:

A Dark Apocalyptic Romance

In A Little While

THE KING SISTERS WORLD

The Wren

The Wild